The Blacktop Champion
of Ickey Honey

· *and Other Stories* ·

But there is always a sense of brokenness to our living. We are destined to lose much that we value. We are destined to feel betrayed at times and disappointed. These things do not happen because we have been "bad" people, nor can we prevent them by being "good." . . . It is one of the conditions of living that we will always have grief in our lives.

The Reverend John H. Nichols
From "Failure and Successes"
The Minns Lectures, 1985

The Blacktop Champion
of Ickey Honey

· *and Other Stories* ·

Robert T. Sorrells

The University of Arkansas Press

Fayetteville · London · 1988

Designer: Chiquita Babb
Typeface: Linotron 202 Garamond #3
Typesetter: G & S Typesetters, Inc.
Printer: Thomson-Shore, Inc.
Binder: John H. Dekker & Sons, Inc.
The paper used in this publication meets the minimum requirements of the
American National Standards for Permanence of Paper for Printed
Library Materials z39.48–1984. ∞

The following works have been previously published:
"Charley Billy," LSU Press anthology *Southern Writing in the Sixties,* 1966;
"Drowning," *Western Humanities Review,* Vol. XXII, No. 1, Winter, 1968;
"A Mature and Civilized Relationship," *The Arlington Quarterly,* Vol. II, No. 3,
Winter, 1968; "The Phone Call," *American Review* (#19), January, 1974;
"Rookie," *Penthouse,* February, 1974; "Lovers," *Playgirl,* May, 1974; "The
Blacktop Champion of Ickey Honey," *American Review* (#26), 1977. Reprinted
in *Best American Short Stories,* 1978; and "A Fan of the Game" (unpublished) was
the winner of a PEN/NEA Syndicated Fiction Award, 1983.

Library of Congress Cataloging-in-Publication Data

Sorrells, Robert T., 1932–
The blacktop champion of Ickey Honey and other stories.
I. Title.
PS3569.069B57   1988   813'.54   88-14311
ISBN 1-55728-045-2 (alk. paper)
ISBN 1-55728-046-0 (pbk. : alk. paper)

For Dillman, who has always said Yes *to life;*
and for Walter and Ruth, sweet children of our love.

Contents

The Blacktop Champion
of Ickey Honey

· *and Other Stories* ·

The Blacktop Champion
of Ickey Honey

• • I try hard to be optimistic about life, but when Hoke Warble came to me and told me he had agreed to a one thousand dollar grudge match with Newton Slock, I said, "Hoke, why don't you just go on and give Newton his money right now and save all of us, your friends, the embarrassment of having to sit out there on those splintery bleachers at the Ickey Honey Country Club under what will no doubt be a broiling August sun and watch you get your ass whipped?"

Or words to that effect.

But first, Ickey Honey. It's a hamlet in Punkin County, South Carolina, and though now called "The Gateway to the Blue Ridge," it is not quite far enough up in the mountains to get more than one snow every four or five years that doesn't melt by noon. It's really more "out from" than "up toward."

Too—contrary to whatever those slack-jawed kids over in Clemson might say about it—the name is not what you might think. Honey, for instance, is a corruption of an old Indian word, *Honea,* which in the Cherokee means *Path.* Ickey is another corruption from the Cherokee, *Ikeowaywa,* which, imperfectly translated, means *The Place From Which One Leaps Out.* So those Clemson people delighted in telling each other that Ickey Honey was the jumping off place, the end of the earth. In fact, however, to the Cherokees *Honea Ikeowaywa* was the Point of Beginning, the place from which the hunters went to hunt, the warriors to make war, and so on, with the implication that they were the actual center of things, the place where all paths come together. Something like Rome, I gather.

But what can you expect from a corrupt people if not a corruption of language?

However, the old-line natives retained the history, after a fashion, and that is why our high school athletic teams call themselves the Warpathers. We kept the high school, by the way, because when all that consolidation got started twenty years ago, we fell off the county superintendent's list. So, by being lost, we managed to retain our integrity, unlike most of those new schools which ended up in the middle of some junky hunk of land without even a dusting of topsoil: schools juxtaposed to nowhere and neighbored by nothing but parking lots for the buses.

In Ickey Honey, at least, you had to walk past the school every day of your life, and you knew it was where you had to put in your time, like it or not, and you knew it was a part of the whole Ickey Honey scene—just like the church you had to go to. I am not saying that everyone liked it. I am simply saying that *it* was there and so were *you,* and the result was that you grew up with a very personal one-to-one relationship with things.

As to Hoke Warble, he was less what you'd call a *friend* than a part of me. Neither friend nor enemy. Just always Hoke, the derivation of whose name I will spare you the complex though fascinating details. Hoke was as native to Ickey Honey as cones to our pines or red to our clay or shotguns to our weddings.

At the same time, though, it must be admitted that Hoke had certain desires in this world, one of which was to rise. Hoke even wanted to excel. Now you must also understand this: coming from Ickey Honey can do things *to* you as well as *for* you. If we grew up rich in deep and abiding relationships to our buildings and our people, we grew up poor in vocational models. A few gas station attendants, some feed store people, a grocer or so, and the preachers twice a week. That was it. When I was growing up, we didn't even have any rednecks in town on Saturdays. *We* were the rednecks, and every Saturday you'd find most of Ickey Honey hunkered down chewing and whittling and staring bug-eyed on the sidewalks of such big towns as Six Mile and Ninety-Six.

So either you praised the virtues of living crimeless in Ickey Honey, or the minute you set eyes on a real town you started plotting your escape. But if you were Hoke, you dreamed on a grander scale. Where most of us decided to stay or leave for the wider world, Hoke decided he could both stay and leave by bringing the wider world into Ickey Honey. After finding out that other places were far brighter and more inviting, and after dutifully toting his slide rule around Clemson for four years, Hoke wanted Ickey Honey to be worthier of him than he figured it was. He wanted Ickey Honey to improve.

So he established, subscribed, and built the Ickey Honey Country Club, the first step on Ickey Honey's forced march into growth and development. A disinterested observer, however, might have concluded that the Country Club was really something else. A city park, say, with an imposing gateway arch to belie what was on the other side: a pool, covered over after six drownings (though no people); a memorial plaque to Hoke; two outdoor basketball goals, their metal nets missing; and the tennis court.

Hoke built the tennis court fifteen years ago, long before tennis, like golf in its time, had become a game of the masses. Hoke, some said, had always been a man of vision. As a matter of fact the last time I heard that said was the day Hoke came in to talk to me about the best-two-out-of-three-set grudge match. As another matter of fact, he said it himself.

"What do you mean, 'Get my ass whipped'?" He extended his head as far as he could from his neck and glared up at me. I am five feet ten.

"Of course I will beat him," he demanded, and swabbed his sweating face with a huge handkerchief. It was late June, but summer had come early.

"Huh!" he bullied further, a forefinger jabbing right between my eyes. "I will destroy him. Newton Slock. Yech! That's not even a name. What kind of name is that? You know all about weird things."

The implications of his questions fanned the fires of his own inventiveness.

"I'll tell you about weird. Newton Slock. *That's* weird. Do you know how big a freak he is? Let me tell you about Newton Slock . . ."

"No, Hoke," I interrupted. "You don't need to tell me about Newton Slock. I know about Newton Slock. Newton Slock attended Presbyterian College for Gentle Men, and in his four years there he was president or editor of everything from the minor sports club to their yearbook *The Guiding Light.*"

"Huh!" Hoke said, his red face cracked by a sour smile. "Huh! It's easy to see you've been around him for a minute and a half. I'll destroy him," he said by way of getting back to basics, and he wadded his handkerchief down into a pocket of his blue shorts.

"Listen, DB," I said. DB stood for *Drag Butt,* a nickname Hoke hadn't much cottoned to, but which stuck anyway because Hoke was built like . . . well, like a toad, maybe. Or a fireplug. Or a sack of corncobs?

"DB," I said, "first off, Newton Slock is your friend. You got him here to help improve the town by making it into a subdivision—for which I don't much love either of you. And he has helped you make a passel doing it.

"Also," I went on quickly before he could stick his finger back between my eyes like the barrel of a Saturday-night special, "Newton Slock is a very competent tennis player who was captain of his team in college and who has played a lot of tennis since.

"And who," I hurried right on, "has not spent nearly so much of his leisure time as you sitting and *watching* tube tennis whilst drinking cases of beer and consuming plastic snack-slops by the crate."

"You don't understand a thing," Hoke said. I had run out of breath. "There is no way that weirdo can beat me."

"How about by playing better tennis?" Forthrightness compelled me at least to put it forward as a possibility.

"And he can't because first off," he shoved that salami-shaped thumb up at me, "he is a freak! Second off," and he pulled his index finger up from his fist, "he is *wrong*. Third of all . . ."

Now it looked like a salami and two Vienna sausages. I wondered how he ever managed to hold a racket with a hand like that.

". . . I'm right."

His hand stayed bunched near my chin, so I had a chance to look at his fingers for a minute before I answered.

"Hoke, it occurs to me that all the right in the world will not make you as good a tennis player as Newton Slock."

He looked crushed, not because it occurred to him my judgement might be sound, but because he must have suffered a sense of betrayal.

"Lookee," he said to me.

I looked at his hand. So did he. He even started to point at it before quickly stuffing it into his shorts pocket.

"You don't even know what he's done. How can you talk like that and not even know what he's done?"

I had wondered what had happened, but I knew Hoke well enough to know that he would never answer a direct question.

"He cheated you," I said and turned as if to walk away.

He grabbed my arm.

"You're gonna hold the stakes," he said.

"Fine," I answered real quick, figuring I'd gotten off pretty light if that's all there was to it. But I smelled the rat when I looked at him.

"You're also gonna get me in shape," he said with what I took to be a leer.

"No way."

"Lotsa ways."

"Hoke, you idiot. I don't know a durned thing in the world about tennis or how to get in shape for playing the fool game."

"I'll teach you. There's nothing to it. Honest. All you have to do is keep your eye on the ball and return their shots. Let them wear themselves out. Simple."

"I'll tell you what's simple," I said. "What's simple is that I can't even be out in the field as a county agent nearly as much as I'd like because I got no knees, what with arthritis from old Warpathers football days. And that means I have to ply much of my trade in an office which doesn't keep me very even-tempered, which means in addition that there is no way I *can* go hoppitying around a macadam tennis court like some twenty-year-old. And neither can you because you'd drop dead from cardiac arrest and heat prostration—especially in this kind of weather."

"One more thing," he said, just like I'd never opened my mouth. "You're going to referee, too, so you might as well start boning up on the rules."

I did not respond. He knew I could be as hard-headed as anyone—including himself—and that when I clammed up he'd better talk fast because I never bothered to spend much time arguing cases. You get so you mean it or you don't in this world, and there's no point in standing around jawing. Now Hoke, being what he called an entrepreneur, was nothing but a sack full of arguments.

"All right," he said. "I thought you were a friend. All right."

He looked like he always does when he busied his mouth to work his brain. I still wasn't going to ask him what this mess was all about.

"Then I'll tell you," he said. "Tell you short and sweet."

"All right," I said.

"It's really very simple," he said, giving all the appearance of being calm and in control under intense emotional pressure.

I gestured for him to please go on.

"He's a cheat."

"A cheat?" I said.

He looked confused. Then, "Land," he nearly whispered. "Land is the wealth of a nation."

I said nothing.

"He has been robbing me blind and I intend to beat the bastard at his own game, Lodi. Then I'm going to kill him."

It was the first time all day he had called me by my name.

As for myself, I'm a County Agent. An entomologist, really, who got into county agenting so I could eat regularly. Too, the job let me stay in or near home, which suited me just fine.

Lodi Poidle. I was drafted to fight the Korean War, but ended up in Austria, realized that *Poidle* was a corruption of *Peutl,* and that it was from Austria we came some hundred and fifty years ago. But that was through my father. Through my mother, a Scot, we have been here God only knows how long. Also through my mother we have been here more or less forever, since she was part Cherokee. When I was a child and asked which part, she only laughed, but when my father asserted at the dinner table that he knew which part was Indian, she would just smile sweetly and say, "The princess part."

So in Salzburg, Austria, I learned to skate and ski, to speak a little German, and to be dissatisfied forever with American bread and beer. Then back home to finish school, take the county agenting job, marry, and accept my place as a stable member of the Ickey Honey community. And all because of bugs.

When I was little, I remember, I loved the pines: loblolly, slash, white. I remember sitting in a plantation of them once, listening. *Crunch, crunch.*

I finally asked my father what it was I kept hearing. He sat down beside me, listened carefully, and said, "Pine borers. They are eating the trees. Look," and he showed me their holes, even got his knife and dug out a few of the varmints.

I said, "They are eating up all the trees?" He said, "Yes, Lodi." I wept, then spent years hating the pine borers with all the passion of my youth, determined to learn how to save the world from them. That's why I went to college in the first place. But there I learned to love bugs. The fruit fly, for instance. You have to admire him after a while. And nits and newts and mites and all the rest.

"Buggy!"

It was Hoke shouting at me. I rested my racket on my toes. He was unhappy with my play.

"Damn, Lodi. You got to go after the ball. You got to chase it to hit it back. Isn't anyone going to hit it right to your forehand every time. You're not giving me the first sign of a sweat."

"Sweat! All I have to do is stand here and I sweat."

"Well if you'd wear shorts and a T-shirt instead of those khaki trousers and shirts you wouldn't get so hot."

I pointed the racket at him. "Hoke, you're stupider than you look if you think I'm going to walk around this town in short pants that look like underwear."

"Get ready for another serve, Lodi. If I can get my power up for the serves I can take him."

"Hoke, if there's anything Newton can do it's return serves."

Hoke glared across the net at me. "Oh yeah? Well if there's anything else he can do it's foot fault." His face was a ball of red, wet hatred. "You got to watch him careful on that or he'll foot fault on me all day long if you don't catch him and call him on it."

I walked off the court toward the bench and started to button up my shirt.

"Hey!" Hoke yelled, racing around the net. "Where you going? You promised me two hours this morning. We only been out here thirty minutes."

"I think it probably isn't right for me to train you if I'm going to have to referee the match, Hoke, because I'll have to call your foot faults, too."

"I don't foot fault."

"You do."

"I don't."

"Do."

"Don't," he hollered.

I stood quietly and stared him down.

"Much?" he asked.

"Every time," I answered.

"Well, hell, Lodi. You mean you'd call something like that on me after what he's done? Would you?"

I finished tucking in my shirt.

"Lodi?" he whined. "Man, I *need* you. You got to *help* me. You got to tell me things like how does he serve? And, how does he play the net? And stuff like that. Lodi?"

I faced him. "Hoke, how many years have you been playing tennis with Newton Slock?"

He shrugged. "Ten, maybe. Why?"

I could only shake my head. This was beginning to surpass wonder.

"Then you have probably played two thousand games with Newton Slock, since for the first five of those years he was the only other person in town who knew how to play."

"So?" he shrugged. "What's that got to do with foot faults?"

Even I was stunned. "It means I'm going to call them," I mumbled.

"Good!" he shouted, beaming at me like he meant it. "I just had to make sure you were still Mr. Incorruptible. Get your racket and let's go."

I did, too. I was a good example of how Hoke Warble—slide rule dangling jauntily from his hip, wearing his civil engineering degree on his sleeve like some wear their hearts—was able to borrow money enough to buy land, hire surveyors, rent bulldozers, and, by whispering the sweetest of honey into the ears of conservative builders, turn them into daring speculation contractors. He could talk people into things. Part wheedle, part bully, but mostly a play on your own greed or whatever strength he knew he could grab you by and turn you with. And to give credit, the minute he knew that Clemson Agricultural College was going to stop being a military academy and start being a university with coeds, was the minute he understood the power of wide roads leading from Clemson direct to my home town. No need to guess who owned the best rights-of-way when it all got started.

That was Hoke, but it was almost worth it to watch him play tennis. His serve, for instance, wasn't what you could call good, but it was hard to return. He held the racket in what at first appeared to be the ordinary way, only because his hands were so small, he had to chisel the grip down and then hold it about three inches up from the end. Also, he couldn't hold but one ball at a time in the other hand. But since all the pros had three balls, he did too—in his pockets. I mean you to understand he kept two or three balls in *each* pocket. As I have suggested, Hoke already filled out his clothes. So to stuff all those balls into the side pockets gave him the appearance of a hog with great wens on each hip.

Then he would peer steadfastly across the net at his opponent. With the ball held right up against the bottom of his racket, he would begin to rock his entire body forward and backward while at the same time he shoved his arms back and forth so you weren't sure what to watch. When he had gotten himself all wound up, he would lean way over toward the net, bring his racket to the ground in front of his left toes, rear back, and then with a quick jerk and grunt serve the ball.

As a rule, he served three times. The first went into the net. The second ticked the top of the net. And the third he just pooped the ball into play. When the time came for *you* to do something, you were either worn out watching all that business or just exactly bored enough to be out of the notion to play.

But play we did: I would serve and serve so he could practice his returns. Then he would serve and serve while I shagged balls for him. It was wearing work, but Hoke went at it like a pro. Hours and hours and hours of it.

I thought once that he might lose fifty pounds working like he did with out-and-out hot weather already settled in like it was. But every time he finished sweating off eight pounds (he weighed in before and after each session) he'd drink about a quart of beer with his sandwiches and snack-slops plus his regular meals. So he ended up eating more than usual. And the more he trained, the bigger he got.

"But stronger, Lodi," he'd insist. "And quicker."

Which brings me to Newton Slock.

Newton wasn't a native. Newton was from what is called the "Low Country," a section of our fair state thick with history, plague, cotton, a language called "Gullah," and rich people who can't stand the sight of someone from the up country who can afford to drive his own car to work.

Now there are two ways for people like me to approach an outsider like Newton. One is to say that at least he has seen the light and come to where God intended people instead of sand fleas and red bugs to live. The other is to remain always suspicious. Since he was a good friend of Hoke's, I was at least somewhat predisposed toward the latter, but being me, I was also prepared for the former.

All of Newton's activities in Presbyterian College for Gentle Men were nothing but preparation for the "Life of the Real World," as he phrased it. Committees, activities, meetings, clubs, organizations, service to the community . . . Lord, there was no end to it. He was Hoke's PR man, in short, and the volume of leaflets, letters, flyers, pamphlets, and advertisements he flooded into the mails was worthy of any government bureaucrat. Not to mention the number of dinners eaten or rounds of golf played with university deans, textile mill executives, and editorial writers for the local newspapers—all to help turn Ickey Honey into a subdivision worthy of Hoke Warble.

"Not a subdivision," Newton once said gently some years ago. "What we are creating here is a residential community, Lodi," and he looked at me with those Gentle Man's sincere eyes.

"I see," I said back. "But what's it going to *do*?"

"Do, Lodi?" He never broke stride. "Why, it won't have to *do* anything. It will provide a restful place for people to live in. It will be a retreat where people can reintegrate themselves and so face the next day's challenges."

"It seems to me," I tried, "that people are already integrated if they live more or less where they work."

"Ah, Lodi," he smiled.

"It seems to me, Newton, that when you make a person live away from his work, or when you make him do work he hates so much that he feels he has to live away from it, then you have separated him out from himself so that he *has* to reintegrate. My father never needed any reintegrating because, being a forester and a farmer, he lived where the fruit of his labor was."

13

"Your father lived in another time, Lodi."

"Newton, I live right here in Ickey Honey where my work is."

"Hmmm," he said wisely. "Bugs are ubiquitous, yes, but not all of us in this modern world of today are able to do that. This nation isn't agricultural anymore, Lodi."

He said that very archly as though I probably hadn't heard the news yet. I was going to tell him that people had always lived in towns, and that in lots of places they lived happily and well-integrated right above their shops. But I figured it wouldn't help.

Besides, Newton was a nice enough person. He was not mean. He was not a beast. It's just that I didn't understand how someone who was supposed to be so smart could really believe the things he kept saying.

So we practiced, Hoke and I. We practiced the forehand return, the backhand return, lobs, serves, the serve return, the two-hand grip. He practiced doing like Arthur Ashe, or Jimmy Connors, or Ilie Nastase, or . . .

But through it all, Hoke remained largely his own man. When I had told him earlier that I couldn't go hoppitying around the court it was because Hoke was about the only player I had ever seen, and hop was what he did most. He always seemed to go up and down more than back and forth. That never changed much, either, though I must admit that as the match drew nearer Hoke was able to make his upping and downing more useful. And just a week before the match itself, he had a long and serious talk with me before our practice session.

"Lodi," he said, the sincerity nearly choking him. "You'll never know how much I appreciate your helping me this way."

I shrugged. "I've actually come to enjoy it, Hoke," I said. "I didn't think I would, but I have actually come to like the game. Sort of."

"I will tell you something," he went on. "I am going to beat him."

I waited for more, but there was silence. I looked up and damned if there weren't tears in his eyes.

"Well," I said. "Well, Hoke. I never thought you had a chance four weeks ago. But durned if I don't think you can give him a real run for his money now."

At that, the tears disappeared, and so, too, I think, did the era of good feeling we had been sharing.

"Money!" he snorted, and it did not take a genius to gather he was not alluding to the thousand dollar bet. Had Newton been cheating him? I still couldn't believe it. Couldn't believe, at any rate, that there was something illegal involved. I kept my own counsel and waited for Hoke to reveal himself.

He gave me a man-to-man stare and a professional little pat on my bottom as he said, "Let's hit it, Lodi," his voice quiet but firm with the sureness of a man who knows his destiny is soon to be fulfilled.

As for my own destiny, it was bouncing along innocently enough until one day I was driving back to my office after a visit to look at a garden club president's scaly azeleas. A sporty little Audi had nipped in front of me and on the left side of its bumper was a sticker. It pictured a hand clenched tightly around a tennis racket being held on high. The inscription read: TENNIS NOW! On the other side of the bumper was another sticker. It read: ALL POWER TO THE COURTS. Dawn glimmered slowly in my gut where a voice rumbled lowly unto me saying, *Lodi, Old Bean, someone has been very busy promoting this thing while you were out training Hoke.*

They came in from all around, the natives did. They came in from places that hadn't even been crossroads for thirty years. They came in in their pickups and on their flatbeds rattling, straining against the baling wire that seemed to hold them together. They came in with NeHis, RCs, little packets of salted goobers, peanut butter crackers, Cheez-Its, and dangerous-looking sacks worn soft from constant reusings. They came in in overalls and ankle boots— their sides sliced to give bunions ease; their little children barefoot and knobbly-ankled; their teenaged daughters slumpshouldered against maturity; their boys ballsy but stiff-necked against the alien feel of a town grown smooth and untouchable to the rough clutch of their snag-nailed hands. Their sense of being forever excluded was as heavy and real to them as the heat that hunkered down on us all for the past week.

They found places for their vehicles near the Ickey Honey Country Club, parked, and made their way to the tennis court. There were stands on both sides of the court, and for no reason other than that he had parked nearest it, the first arrival had stepped warily up on the closest set of plank bleachers; followed, then, by the others as they clanked and chugged into town and in their own turns parked near the vehicles they knew, the ones they understood to be like their own and thus peopled by their own kind. They climbed the seats, sat, looked around with care, not wanting to move fast enough to draw attention to themselves.

Across the way another crowd was taking its place: in trousers or shorts and deck shoes, they looked dressed more for sailing on the lake: smoothly tanned all over, lounging, at ease, relaxed and chatting with one another. Yet they sedulously avoided eye contact with the people on my side. Except, that is, by flicking, darting little side glances. Their heads stayed averted. They were the residents.

After not too long the principals arrived. From the residents there came a polite pat-a-pat-a-pat of applause. From the others . . .

I would like to say that I heard groans when Hoke and Newton made their appearances. I would like to say they gasped or snickered or did something outrageous. But they didn't, and I loved them for holding their collective judgement in abeyance. And yet . . .

. . . something of wonder went through them when they saw the two men, when they saw that *those* were to be the contestants they had lurched into town to see, were willing to sit on splintery planks under an already roasting sun to watch as the ancient rituals of man's pride in self and family and place were satisfied.

. . . something of wonder crossed their faces.

To their right was Newton Slock: six feet two inches, trim, dark-haired, fit looking; his tennis shoes were Adidas, a solid suede, a no-nonsense shade of blue with socks to match; his tennis shorts were lighter in color, more what you might call "bonnie blue"; his shirt—its rolled collar very precisely casual—was color-coordinated with the shorts and sneakers, a thin rim of maroon piping around the sleeves of the shirt and down the sides of the shorts. On his wrists were light blue sweatbands. Topping it off was a visor, blue on the underside, a rich, creamy off-white above. A take-charge guy, you could tell right off.

And to their left was Hoke. He too had chosen Adidas, but they were white trimmed in gold. His socks matched, as did his shorts and shirt, with a little alligator emblazoned over his heart. Not only did he have sweatbands on his wrists—bright gold ones— but a gold sweatband encircled his head as well, like a tight halo.

They were a sight indeed. Hoke did squat bends while Newton went through a complex routine of circular arm movements. Apparently they were not going to give each other any warm-ups like every other tennis player in the world does before a match; so the next move was mine. I stepped toward the net, careful not to get on either side of the court lest one of them accuse me of favoring the other. I motioned them to come to me.

"Well," I began.

They glared at each other.

'Well, here we are. I reckon it's time to start."

Newton kept up his arm swinging while Hoke bounced up and down on his toes. They looked like two boxers.

"Hoke, Newton, this is a grudge match for one thousand dollars—winner take all—best-two-out-of-three sets. The first two can be won on tie-breakers, but if it should go to the third, we play old rules and you have to win by two games. Right?"

"That's what we agreed to, Lodi," Newton said, and you could have slid to Heaven on the oil in his voice.

"All right, then," I said. "Newton, since you have been challenged, you serve first. Hoke, where are you going to start off?" He nodded to where he had been warming up. "All right, then . . ." I was about to tell them to shake hands now and come out fighting, but they had turned away and were heading to their respective positions.

What shall I say of that match? Newton served and scored. Served and scored. Served and scored. Served and won the first game. They swapped courts.

Then it was for Hoke to serve. He did, and the ball smashed into the net. He served again, and it bounced off the top of the net to land in the service area. He served once more, pooping the ball over the net toward Newton who returned it with a forehand smash that ripped by Hoke just as he was on a bounce up and thus unable to give chase.

His other three serves met much the same fate. Newton whapped them all back so hard poor Hoke could hardly see them coming, and I wondered why, after he served the ball, he didn't move instead of obstinately bouncing straight up and down where he was. Newton returned every single serve clear across the court from Hoke, who didn't seem to catch on to what was clear even to a gravelly voiced little native son behind me. "Poppa," he asked the puff-eyed, nine-fingered frighty-looking man directly behind me, "oughten that there fat one to do something else?"

And that was pretty much the story of the first set—except for the two games Newton lost or gave away by playing left-handed. I breathed a little sigh of relief: at that rate it couldn't take too long.

However, I hadn't counted on temper. After Newton won the third game of the second set and was starting around to wipe his face at the net before going to the other court, Hoke flung his racket against the fencing behind him and loosed a terrible flow of invective. I was startled, but Newton was stopped in his tracks, and the crowd on my side loved it. A small but hearty bit of laughter riffled through them to make its impact on Hoke, who by then had stalked to the fence to retrieve his Wilson-T-4000-"Pro"-Frame-with-Sensor-Dome-to-Reduce-Vibration-from-Contact. He stared hard at it as though to make certain it had withstood the throwing it presumably was made to withstand. Newton wiped his face and I noticed him looking across at Hoke who swigged mightily several times from a tennis-ball can filled with Crocodile Juice or some such business. It was a green, mostly sweet liquid that Hoke seemed to think would see him through life. I drank some once when I was getting him in shape, but it tasted like Kool-Aid to me.

He drank mightily, I say, and glared unadulterated hate back at Newton. They each finished their refreshments and ablutions and took up their positions once more. It was Hoke's turn to serve, his last serve having been broken, as they say in tennis circles, by Newton.

Hoke may some day in his life be out, but he will never be down. I think we'll have to bury him standing up. I not only had not counted on bad temper, I had not counted on Hoke's basic—well—sneakiness. He quick-served.

Instead of going through his usual folderol of a wind-up, he took his preliminary stance but flipped the ball quickly and popped it over the net. Newton stared at it as it bounced once, then twice, then even a third time before his brain responded to what his eyes so clearly saw.

"What was that?" Newton yelled.

"That was fifteen-love, Dummy," Hoke yelled back.

Newton straightened. Still in disbelief, he looked over at me. Then I realized he wanted a ruling. There hadn't been anything for me to do once the game got underway, and I had almost forgotten that I was supposed to referee. But what did I know? Newton had been ready. Hoke had been ready. They had both been where they were supposed to be.

"Fifteen-love, Newton," I called back, and held my hands out to let him know there was nothing personal in it from me.

"Serve it up like that again, DB," Newton dared. "Serve it like that again." He looked ready for tigers.

Hoke was craftier than that, though, and what he did was to throw the ball up in the air. Then he gripped his weapon with both hands, and as the ball descended, he took aim on it like a batter would on a hugely arcing, slow Ephus pitch. The ball hung high in the air hardly rotating enough to have any kind of spin on it at all, floated so slowly you could count the puce hairs on its hide. Then at just the right moment, he slashed as viciously as ever any medieval knight slashed at the juncture of an enemy's neck and shoulder. It cleared the net by a fraction, hit just in the service area, and spun off the side of the court so hard and fast that even if Newton had been ready for it there was no way he could have gotten to it.

Hoke cackled, positively jumping up and down at the spectacle of Newton standing bug-eyed.

"That's thirty-love in case you were going to ask." He whickered and fairly danced into position for the next serve . . .

. . . which Newton returned out of bounds, losing for the moment the cool which was his hallmark in the tennis world of Ickey Honey.

So that for the next serve, Hoke was in a position to win his very first game of set two. He readied himself as Newton gripped and regripped the handle of his nylon-stringed, high-tensile, steel Wilson T 2000. Around came Hoke for the serve. *Smash!* into the net . . . *Pop!* off the top . . . and while Newton eased up to blitz the *Poop* that had to follow, Hoke himself, after pooping, rushed the net with a scream and a whoop that caught Newton unaware just enough for his return not to have very much on it. Hoke caught it on the run and blasted it with a leaping two-handed *Splat!* that sent it careening, not only off the court, but over the restraining fence behind Newton as well.

"No!" screamed Newton Slock, looking now again to me for official confirmation of his protest. "No fair. Foul. You can't scream like that."

I hadn't read that you couldn't scream like that. As a matter of fact as an old Warpather I had thought the scream pretty good, reminiscent of the times Hoke, a terrifying looking but otherwise ineffectual linebacker, would leap feet first across the line of scrimmage war-crying all the way. It often got him kicked out of the game, but by that time it would have worked its purpose of scaring the opposition and getting him kicked out so he wouldn't have to play any more that afternoon.

"No fair," Newton kept insisting. "You're not allowed to distract your opponent that-a-way. It isn't cricket." His normally dulcet tones had become peculiarly shrill.

All the while Hoke cackled to himself and strutted up and down the backline of the court. He wiped a trickle of Crocodile Juice from his chin.

"Come off it, Newton Shlock," he called. "You're still ahead three games to my puny one. Can't you stand that? Heh heh heh," he finished. "Heh heh."

That seemed to calm Newton down a bit as he took up his position. He looked ready to serve, but then turned and walked away a few steps talking to himself.

Come on, baby, we could all hear him mutter. *Let's put this joker down and get on back home.*

He apparently did himself some good, because he got back to the line and served one of the most bully fast serves I ever saw.

The crowd on both sides *oohed* at it, but Hoke stood there calm as pie.

"Out," he said very politely and very softly.

"What? What do you mean out? That serve was fair by six inches." Newton looked over to me.

I was in for it.

"I didn't see it," I said, hoping it was loud enough for them to hear without being so loud as to let everybody know I hadn't watched where it hit.

"Better play it over," Hoke mewed.

"Play it over, hell," Newton bellowed. "It was in."

"Rule says," Hoke went on calm as a sleeping cat, "you got to play it over if it is contested and the judge can't make a call. Heh heh heh."

It was, and I couldn't. I shrugged to say I was sorry. Newton talked to himself again for a little while, then went back to the line, but Hoke had gotten to him and he double faulted. Love-fifteen.

Newton started putting himself into it now. He wiped the sweat from his brow, blinked twice, and served again. Hoke held his racket out and let the ball return itself. Newton hadn't expected him to be able to return that hard a serve, or was starting to wear down mentally a little, because he never tried to make a play on it.

Love-thirty.

With the next serve, he heaved mightily once more and got off another blistering serve, but just as last time Hoke got the racket out to it and let the ball return itself. Newton managed to return that return, but Hoke fed him a high, deep lob that Newton had to run back for. The sun was high by then and the sweat was rolling fast off everybody, so Newton didn't get as much string on the ball as he should have. It got back over the net, but Hoke pounced on it and placed it out of reach.

Love-forty.

Newton's first serve was laid in with great strength, but it caught the net for a fault. The second serve was milder. Hoke got to it and lobbed it high and deep again. Newton ran back and smashed a return, but Hoke caught it at the net and made Newton run up fast to get it back over. Another deep lob, another pop over the net, another run by Newton, another deep lob, another hard run to the net where he smashed it past Hoke for the score.

Fifteen-forty, but Hoke had worked very little and Newton had worked a lot.

Even I had to admire Hoke at that point. He was playing what's called a "very smart game," and I started to wonder if maybe he had a chance after all. I also started to wonder whether Newton didn't understand what was going on yet. He lost the next point and the game on exactly the same kind of *I'll-hit-it-while-you-run-after-it* play of the point before.

They swapped courts once again, pausing longer at their rest areas to drink deep and sponge off. It was hot. I heard cans getting popped in the stands behind me, and the deep, soft sounds of slurped foam came trailing on the sweet smell of hot beer.

Score, Set Two: three games to two, Mr. Slock.

The natives had finally warmed up to the game as well as to the day. Though they were even more ignorant about it than I had been, they began to understand the basic points, though in truth the thing they liked best was the way the players urged themselves on.

Newton's favorite routine was to wheel around from the net when he had made a particularly bad play and stalk away where he would set one hand on a hip and talk—actually to himself, though it looked like he was trying to reason with the fence. He would gesture and gesticulate, then shake his racket at it as if threatening to raise a lump on its mesh if it didn't start doing better.

But there were more violent moments, too. His standard form of mayhem was to stare across the net at Hoke after a goof, then swirl around and fling his racket at the fence. When he did that, a nice, large murmur of approval would well up from the stands on my side. Once, I heard someone—whose voice came from very near where most of the beer popping came—holler out that he ought to have "flang the racket at Hoke, heh-heh-heh." That brought even louder murmurs of approval from his friends, and I heard three cans pop nearly at once.

Hoke, on the other hand, was constantly in motion anyway, and his usual sign of disgust was to skim his racket across the court at the fence behind him. If that didn't do any good on the next point, he would take it in both hands and approach the post that held the net up, and there he would pop the strings on the top of the post as though not so much to see how really and truly well-built the Stratabow construction was (he had changed from his Wilson-Sensor-Dome to a Wilson-Chris-Evert), but more to let it understand that another bad miscue would bring it instant ruin. Beyond that, he would slam the flat of it against the top of the net, smash the edge of it into the fence behind him, or toss the whole thing up into the air as he walked away from whatever had disgusted him . . .

. . .such that when Newton and Hoke both were going hot and heavy at themselves, it sounded less like a tennis match than the preliminary clash and rattle of muskets as advance scouts began feeling for enemy pickets to discover the whereabouts and strengths of an entrenched foe.

The heat was getting ferocious. Each serve took more time. Each return required more effort. The stops at the refreshment areas between court swappings lasted longer. The cans popped more often behind me, and the paper sacks were getting plopped down under the stands, empty now of their contents.

Once, even, play had to be stopped a minute as a fan—caught in the heat and believing as Newton had earlier that the match couldn't last too long and having sucked more beer sooner than he might otherwise have, and having friendly nips from the soft sacks around—fell not only asleep, but down as well; fell from the top row of the bleachers to the ground beneath, much to the huge delight of his friends, whose thorough-going and hearty laughter disturbed Hoke right as he was about to serve. Though it bothered Hoke—who wasn't about to say anything to them about letting the players be the ones to scream and shout—it didn't seem to bother the fellow who had fallen. He grunted once when he hit, belched, and lay quietly the rest of the day, except for his snoring.

But as the play wore on, it became apparent that Hoke had put the hex sign on Newton, who just couldn't manage to get any sort of real lead again—Hoke had taken the second set seven-six. Newton was still winning his share of games, but he was taking longer and longer to do it, and it appeared to me that he hadn't planned on having to stay out in this August sunshine for as long as we all were. The number of deuce games and the number of deuces in those games was telling on him. How Hoke managed to stay on as long as he did, I don't know. Greed probably. And I suppose a certain amount of pride, too.

But it was not until Hoke tied the third set at six games that I really noticed how much slower on their feet they were. Newton was preparing for the first serve of the thirteenth game. It was one o'clock in the afternoon and they had been playing steadily since ten that morning. By now about four more people had dropped from the stands, each with a kind of soft thud and grunt. The ones who could stick it out with the beer, and with the air thick enough to chew, it seemed, grew more and more interested in the game, though their outbursts were reserved for the more spectacular plays.

Newton served right to Hoke who returned it—there had come to be a good bit of extended volleying by now rather than the attempts to dominate every point—and after a bit Hoke managed to put the ball out to where Newton had to make a little run for it. Earlier in the day it would have been nothing, but Newton never got to the ball. He had begun making chase and even had his racket

extended, his arm and him leaning way out after it, but his legs hadn't been able to follow. It was like his body was outrunning his feet such that he simply fell down. I even wondered, I hate to admit it, how Hoke had gotten over there to weight Newton's shoes like that.

Then I glanced over at Hoke and noticed something about him, too. His fancy sneakers had long, ugly black streaks on them which at first I took for slits, but which I finally realized was tar. Then I looked at the court itself, and there I saw great ripples that hadn't been there at the start of the game. It was like looking at a relief map of Appalachia, great crinkles ridging up all over.

Then Hoke, reaching up high after charging the net, fell flat on his ass. His feet just purely slid out from under him. It was the court, I realized, even with the stands clapping and whistling behind me at Hoke's comic fall. They were playing on what was quickly becoming a lake of tar.

"Stop," I shouted, and jumped to my feet.

It was too sudden a move in the heat, I suppose, because the next thing I knew, Hoke was pouring that sticky Crocodile Juice all over me.

"You all right?" he asked.

"I think so."

He didn't even say *Good* or anything, but started right back to the tar pit to resume the game.

"Wait," I shouted again. "Newton, Hoke, come over here."

"What for?" Newton panted.

"Because I'm the durned referee, Newton. Now get over here. Hoke, you too."

They approached and I said, "This can't go on. That tennis court of yours is melting, Hoke."

"What do you mean, 'That tennis court of *yours*'? What do you mean by that?"

"Hoke, you built the durned thing and it is melting. There is no proper way to finish this match today. Neither one of you can stand up." I tried to appeal to their softest spots. "Neither of you can play up to your finest capabilities. It's all tied right now. Call it a draw and each of you keep your money. Or finish it up tomorrow after the court has cooled."

"Tomorrow is Sunday, Lodi," Newton felt inclined to inform me.

"Sunday, Schmunday," Hoke wrinkled up his nose at Newton. To me he said, "Lodi, durn it, you don't interrupt tennis matches. It ain't cricket, you know," and he laughed in a labored and wheezy kind of way.

"But if it rained we'd postpone it until there wasn't any more rain and until the court was dry, wouldn't we?"

"This ain't rain, Lodi. This here is nothing more than tennis weather."

Tennis weather? I thought.

"But Hoke . . . Newton . . ." I tried to plead for good sense, but the onlookers started stomping their feet, started shouting questions as to whether or not someone had won and weren't they going to get to see the rest of the thing.

Hoke, his Stratabow in one hand, opened his arms up toward the stands and said, "Lodi, you wouldn't want to disappoint *them,* would you?"

I looked back and saw the soft paper sacks getting softer and softer, and I saw fresh reserves of supplies being carried up from the local markets.

"All right," I said. "But it's dumb."

I sat back down, weary from trying to make fools act sensible. There I was sitting out in God only knew what kind of heat; there they were running around smacking puce and mint green and baby blue balls back and forth at each other for reasons that still remained obscure and suspicious to me; and across the way was a handful of soft gulls, anxious to believe people like Newton Slock, willing to be ashamed of little old hamlets like Ickey Honey that hadn't ever done them any harm by being there, delighted to know nothing of my town's past, perfectly programmed to accept that prior to residential communities there had been nothing but chaos; while to my rear was a surly wad of retards and mean things waiting in a sad and desperate way for some blood to flow.

"Serve it up," I hollered. "Hell on it. Serve it up."

And as they resumed their stances, Poppa reached up from behind me and slapped my arm. I jumped.

"This thang gonna keep on a while?" he asked.

I nodded. "It looks it."

"Then here," he said. "You look to need it," and he slipped a tall can of beer into my hand. I could have kissed him. Instead, I tilted my head back and drank that beer down in gulp after gulp after gulp. God, but it was good. I never took the rim away from my lips until it was empty. Then I belched once and felt lots better.

The play went on without me, but I tried to follow what was happening just in case they were to make me decide an issue. The fact is, though, they had begun playing for real and they had too much to worry about just staying on the court without wasting a lot of energy being snippy with each other. In the meantime, I got madder and madder.

They could hardly move any more. Their shoes were clogged with tar; they slipped constantly; and the natty outfits they looked so prancy in earlier were beyond redemption. Talk about your deep-down dirt, I'd like to see a washing machine get those duds clean. Ha! And there was another beer in my hand.

Soon I even noticed that their rackets were getting gummed up. And the balls would hardly bounce. And the more beer I drank, the angrier I got about it. But I did have to admit that it was funny. Once, Newton just plain could not lift a foot from the court. He was reaching and stretching, and—of course it could have been partly the beer by then—it seemed like slow motion as he fell the length of himself onto the court. The crowd appreciated that as did Hoke, who coughed and wheezed and managed to let out a little bleating laugh of his own.

But on the next play, Newton—not to be outdone or shown up without a fight—caught Hoke prancing slowly along the line of the net, delayed his swing by a fraction, and placed the volley with tremendous drive and accuracy right in Hoke's balls.

Down he went with a squawk like Daffy Duck winged in mid-flight. Oh how my natives loved that. Poppa pounded me on the back.

"What happened?" he demanded, his face a terrible crimson.

"That air feller he clipped him right in the balls, Poppa," his son answered, "and down he went. See there?"

Hoke was indeed holding himself near the afflicted area, but seemed to be all right, more or less.

"In the balls?" Poppa screamed. "In the balls?" His face cracked into something that must for him have approached a smile, but it was hard to say, because it gave way almost directly to a look of pain and loss.

"Goddamn," he said. "Goddamn. The only thing interesting to happen out there the whole day and I miss it. Goddamn it, boy, whyn't you tell me? Whyn't you *tell* me?" and I thought he was going to clip the boy across the mouth. Instead, he popped two more beers and gave me one.

"Durn," he muttered, by then too heartsore even to curse.

Hoke was back up on his feet ready to go. The games by then were eight and eight.

I think.

Yes, they must have been. Eight and eight with Newton about to serve yet once more. He took his time about it, even managed again to go back to his friend the fence and talk to it a while. Then it was back to the line.

I drank another can of beer. Entire.

It was just like the very first serve of the game. As a matter of fact, I was thinking it *was* the very first serve of the game, because Newton looked exactly as he had, except for the oil and tar he had dredged up from the macadam court, of course. But he wound up the same way, and I finally understood that he was out to win two games in a row so he could put all this madness behind us.

Good luck, Newton, I found myself saying as I chuckled into despair, knowing as I did that he would never be able to do it. This match, I had come to understand, was like the rock of Sisyphus: there was no end. No matter who got an advantage, it would be deuced the next time around. We were all damned. The world had come to an end the night before, only none of us understood it. For reasons unknown to us all, we were here for Eternity to watch Newton Slock and Hoke Warble battle each other in a tar pit with balls that bounced less and less, on feet that stuck more and more, under a pitiless sun that was to grow hotter and hotter with the passing of each millennium until our brains were seared and scorched beyond the redeeming power that any further harrowing could possibly bestow. Me and these careless nine-fingered folk and their children . . . and the beer would get foamier as the air got heavier . . .

Newton served.

. . . and we were all in it together for no reason under the sun except that we had planned our own destruction this way. We had all planned to be doing what we were doing, and the world was stopped right then and we were cursed and damned to keep it up until the very edge of time itself . . .

Hoke got his racket out with just enough of a push behind it to get the ball back over the net.

. . . and if I had been doing what I was supposed to be doing when God placed his mighty finger on our little spinning ball and said, "Stop. It is enough," I would now be out in the pine groves listening to the cooling breezes soughing through my beloved trees. I would be noting with loving interest the progress of the borers and listening to their little *crunch-crunches* with both the sadness of the tree lover as well as the admiration and awe of a true bug man. Or I could have taken that trip back to Austria that I had wanted to take for so long, but for which there simply never had been the money or the time—or so I had kept telling myself.

Newton made a beautiful play on Hoke's return and drove it deep into the corner.

Instead, here I was with these people I did not love, though I might have a grudging admiration for their ability to survive; instead, here I was having to watch that which I did not love, though again I had learned to have a modest admiration for it; instead, here I was exposed to all, having to judge that which I knew so little of . . .

But it was higher than he would have preferred, and with the increasing heaviness of the balls, it bounced stolidly up rather than skittishly off and out of reach.

Instead, I had not lived my life as we are admonished to do: as though each moment might be our last and that therefore each moment should be lived as the moment of greatest good, because if God wearied of watching us spin and spin and spin . . .

So Hoke got to make a play on it. He returned it. Newton had to make a run and answer with a high lob.

He could end it all at any time. Which it was more and more apparent He had already done. He was the Final Arbiter, the Last Word, the Judge . . .

But it went right to where Hoke was.

The Great Referee in the Sky . . .

And he had it played perfectly.

The Great Referee can just stay STOP! and it stops . . .

He timed it all, screwed his nerves and wind and Head-PBI-High-Tensile-Aluminum-Framed racket all into a single piece of fury, brought his arm around in his most convincing swing of the afternoon, and smashed it into Newton's court. The ball was more a projectile hurtling with blind rage and savage speed, but Newton, knowing he had to take this point to keep himself going, was up to the moment; he was prepared; his arm was already drawn back to deliver a telling, highly-controlled blow for superior competence, when the ball hit.

SLUUURCK!

The sound of it echoed, reverberated forward to Eternity and back into the fastnesses of pre-history, and forward again to our own blink of time. It was an answer to prayer. That's all I could think of at the time. An answer to prayer. And I remember wondering why God had deemed my charred soul worthy of salvaging for yet a little longer. The ball—charged though it was—went slurking directly into a thick, gooey tar bubble, tried to bounce up as is its nature, and though it managed to proceed some two inches on its destined course, remained, finally, where it was, like a fly foolishly buzzing into a spider's web, a captive like the rest of us; a thing caught forever in the wrong place at the wrong time.

Until—with the clarity of vision we all hope Deity surely must have—I sprang to my feet, beer can clutched in each hand, arms spread in the benediction of salvation, and pronounced:

STOP! IT IS ENOUGH.

And with that, I collapsed giddily, face down, eyes wide, my lips spread in a sanctified smile, my brain purged forever of trivia, it now being heavy with the insight and inspiration of Deity; collapsed, I say, into the slick pool of Hoke Warble's rapidly melting tennis court.

My head almost started hurting all over again when I read the weekly paper and looked at that picture of Hoke Warble and Newton Slock grinning like jackanapes, shaking hands, holding out those thousand-dollar checks they were donating to the Ickey Honey Country Club and Recreation Center to have more tennis courts built so all those residents and nine-fingered folk could come play tennis with each other and spend their hard-earned money in the Pro Shop on expensive rackets and sneakers and alligator shorts and warm-up togs and colored balls and . . .

I spread more goo across my flaking forehead to ease the sunburn which was still pretty uncomfortable, but I had been put to bed for heat stroke. That's what the doctor called it. I suppose he was right as far as he knew, but I'm not so sure that that's what really put me down. I think it was the knowledge that I had been taken in and that the entire Thousand-Dollar-Winner-Take-All-Grudge-Match was a put-up job from the start. To create some lively interest in the sport, is what the paper quoted Hoke as saying. And it was to become an annual thing, Mr. Warble had strongly hinted. It would attract visitors, he said. They would spend lotsa money, they did *not* quote him as saying. It would put us on the map, he *did* add. It would put us on the map.

It was enough to make a grown man sick.

My trouble, I'm sure, is that I try to be straightforward about things. So it seems to me that they could have gotten that interest by fixing up the court they already had and by getting the people who wanted to play to build a new one. But as I say, Hoke always was one to see things on a grander scale than the rest of us. He always needed a little drama in his life. As for me . . .

Well, I don't mind there being more tennis courts. And I don't mind there being a club house. And I don't mind them taking the cover off the old swimming pool and fixing it up so it can be used again. That's all nice enough. I guess I don't mind things changing and growing, really. It's just that I like to see things grow where they will grow. Maybe I've been too favored by the natural flow of our small streams and the twists and turns of the gullies and draws, the odd profile of a mountain face, or the startled explosion of a deer flushed from hiding when you weren't looking for it. I guess I like for streets to follow the natural bend of the land. I guess I still like towns that have kinks in them, kinks and little odd places that are there because there were some kinky and odd people around who put their marks on the place at one time and another. Kinks and odd corners: *that's* what lets people know they are in Ickey Honey—or anyplace else that is still somewhere. Kinks and odd corners on the maps of our hearts.

Rookie

• • The sub-assistant coach tootled his whistle twice. Quickly. The Kid snatched one last time at the loose tops of his socks before he began to lean into the man next to him on the circle. The coach set one foot into the small inner ring and smartly tossed the ball high. Four hundred and fifty or sixty pounds of muscle and nerve ends smashed together at the thigh. The tips of three fingers slapped the ball back. High in the air the forward Coco pulled it in over the out-jumped hand of his blue-shirted opponent, spotted the Kid flying down court toward the goal, faked once, then hooked hard over his head. The Kid took the pass over his shoulder in stride, bounced it once, twice, dragged his foot on the third dribble, and twisted as Bonelli shot past—totally faked out. He leaped, turning in midair, and in the old familiar motion laid the ball up and off the backboard.

The hoop trembled as the ball batted about just inside the rim. Then it spun out, and Jasmo, still pushing hard in his eighth year for a real All-Pro slot instead of his annual Honorable Mention, had the rebound down court before the Kid could quit looking at the hoop.

WHAT THE HELL YA WAITIN FOR? the head coach hollered into his bullhorn from the desk on the side of the court. YOU BLOW THOSE EASY ONES AND L.A.'LL HAVE IT CINCHED IN

THE FIRST QUARTER. His voice echoed through the empty auditorium at the Armory.

By then the Kid was down on defense trying to keep his teammate-adversary—who *was* All Pro—from driving straight past him. He tried hard to force him into the center where he might be intimidated by Orville who'd often spin out from behind his own man to raise the longest, widest, thickest hand in pro basketball over his head and start it downward right at the face of any guard stupid enough to drive the center lane on him.

But the Kid wasn't quick enough. Bonelli twitched his right shoulder, lowered it, and drove the line.

The Kid did what he could, but the coach-referee's whistle screamed in his ear.

Number forty-one you're on the HIP! and he made an exaggerated copy of the Kid's last-ditch attempt to save the basket. *Two shots. In the act of shooting.*

YOU WERE SNATCHIN YOUR GODDAM SOCKS AGAIN, FOR CHRISSAKES. The bullhorn's echo rocked across the empty seats.

The Kid strode away hands on hips to take up his position near the backcourt line.

I TOLE YOU AND TOLE YOU, the bullhorn sounded again. *NEVER NEVER NEVER* TURN YOUR GODDAM BACK ON A PLAY EVEN IF IT'S JUST FREE THROWS.

The Kid blushed.

DO THAT AGAINST WEST AND HE'LL *KILL* YA. WE OPEN IN *THREE DAYS!* OR DON'T YOU REMEMBER? He was on his feet now and out from behind the desk.

Bonelli plopped the first one in. Automatic. The Kid wiped his face on his red jersey.

Bonelli plopped the second one in. Automatic. The Kid flipped his mop of hair out of his eyes and stepped up to take the pass from his guard Brown.

Brown was holding up three fingers to signal the pattern he wanted as he whipped the ball over to the Kid who took it easily, whipped it behind his back in a beautiful look-away pass to Coco who had come way up from his usual deep position. Coco whipped

34

it into Orville who shot it quickly back out to the Kid who had dashed in to get his pick. All he had to do was leap and pop it home—the shot was made for him. In college he'd averaged forty points a game on this play for three years.

But Bonelli had hooked a finger ever so lightly into the Kid's waistband. Not much. Just enough to break the rhythm of his reflexes. He could feel the shot sliding just out of control the second it started to leave his hands. When he came down he rushed in to scramble for the rebound, but Jasmo had it: in one hand, then out the other, and Bonelli was laying it up at the far end of the court before the Kid ever got near the basket.

FOR *GOD'S* SAKE, KID, came the bullhorn at him again. WHEN YOU GOT A JASMO IN THE CENTER, LEAVE HIM TO COCO AND ORVILLE, FOR CHRISSAKE. YOU THINK *CHAMBERLAIN'S* GONNA GIVE YOU THE BALL? THAT AIN'T KENTUCKY OR VANDERBILT OUT THERE NEXT TUESDAY, SONNY. IT'S THE BY-GOD LOS ANGELES LAKERS.

But the Kid was back-pedaling defensively as fast as he could— and in good position, too—but only because the pass to him from the fast break in-bounds play had been intercepted. He'd missed the signal for it, and was heading back up the court in the wrong direction when the ball was chunked the length of the floor to him.

Bonelli started driving on him again, but the Kid faked with his left hand and Bonelli drove to the outside where the Kid suddenly had him blocked out. And in trouble, too, because the Red team's other forward—Matson—finally decided he'd help out a rookie in a game scrimmage. Bonelli tried to pass the ball out, but the Kid stuck so close to him he couldn't get it away. The Kid finally reached under and between Bonelli's legs and batted the ball loose. It spun away just out of Bonelli's reach. Matson reached down nonchalantly and passed it quickly to Coco who shoveled it to Orville who stuffed it through at the other end.

GOOD PLAY, MATSON, the bullhorn bellowed. THAT'S THE WAY TO LOOK ALIVE.

At the end of the first quarter the score was 13–14, Blueshirts.

During the break, the assistant coaches in charge of the two squads amended game plans they wanted for the second period and started outlining patterns, while the Head Coach—now up in the stands with his bullhorn—kept up a constant commentary.

DISGUSTING. THAT'S WHAT. FOURTEEN GODDAM POINTS, REDS. FOURTEEN. BONELLI, YOU SHOULD HAVE HAD THAT MANY YOURSELF. YOU AND COCO. EACH. HEAR? DO YOU HEAR?

Coco looked up in the stands toward the Head Coach. Bonelli, on the other side of the court, was massaging his right hand. It hurt where the Kid had stepped on him after knocking him down on a charge. Jasmo, at six feet eleven and three-quarters inches, stood slouching above the bald, sweating head of his coach. He was looking out at the seats, his jaws slack, the sensitive finger tips of one hand playing slowly off his lower lip so that a series of *plup plup plup plup's* kept coming from him.

HE'S BEING NICE TO YOU, KID. YOU HEAR, BONELLI? STOP BEING NICE TO HIM. YOU HEAR? KID?

The Kid stepped out from the huddle to acknowledge that he'd heard.

"Whyncha lay off him, Boney?" Andrews, one of the Blue forwards said.

Plup plup plup.

YOU HEAR?

"Screw him," Bonelli said. He flexed his hand.

Plup plup.

His coach went through the defense once again.

"He's after my job."

Plup.

YOU HEAR? AND ANOTHER THING, KID . . .

The assistant coach in charge of the Redshirts looked up at the Kid who was looking up in the seats trying to hear the Head's instructions over the echoing of the bullhorn.

"Hey, Kid. You want to play ball?" the Assistant asked.

"Huh?"

"Then would you please mind listening to what I'm trying to instruct . . ."

36

YOU HEAR, KID? A QUARTER MILLION DOLLARS GETS
SIX POINTS A QUARTER? YOU THINK THE OWNERS GOT
NOTHING BETTER TO DO WITH A QUARTER MILLION?

Plup-plup-plup-plup-plup-plup.

"Screw him."

"Does it matter if your pecker drips?" Andrews asked no one in
particular.

"All black peckers drip," Bonelli answered.

The Assistant's head bounced and jabbed, red and shiny.

Plup pl . . . "Look out, Wop."

"Up yours, Spook."

Tootle tootle went the whistle, and the Redshirts and the Blueshirts set themselves up in position for the second quarter.

The Kid and Bonelli leaned into each other hip to hip, thigh to
thigh. The ball went up: smash, tip. Coco got it again, shot it
quickly to the Kid who wheeled to fly down court. Only he ended
up on the floor next to Bonelli, both of them clutching their
foreheads.

GREAT, KID. THAT'S JUST ABSOLUTELY PLU-
PERFECTLY *GREAT!* YOU SNATCH THOSE SOCKS AGAIN
AND I'LL KILL YOU. I'LL FEED YOU TO JASMO. JASMO,
YOU WANT SOME FRESH MEAT?

Plup plup.

CLEAN THAT MESS UP OFF THE FLOOR, FOR
CHRISSAKE.

The two men were up and seemed to be all right. All of the
Blueshirts and most of the Redshirts were gathered around Bonelli,
looking at his forehead for any tragic evidence of fracture or brain
damage.

Coco lumbered over to the Kid who was trying to break into the
circle around Bonelli to see if he was all right.

"Stick your head in a All Pro's face again and you're in *bad*
trouble, boy. *Real* bad trouble." And he stalked off, legs stiff and
menacing.

QUARTER OF A MILLION BUCKS AND YOU JUST BLOW

IT LIKE THAT, SONNY. NOT TO MENTION AN ALL PRO. CAN *YOU* TAKE HIS PLACE THIS YEAR, SONNY? CAN *YOU* AVERAGE TWENTY-SIX A GAME THIS YEAR, FELLAH?

"Fellah . . . fellah . . ." the words ricocheted and echoed through the Armory gym.

"You all right, Bonelli?"

"Screw him. He wants my job."

The Blues took it in from out of bounds, and they tried the second quarter again.

Midway through, the Head smashed the seventh bullhorn of the practice session. Bonelli heard and called a timeout.

"You ain't passin off, Wop," the other guard, Smith, said.

Plup.

"Screw it."

"You tryin to play a one-man game, Peckerhead."

"Up yours, Spook."

Plup. "Watch it, Guinea-Wop."

"Up yours, too, Spade."

Plupplupplupplupplup.

"You ain't drivin," Coco yelled at the Kid, and jabbed him hard in the sternum for emphasis. "You not *help*in'" (jab jab *jab*jab) "anybody at all." Jab jab.

"I'm trying, Coco. Christ! What's everybody so badassed for today?"

"I've fed you ten times more than I *ever* feed Bonelli, and you haven't done a damned thing."

"They're not falling, Coco. What can I do?"

"Hey, man," Orville put in over the coach's head. "You're taking shots when there aren't any. I set you picks and screens till I'm about white and you don't use them. You pass off when you got a good shot, and shoot whenever that dumb, olive-brained foreign Italian Wop bastard yells 'shoot' at you."

"Why's everybody so tight-assed today?"

WE PLAY L.A. TUESDAY, LADIES. TODAY'S SATURDAY, GIRLS.

"Hell, it's just an exhibition, Orville."

"Just," screamed the Assistant. He stopped in the middle of a complex explanation of a one/three/one offense he had been working on just for today's scrimmage. *"Just?* Jussst? Keee *Rist, Fellah."*

Both teams seemed to settle down a little until halftime. Then: Blues, forty; Reds, thirty-six.

THAT'S A SWEET HIGH SCHOOL SCORE, the Head spoke gently through the eighth bullhorn of the season. VERY NICE AND SWEET.

During the half each squad went through the entire rigamarole of leaving the floor, going down to the dressing rooms, sucking oranges and oxygen, changing socks, rubbing linament into cramping calves, and listening to the coaches analyze the first half of play.

The Kid felt as though he had breathed deeply only about three times before they were up and back out on court. During the warm-up, he got a ball, shot, reached for another one coming toward him. But Coco intercepted it. And the next. Then he chased after another one, but Matson snatched it away. Thud. Thud-thud. Thudthudthud. The balls bounced all over the floor. The Kid, hands up and out a bit in front of his face, kept waiting for one of the balls to bounce his way so he could take some more practice shots, but none managed to get past his teammates.

Tootle went the whistle. Brown bumped into the Kid hard as he trotted to the bench.

During the third quarter, the Redshirts caught up with the Blues in a ragged, free-lancing, shoot-and-run twelve minutes with lots of body contact and bumping and pushing off out front as well as under the basket. Orville, at seven feet one-quarter inch, was starting to push Jasmo and out-rebound him by that extra inch and a quarter. Jasmo kept thinking about Chamberlain and Russell. Year after year it was Chamberlain and Russell. And Honorable Mention for him. He scored over Russell and held Chamberlain below his average practically every time. But it was always Honorable Mention for ole Jasmo. Even after an article in *Sports Illustrated* about him entitled, "Mr. Consistent." After Russell quit, he thought for a season there would be a chance for him, but then there was young Alcindor jack-rabbiting all over the court. And Chamberlain going on it looked like forever. And even now this second-year bull Orville hawking all over him. Russell gone and ole Jasmo getting too old to cut it. When you got to be canny because you can't be quick . . .

. . . and Bonelli. Never got to play against Cousey. Never got to play against the best guard ever in the whole world history of basketball. Cousey who was so goddam good he even faked his own teammates out of their jocks. Cousey who could fake three times from when he left the ground to when he dropped the ball in the bucket. Cousey who was so goddam good he could pass off a hundred times more than he ever shot, because he could always get a shot. Always. Cousey could get shots because Cousey always knew where the basket was. And if he had the ball, he could keep it away from anybody. *Any*body. And he could fake three men out so fast and have a shot away if he wanted, he could just pass off all day long and make a great scoring guard out of his own grandmother. Cousey who had more moves and body English than Elgin Baylor, even—which is saying plenty, because he scores more than Cousey ever did—but wasn't Cousey no matter what. Bonelli, three years All Pro, but never got to play against Cousey and show him how good he was, too. Bonelli, who never got to play *with* Cousey, either, for that matter. If he'd played with Cousey, those Jones boys for the Celtics would have warmed the benches till they rotted out from under them, because he and ole Cous . . . . Why, he'd have scored forty points a game with ole Cous, because he's about the only guard he'd ever known who could even begin to keep up— really and truly keep up—with Cousey . . . .

MOO-WONK, the buzzer sounded, and there were just twelve minutes left.

Bonelli and Smith were the first-string guards.

Jasmo was the first-string center.

Coco and Matson were the first-string forwards.

. . . last season.

Now there was the $250,000-bonus-baby rookie who averaged forty points a game for three varsity seasons in what had to be the best, take it all in all, the best basketball conference in the country. The Kid wasn't going to put Bonelli out of a job, but there were Brown and Smith. And Jasmo had had problems feeding him in time for him to get his best jump shots off. And even if the Kid had had problems with totally different styles of play when he was *with* Bonelli in a scrimmage . . . Bonelli could shoot, drive, and pass. But the Kid! The Kid could do all that and *handle* the ball, too. Really handle it. At night Bonelli had started having dreams, in which he gnashed his pretty, white teeth, because the Kid reminded him of Cousey. A little. But the Kid was six feet four inches and could leap very high in the air.

. . . and he'd put more pressure on Coco and Matson, too, because he *would* crawl around in the center and bother Jasmo. Throw him off his stride just enough, just enough to give Orville the quarter second he needed to take rebounds from Jasmo. Lots of guards were swapping as forwards now. You could never be sure.

Jasmo never got any quarter-million-dollar-bonus, either. Plupplupplup.

"Screw him."

Score: Blues 86, Reds 87. Bonelli had twenty (but only three in the third quarter); the Kid had twenty-four (with fourteen in the third quarter.)

THAT'S A LITTLE BETTER, BOYS. BUT YOU'RE PLAYING FOR JOBS, NOW.

Jasmo cast a baleful look across the floor at the Kid who had been helping Orville get all those rebounds. And the man up there yelling at him to keep his scrawny little ass out of the center. Plup.

Bonelli flexed his hand.

Andrews and the other forward, Kelly, a second-year comer, looked across the court at Matson and Coco who were looking hard back at them. Everybody breathed heavily as the whistle for the last scrimmage quarter sounded.

FOR JOBS, NOW.

Tootle!

It was good, hard, but more or less slightly roughneck basketball for eight minutes. Everybody was very careful to get his good shots, to work his best defense, to stay clear of fouls.

Then the Kid, crouching in youthful exuberance, watched a shot by Matson from deep in the corner bounce high off the rim. It seemed to go up and up forever, then come straight down very slowly. He plotted its angle of ascent, gauged its angle of descent, computed the degree of spin it was collecting, and accurately concluded where he should put himself to get the rebound. Coco— and Matson himself—were out of it, just about: Coco was screened by Kelly, and Matson was still out on the edge, apparently confused because the shot hadn't dropped for him. Orville was shut out by Jasmo. The time was propitious, the calculations precise. The ball finally hit, skittered, and the Kid was there reaching up with everything figured.

Except Jasmo.

Jasmo was there, too. And though not first, he came with more guns. The Kid had one hand on the ball, but Jasmo swept it away from him. The Kid twisted to avoid that awful forearm and hip as the Jas curled his body down in a short, tight, controlled arc. The Kid was quick. He made no contact. But he hadn't noticed that Jasmo *had* noticed him. He wasn't prepared for Jasmo's clear-out move. With the ball safely in the vise of his hands, Jasmo straightened and swung his body from the hips up, his elbows out like scythes looking for a field to clear. He got the Kid on his first sweep to the right, but missed Orville—who knew what was bound to come—by a good three inches on the sweep to the left. Even as Orville was blocking Jasmo's clear-out pass, the Kid was crumpling to the deck like the Big Max the second time Mr. Louis met him in the ring. Down and out. Coocooville.

Tootle.

Jasmo's elbow was as big as a child's head.

Tootletootle!

CHRIST.

Slowly the Kid rolled over on his face. Then he stopped moving. Then he rolled over on his back and stopped moving again.

His nose probably was not broken, his teeth most likely not cracked off. But his lips were shredded and his teeth were loosened plenty and bleeding at the gumline, and his nose looked like a mushy beet.

IS HE ALIVE?

Coco peered down at him.

"Jesus, Jas," he said.

"Your elbow okay?" the Blueshirt's coach asked.

Jasmo screwed up his mouth in pain.

"Take a few shots, Jas, and make sure that elbow's okay."

A QUARTER A MILLION dollars

". . . dollars." The Head Coach was down on the floor by the time the Kid managed to push himself up to a sitting position. The trainer took the smelling salts away and covered the Kid's face with an ice bag.

Jasmo muttered that the Kid had the hardest face he'd ever knocked into. "You sure it wasn't his head?"

"Nah," Bonelli answered. They passed a ball back and forth to each other. "He'd be dead now if it was his head."

The Kid got up in stages: first to his knees for a while, then finally to his feet. The head kept pawing at the ice bag trying to get it down from his face, but the Kid and the trainer kept putting it back up.

"I wanna *talk* to him," the Head fussed.

The trainer nodded to the side of the Kid's head. "He's got a ear over there," he reminded.

"I tole you and *tole* you," the Head screamed in one of the ears. "When you got a Jasmo in the center, leave him to Coco and Orville. Right?"

The Kid nodded.

"If it's Alcindor, you leave him to Jasmo and Coco. Right?"

The Kid nodded.

"If it's Chamberlain, you leave him to Jasmo and Coco. Right?"

"Yah, yah," the Kid said. He took the ice bag off for a second. "Yah. All right. All right!"

"Well don't you go getting prima donna with me," the Head

screamed at the Kid who had covered his face with the ice pack again.

"Murmwrmur," the Kid said.

"What?"

He took the ice bag from his face again.

"I said I'm just trying to play this damn game, is all," the Kid snapped. Still, there was more confusion and hurt in his voice than violence.

AWRIGHT, THEN. THEN PLAY!

They played another two minutes. Ragged. Very ragged. The bullhorn never once stopped. The assistant coaches from the side-lines never let up. The players were punishing each other merci-lessly. The body contact for a minute and a half was brutal. Smith held on to Brown who was trying to dribble. Then Coco had the ball. Trying for a hook shot with his right hand, he shoved off with his left by sticking his fist in Kelly's throat. And Jasmo finally pinned one of Orville's arms to his side while Orville whammed and whammed with his other elbow trying to find the Jas's head.

The Head was back down from the stands bullhorning every step of the way to the scorer's bench where three sub-assistants had finally quit trying to keep stat sheets on the players.

"Screw him," Bonelli kept muttering when he could draw the breath. His legs stayed under him only because he refused to col-lapse on them. You don't run All Pro's off the floor, his training and his pride kept telling his legs. "Screw the son of a bitch."

"Screwhimscrewhimscrewhimscrewhim*screw*him," he shrieked as the Kid finally drove past him. Hard. And leaped fourteen feet from the basket, heading to it like an electronic homing rocket after a bomber.

Bonelli reached out and grabbed at the Kid and got a death grip on his shorts. The Kid was driving so hard he literally pulled him-self out of the pants as he leaped, legs still pumping, knees flailing as he soared first through Kelly who hit the deck to get out of the way, and then through Jasmo who tried to, but wasn't quick enough and was knocked, finally, clean off the apron and into the seats where he looked like the come-back Louis after Marciano was through with him.

44

JEE SUS GOOD GODDAM CHRIST . . .

. . . and the Head was on the floor storming toward the Kid through the carnage: Bonelli—stretched out face down with a pair of men's shorts in his hand; Kelly—lying very quietly on his back, breathing very hard, and looking whiter than ever; Jasmo—managing to right himself, his eyes wide, his mouth hanging slack as he crawled slowly on his hands and knees back to the playing floor. And the Kid himself had miraculously landed on his feet, sunk down to his ankles, and sprung back up.

"You by-God . . . ," the Head stormed. His eyes bulged, the veins in his neck and at his temples looked as though they would explode in a paroxysm of . . .

"Can't you do anything right? Look at *that:* All Pro. And *that:* Honorable Mention for eight years in a row. And *that* . . ."

But the Kid had reached down and taken off his athletic supporter, so he was clad only in sneakers covered by his fallen socks, and his red jersey. He held his jock strap under the Head's nose.

"You want that, too?" he screamed. "You want this, too?" he repeated half a dozen times. Suddenly he wheeled and flung the strap toward the basket. It sailed awkwardly in a none-the-less neat arc and fell on the rim, then nicely through the net. Everyone saw it. Then everyone looked at the Kid, and even though they saw tears pouring from his eyes, they heard something else: a giggle. He choked on it slightly and half coughed it out, but it was clearly a giggle.

He giggled again. Jasmo had finally gotten his breath and his footing in time to see the young man—looking terribly vulnerable and young—standing in the middle of the basketball court with his prick hanging long and limp. And it occurred to him that the Kid's cock looked a bit like he felt. He giggled at that, pulled his jersey off, and threw it at the basket too. But missed. Then Coco had a sneaker off. He charged at a hobble and dunked it with a great whoop of joy.

The next thing anyone knew, there were shirts and jocks, socks and sneakers, bandages, tape, wrist and forehead sweatbands flying through the air. And there on the basketball court of the Armory were thirteen grown men, buck naked, playing with basketballs. It was much like the warm-up periods before games and second halfs. Except there were great grins and smiles now. The air was swept with the bodies of men: black thighs, brown butts, white calves, arms, backs, bull-like necks. Sweeping, pirouetting, cavorting: a veritable ballet of motion and grace, of preen and— once again—real style, of cock-a-doodle-do and cakewalk and Delta Shuffle on the bounce and pass rhythm of the game with the solid thump-a-thump beat of the balls on the floor. No one played against the other. It was pass and feed, hand off and assist, jump and shoot, drive and dunk. It was approval in dozens of smiles and nods and loving pats of flesh on flesh . . .

At the other end of the court, lined across it like football referees at the ready for the pre-game-toss-of-the-coin-introductions, were the coaches and assistants and trainers. They stared. In the doorway behind them was the assistant equipment manager, toothpick rocking slowly in the wet corner of his mouth. He also stared.

. . . and as suddenly as it had started, it stopped. It was as though a *tootle* had sounded in their heads all at once. They left the floor, quietly joshing, gently chatting with each other, a calmness of civility permeating every sure step of their feet. In the locker room they showered, shaved, dressed, combed their hair neatly, pulled their ties into place deftly, and left.

Back on the court, the coaches broke rank slightly to stand, hands still behind their backs, to mill about aimlessly while the Head, one hand covering his face at the scorer's desk, shook from the sobs no one was blaming him for. The sub-assistant equipment manager quietly make the rounds to pick up the spent uniforms— the odd sneaker in the stands, the blood-flecked elbow pad under a bench. The Head sat at the scorer's table a very long time. Very long.

Tuesday they opened their exhibition season against the Lakers in L.A. The Kid scored twenty-two. Not bad, as they say, for openers. And they hung in to take Los Angeles by three in the last two minutes. The Los Angeles sports writers, looking a bit stunned and confused, kept shaking their heads after the game was over and the out-of-town writers were filing their stories.

"They looked psyched," one of the locals braved. "All night long they looked psyched," as he riffled back through his game notes with awe.

A Fan of the Game

• • Dear Henry,
I would call you "Hank" except I think that it might be too much
of a liberty, and God knows there is too much liberty loose in the
World today as it is already without me. But by the time you read
this you will probably already have received a million letters and
telegrams from all over the world at least saying you're one in a
million and congratulations for breaking Babe Ruth's home run
record that stood for thirty-nine years. And when he did it nobody
knew or very much cared anyway, and they sure didn't put a bust of
him outside Yankee Stadium that afternoon either, with maps of
the country and balloons and people singing the Star Spangled
Banner and all. But you did it even with all that hoop-la-la and it
was beautiful, too, even if I didn't get to call you from Washington,
DC, that night and get to say so like some people I could name who
have a habit of calling up Sports Stars like yourself. I never got
invited to anybody's college football locker room after a game, either, like some people I could still name. Yet I am a loyal fan of
yours anyway, Henry, and I thought you ought to know.

48

But that isn't why I am writing you this letter, exactly, because a lot of things have changed since the "Bambino" clouted his now second-best record out way back then when I was just a kid in my third year. And my wife doesn't understand why I would bother writing you a letter about anything anyway, since she doesn't understand Sports or Stars or Fans either one, which is a source of some friction between us in an otherwise very fine marriage with no more than the usual ups and downs which you certainly know about, so there's no need my saying anything further.

But I am writing you because after you hit ole Number Seven One Five, the Braves announcer said that in years to come people will ask, "Where were you on the night of April 8, 1974?" and went on to say with a laugh that about 500,000 people will claim they were there in Atlanta stadium with you and Pearl Bailey and Sammy Davis Junior and Bowie Kuhn's *representative* (about which there is no need for me to embellish since what's done is facts) and all the rest, when there weren't but 53,775 people there. Officially, at least, but even that can't get stretched into a half a million since there aren't but 51,383 seating capacity in Atlanta anyway and it was Standing Room Only that night.

Anyway, when he asked that question with a laugh in his voice I could have cried if I had still been a kid like I was with Ruth. Because if you look very carefully at the beginning of this letter you will see that it was written at a quarter after nine. Your big Number Seven One Five was officially clocked at 9:07. Get it? And just so you'll know, Henry, on that spectacular Night of Nights for you and for all *real* baseball fans, I was in the kitchen putting away the clean dishes out of the dishwasher and then scrubbing up the dirty ones after supper to put in. I thought I would be helpful, if you know what I mean.

Understand, I don't blame my wife. It's just that some things are important to me that she doesn't care all that much about. And vice versa, to be fair about it. Vice versa. She's got her own little TV set which she keeps in the bedroom where she goes after supper lots of times to read the magazines she buys, and there she watches the TV with warm water in a hot-water bottle around her neck and reading. I don't like the thing myself, actually. I never have, either. I'm still a Child of the Radio, I guess you could say. Like you, because you and I are the same age, Henry, although actually I think I am a year your senior.

But I was very tempted on that Great Night of yours to watch it, because I listened to your 500th, Henry, and I heard your 600th, too. And so you see, I have been keeping up as much as I could. And even if we are the same age, give a year, you have to admit that you have done more in your lifetime so far than have I. Or probably will, I have to be honest and admit. After all, I don't get to call George Allen and tell him what plays to use against Joe Namath. And what would have been the chances of a phone call from me getting put through to you on that Glorious Night? We both know the answer to that one, Henry. But all is not lost, because I don't have to live in Washington, either. And he does, which is his problem.

I even hinted to my wife about sharing the TV that night, but though I love her very much and am as devoted to her as the Lone Ranger and Tonto ever were to law and order, she sometimes doesn't catch hints too well. Of course I have to admit I lots of times have handed her a lot of stuff about the TV and it being a Boob-Toob and all like that. Still, she never got the message that I would really like to have watched the game that night. Not all the ceremonies at the beginning, understand. Deserve it all as you did—and much much more besides—still, I am a Fan of the Game. Like I hate halftimes at football. And I had to laugh because Downing was really an American league pitcher, and he's the one that served up ole Number Seven One Five to you. And your first swing of the night. I mean I was glad they put on the Dog for you and all, but you have to remember who Ruth was playing for that sad day in May when he hung up his bat because he couldn't help his team any more. He was a Brave like you, Henry. So much for the Yankees and the American League. Which, I grant is a little unfair, a little unfair. But being a Fan of the Game I was glad in myself that you got the Biggie off a Yankee now with Los Angeles. I may not have made it in baseball myself, Henry, but my faith as a Fan runs very deep when allowed to be.

But I was making this pot of tea and missed it after the dishes.

I would have been heart broken if I had been a kid. It was like Durocher going to the Giants way back when. And more than that, even, when Brooklyn moved to L.A. So I'm glad you broke the record book over their heads, I must say, even if New York isn't fit to live in any more. But you can see the point is my heart is with the National League, and being a NL Fan from out of the past in *Brooklyn* Dodgers days and—can you believe it?—*Boston* Braves days, you can understand my disappointment even if Marilyn didn't. I mean what happened was they both left for the Coast leaving us with nothing but the American League and then what do they do but make up a new team to take their place which everybody cheered because they kept losing. Why couldn't they have stayed where they were and made up the new team on the Coast? I can't explain it.

"Why?" she asked me once. "Why do you shut yourself up in a room with that box of static and listen to a voice telling you something you could watch on television, even? If you need to do that sort of thing."

Like it was dirty, listening to the radio, you know? Anyway I tried to explain that I liked the radio and besides the TV baseball is only on weekends.

"What do you want it, every day?" she said.

"Sure," I said. "As a matter of fact it *is* every day, nearly. A hundred and sixty-two games. More if you're in a playoff or a Series." To which she just looks away with a very obvious shake of her head which she thinks looks knowing. But what does she know? I mean she thinks it's kinky because I like tea instead of coffee. She actually said once it was the same thing as being un-American at breakfast. "What do you know?" I said back quick as pie. "You don't even like baseball which is *the* All American Game." And she's this kind: real sneaky she says, "Pro football's had bigger crowds *and* gates the last few years than baseball," and quotes a lot of garbage out of the *World Almanac* or God knows what. What's she know? And the radio, too. I tell her you can always get a game on the radio. Not like the television where all there is is dum-dum so-called comedies and jerks on quiz shows. Who needs that? Besides, the TV's only weekends and Mondays. And you can never get the color right anyway. All orange grass and green sky and you look actually green or pink, Henry. Like you're sick or something. It's awful. And it's so loud. And public. And a radio you can listen to and still read *Sports Illustrated* or *Playboy* or something. And you can turn it down and still hear it, see? And when you turn it down, you can see Ebbets Field—which strange to say I never went to—or Yankee Stadium again. Only they have long since destroyed Ebbets Field after those bums went to Los Angeles. Snyder never was the same after that. And it nearly killed Campy. And Furillo retired and Jackie got to be an old man even if he was back home. And Big Newk wouldn't fly. And old Gil Hodges dead now. No, Henry, it's all changed since we were kids. It's just not the same any more.

Like tea. I like tea better than coffee. Don't ask me why. Maybe because my great grandmother was Irish or something like that and her daughter-in-law was a Russian or something. But coffee gives me the jitters and tea keeps me calm like the Big Night I missed your home run because Marilyn was in bed and I was in the kitchen even after I told her I was listening to see if they played—tornadoes or not, rain or not. And of course they did, which I knew they would because that's how the National League always was. Scrappy, you know?

But I was calm because I drank tea. Very disappointed, of course, with Marilyn in the bed with her warm-water bottle going gurgle-gurgle behind her ears all night long. But calm. I didn't even get upset until way later when I found out she wasn't even looking at the tube. She was reading *Playgirl* magazine if you can imagine. And she's my age if anything. You'd think she would know better than that. And she never said a word to me, Henry. That's what hurt so bad. I heard the 500th and the 600th and the 713th too, for that matter. So this was just another home run in a way. If you want to look at it like that, I mean. I mean, I don't tell her not to read *Playgirl*. Or *Cosmopolitan* either, for that matter. So why does she have to hassle me about the baseball games? See what I mean?

Not that it's all that big a thing, really. She can be as liberated as she wants, right? As a matter of fact it's never even come up in our house, because Marilyn has lived a pretty liberated life with me all along. And that's been over half my life now, since I was twenty when I got married and then right overseas, but luckily to Europe instead of Korea which may be why I am alive and able to write you this Fan Letter now at all. But she could never understand what I saw in Austria where I served my time in the Army honorably. And even when I tried to tell her about how pretty it was with the snow on the mountains and how the coal they used smelled so different and so good and about the fields with the cows she just said, "So you got the Catskills in February with snow. What's the big deal?" Of course that was way back when I first got out and was starting to settle in to my job and all. Back when we still lived up there which thank God we don't any more.

But I never raised my voice when she talked like that, and I finally quit trying to explain. I don't know. Maybe like with baseball she just wasn't interested. But I let it be, because I like to think that I understand that people are different and because I am a Sports Fan doesn't mean she should be too. After all, she has been a faithful wife as I have been a husband, and she has been a wonderful mother to our child who is grown and who is in college now. But I must say that I was glad for the tea which helped me to stay calm, because I felt betrayed when I finally understood her to say she couldn't get anything on the TV but some old ball game and, Henry, she must have known how I would like to have seen it. That Game of All Games, as it turned out. But not only did she not even offer, she didn't even do the dishes after supper.

What happened was I listened to all the first and third innings—and had to laugh in the first when you got walked because everybody booed which just went to show me what I already could have told you which is that too many of those so-called fans aren't really Fans of the Game like me since they don't understand how those things work and they left after you hit the Big One anyway. Anyhow, since Lum was the last out in the third, it followed as night the day even to a jerk that you would be up second in the fourth. Right? Unless you slipped a disk getting out of the dugout or all that rain went straight to water on your poor knees. So I figured L.A. had a minimum three guys after the commercials, then more commercials, and then Evans would be up and then you. Plenty of time to make a small pot of tea, right? Right. But not when the dishes were there to be done. Oh I could have left them. But you know me. Mr. Clean himself. Mr Paint-up-Clean-up-Fix-up himself. So I put up the clean dishes from yesterday and then scrape and rinse and load the dirty ones from today.

But don't blame Marilyn, Henry. Because the truth of the matter is I should have put the hot water on to boil when I first went into the kitchen. Then it would have been ready to pour and I could have gone back in and probably even heard the ball one pitch to you. But I can't stand a mess and I forgot. I have to admit that. I just plain forgot to start my tea first thing. I even asked Marilyn did she want a cup, because she likes a cup sometimes at night. Don't ask me to explain my wife, Henry. I can't. I can not, for instance, explain to you why it is all right for her to have a cup of tea sometimes at night when she's got that damned water bottle tied around her neck while she's looking at pictures of naked men with her in bed, but it is kinky for me to want tea most times when my Grandmother was Russian. I don't complain, you understand. It's just one of those many things that "Surpasseth Understanding," as the Good Book puts it.

Which I mention only because from everything I have read you are a good man, but I don't think that living the life you have led you would be too offended at my single use of a profane word like I just did. I mean, I would imagine that you would have heard far worse from Tarzan or Selassie from the old Ethiopian Clowns days when you first broke into baseball, only I guess they were the Indianapolis Clowns by the time you got there. But she never even mentioned that she had turned off the game. Not even when I took her her cup of tea which delayed me even more getting back to the radio. Later when she told me—we were in bed, me trying to get to sleep, but her gabbing like women will—I could have cried if I had been a kid. Like I did that day on Stink Field.

But I was a kid then, and besides, I didn't cry because I had fallen into Stink Creek like everybody thought, but because I didn't catch that ball that that crumb hit to the opposite field. A lefthander like him and a loudmouth, too. We were just a bunch

54

of kids in the neighborhood and played on Stink Field which was no big deal, but like you must have done lots of times in Mobile. And over a little hill from that field was Mt. Vernon and a bunch of tough kids who'd come over sometimes and tough around, you know?

But there was this creek. It really had been one to start, only it was practically a very slow-moving garbage dump by the time I was playing over there. And we called it Stink Creek. That was its name and so the field was Stink Field. And that's where a lot of the neighborhood kids played their games in summer. And Stink Creek was out in left field where I played, but it ran pretty much away from the field after that. So it was only the left fielders who really had to worry much about it. Which was me. I also batted fourth on our team because once I hit a triple out over everybody at the high school field and it would have been a home run except I never played shortstop like you and wasn't what you could call the speediest guy in town. But like you, Henry, if I once got ahold of the ball, don't look for it to come down any time soon, because it was off on a trip.

Anyway there was this kid named Louie Maraschino with the big mouth who was so dumb he couldn't say anything but, "Babe Ruth," or, "Bambino," which I personally doubted he even knew what it meant he was so dumb, and he smoked just like he thought he was the only kid who ever did, or "King of Swat," and trash like that. And he was big. Not only for his age, which I have to admit he was, but I also had good reason to suspect that he'd been held back from sixth grade at least twice. I mean we had to borrow a few from out, but that was OK, because they used to live in our neighborhood. And we hadn't lost more than five games in the fifteen we had played.

I swear to God, Henry, we used to play two games in the morning and another in the afternoon. And none of that slapsy-dapsy Babe Ruth League or Little League junk, either. I mean we didn't always have nine guys on a side, but we just changed things if we had to. Like we'd have it two bases. Or the pitcher'd pitch for both sides. Or the catcher catch both teams. Who cared? We were playing baseball, you know? And we still had a core of a team. And we hadn't lost more than five games, because we had to get in as many as we could before half the kids were sent up to the Y camps and day camps and stuff to have fun. So we had what you might call a pretty good win streak going, see? And we were pretty proud of it. Oh, it wasn't anything like DiMag's fifty-six game hitting streak or anything super like that. It was just us kids, right? But we had our pride, too. Just like you have had yours coming up from the Newark Eagles and hitting such great home runs on what I guess you would have to call two opening days. But I never did get on too well with that kid.

I suppose I was sort of scared of him, too. You know how kids are about other kids sometimes. Well, he liked to think he was so great because he was an Italian loudmouth and because Ruth was called "Bambino." And he hit left handed, too. So he thought he was pretty great, which he wasn't except that I have to give credit, he got lots of hits and probably had more extra bases than any kid in town. Still, I was playing deep and nearly in center field because he really usually laced them over the bag at first, and on Stink Field they'd roll clear to the fence that kept us off the Parkway. And he was a third baseman and had made two really lucky plays on me that day. Sure hits and extra bases one of them, except he gets lucky. Honestly. One save was out of sight. I'd hit the stitches off it and in a desperation grab he leaps . . . and look what he finds in the webbing of his mitt? You guessed it. And he tosses the ball around the horn shaking his own head the whole time because he knew he should have wiped it off before he put it back into play, he was that lucky. And the second time was the same thing, because he was laying back for me, only I got a topper he has to charge like crazy. And if I'd been what you might call a less hefty kid I'd have beat it out, too.

Still, I had him played where I thought he was able to hit it, only when he finally got the bat off his big fat shoulder, it headed out to me. Only I wasn't there, remember, where I normally am, but was pulled way over like any left fielder would have done against a leftie.

I took off. I knew it was going to go a long way, but I took off after it just like I had a chance, which all along I knew I didn't, because unlike you, Henry, I was never what the sports writers like to call a skinny kid all the time. But I went after it. And do you know what? I got my glove on it, Henry. I knew this: that if he homered, we lost the game, and if I could catch the ball—or even knock it down and keep two of them from scoring, we'd beat them. Because it had to be a home run, see? And I got my glove on it. I guess I should have been glad to get that much since being slow and playing him way over where I was supposed to, there really wasn't any chance at all anyway. And I am still proud of what I did manage to do, as you can no doubt tell. That I have to admit, even though I am not usually a brag. But at the same time all I knew was that it scooted off my glove and the next thing I knew it and I both were head first into the muck of Stink Creek.

So I fell into the ditch and cried because it was a home run that beat us and also because it was hit in my field by a fat lip who couldn't talk about anything except "The House that Ruth Built." Well, I guess you never built any houses, Henry, but that's not your fault, because for one thing I'll bet you grew up knowing more about Satchel Paige or some of those guys than you did about Ruth. Right? But for another they kept changing everything, and even when you got to be a Brave it was Milwaukee instead of Boston where they started and should have stayed, if anyone was to ask me. But Ruth didn't stay with the Yankees like you stayed with the Braves, Henry. And like me to Marilyn and her to me, faithfulness does mean something yet, especially the way clubs treat players and maybe it's all business like they say and it doesn't matter anyhow.

Which is why real fans have always liked you and Ruth and Ted Williams, because they don't always get much reason to keep on liking the teams. At least to this Fan it does mean something, as I hope you can tell. And see? They change things and then it's all different. Nobody hardly calls them the Dodgers any more. Or the Giants much, either. It's *L.A.* and *San Francisco* by now. Not "Dem Bums" any more like they were to the whole world when I played on Stink Field. We didn't even have any warning track there, either. You just had to *know*. You had to *feel* it coming up on you if you were chasing a deep one. Everybody laughed because I fell in,

57

but the reason I went on and didn't stop wasn't because I didn't know where the edge of the Creek was. Because I knew better than anybody, almost. It was to save the win and because I didn't want to get whipped by that Yankee lover. Not if there was any way on God's green earth I could have had a play on that ball. I never fell in before that, and I never fell in after, either. And I played there lots both times.

But they've got it all fenced in and covered over now, and it doesn't stink like it did, which probably is a good thing take it on balance, I guess. But they've got tennis courts all over now and Hurricane Fencing all around and everything. I mean, there's no chances any more. And the kids never get to play with only two bases or have Big John Jim catch both teams if the other guys are short one. That's why I like the radio, because you can squinch your eyes a little when you listen, and when the announcer is saying, "It's going . . . going . . . gone!" why you can pretend a little, you know? Or when he says, "The left fielder is going back . . . back . . . back . . . . He leaps up and grabs it, Fans. What a beautiful play! He just took a sure home run away from . . . ." Well, you know. From whoever it was. Louie Maraschino, I guess. But you can look away from the radio, is the thing, and still see the play. On the TV you got to keep looking at what's really happening right there on the screen. But with the radio you don't have to look at that at all. You can look out the window at the house next door, or at the grass that probably needs cutting if you're like me, or at whatever there is out there, and it can be *you* for a minute. It can be you going back . . . back . . . back . . . . And still knowing right where that stinking ditch is every inch of the way, because you know every clump of sneezeweed under your feet. Every clump, Henry, and you dare it anyhow. Going back . . . and back. And if you go in, you've dared it, at least, and taken a chance with it at least. And they can't take that away from me ever, Henry. Even if I cried or not, because I'm not a brag, and I know why I cried.

But not with the Boob-Toob. And much as I love her, I don't think Marilyn will ever understand that, Henry. But you probably know that already. And I was just a fat kid till I got my growth.

Well, please forgive me for taking up so much of your time,

Henry, since you have been swell to have read all this so far, as well, I have no doubt, as lots of other stuff from people who are famous like Sammy Davis Junior and all like them. But I had to write you my congratulations too, because I am a Fan even if Marilyn doesn't understand any of that, and what's the use of Fans if they don't ever let you know. Right? You Bet! And because I played ball too, and you must know how I feel.

So I am very truly yours,
A FAN

P.S. Would you believe? I nearly forgot. I also missed Number 714. Five years I waited. Five years I knew you would do it. Not Ted Williams and Joe DiMaggio who were both so great even if they were in the wrong League—at least for me. Not Mickey Mantle whose legs couldn't stand it. Not Willy Mays who was also so good. Not Berra who always killed us with those line shots into the lower right field stands just when we thought maybe the boys from Flatbush would do it *this* year. Not even Jackie Robinson. But you. Five years I waited for those two days, because I knew you were going to do it when not even the Braves had it figured yet. That's faith, if you want to know. And I blew it. Just like I blew the catch on the home run with the ball and me both stuck head first into Stink Creek so long ago. I don't blame Marilyn, but that's why on the eighth day of April in nineteen hundred and seventy four at nine-o-nine in the evening I would have cried if I had been a kid, just like I did that day on Stink Field.

Again, yours very truly,
a fan.

Lovers

• • "Later," Robbie said in the dining hall. He never even looked up at his friends. He was eating his second steak slowly, chewing it thoroughly. "I'll be down a little later." Chewing, tasting the juices from the meat, and now eyeing the platter of avocado sections set out on bibb lettuce, the whole succulent in the simple beading juice of fresh lemons. Ressie had brought it to him. Special. She had promised him something special for senior day. The other boys, also seniors on the football team, were up and through; ready for their day off, their day in town, their whoopee round and about; shuffling their feet; cracking their knuckles; and waiting for Robbie.

But Ressie, dumpy and thick-handed, stood right behind him patting him on the back. It was the day underclassmen look forward to for two or three or four years: special town permission for the graduating seniors. From noon on Friday, until midnight. Whoop-ee. They were free to come or go as they chose. Understanding, nevertheless, that the academy's rules of conduct still applied to them. Even so, it was a benevolence of the institution. And even if it was an anachronism from the time of the academy's founding fathers, still those venerables had understood the compulsion toward and even the necessity for a certain ordering of the self, a certain preparation on one's own for what was to follow.

"Split ends, boys," one of them said. He shook his head sadly back and forth. "They're just born loners." They laughed and were gone to town knowing that Robbie would meet them or not, cross their paths or not. *You* came to Robbie, usually. After so long it was something you understood and accepted: it was *his* presence that graced *you*. Robbie. Who actually figured it would end up being a pretty boring day. He stopped chewing and said, "Where'd you get them, Ressie? They're beautiful."

"Nemmine, you. Jes eat." She patted him again, then as he poised his fork over the plate, tenderly cut, lifted, and ate the soft flesh of the fruit, she ran her hands over his back in the old and familiar gesture. He closed his eyes as her touch worked into his muscles.

"Ressie gonna miss her baby," she crooned to the back of his head.

He turned part way and gave her a half smile. "Ressie, I'm going to die of hunger when I graduate and leave you."

"Um hmmm," she said.

Dumpy and thick-handed, a small wart on her right cheek. Bosomy in her stiff white serving uniform, tough with all the boys in the athletic food line at the academy. But loved them all, she always said. Loved them all.

Especially Robbie.

And crowned—for the years he had known her, had been pampered and fed by her—crowned by a glistening black wig with great sweeping curls that could never have been Ressie's.

Half turned, half smiled at her: black and stiff, the wig; white and stiff, the serving uniform; ashy looking, her legs under the white stockings. He turned back to his food and let her touch him. Four years it had been. Now he would be gone. Ressie would find another pet to spoil and overfeed.

She was gone, then, back to her work. He paused in his chewing for a moment as the slightly sourish odors of the kitchen swirled about his head before they left, sucked into the train of her parting.

Bathed and full, ebullient with the deep spring of the Shenandoah Valley, he strode down the steep hill from the academy to town. He inhaled fully: aroma of apple blossoms and girls in their summer dresses; heat of days and freshness of nights. Newly eighteen, strong, self-proud male cub ready for immortality to clutch him to her bosom.

He laughed aloud.

He had made it, after all. He had made it from the class dumb-dumb to a B-plus/A-minus student; he had made it from special sections for the overweight and posture-poor, to a six-foot-two-inch-one-hundred-and-ninety-pound model of physical fitness; he had made it from the sad shake of the jayvee coach's head his freshman year not only to the varsity's first string, but to the All-Prep League's first string as well; and he had made it from little boy to boy-man.

No wonder, then, the long collars of his wildly patterned shirt flopping against his chest in perfect time with his hair flopping against his forehead as he strode down the hill; his trousers flaring brightly; his knotted tie—fist big—the same material as his shirt. No wonder, then, that bouncing aura of Joseph swept about him, ran before, trailed after.

Favored, he was. Not the biggest of the boys. Maybe not even the best, but the fairest of them all. Favored. The one who stood up at the line of scrimmage in his coach's resurrection of the Lonesome End. Stood while the others bent their backs to each other readying for their primal charges: plated, armored, lacking only tusks, it sometimes seemed. Stood, Robbie did, away from them and remote, his hands resting almost casually on his hips, looking almost disinterestedly down the line to wait for the snap of the ball that turned him loose, set him against the defenders who had no way to overcome his moves: his fakes, feints, leaps, and dodges all looking choreographed and rehearsed for a coaching film on how it's supposed to be done. Further: not only looked it, but did it, too; caught more passes in one season, gained more yards, scored more touchdowns.

And knew what he wanted on that day of senior freedom. A circuit, mainly. A tour of the places where it had all happened. A quick glance at himself in the mirror of his past.

Downtown: There was Chris's, the Greek restaurant with the good Italian food and the beautiful daughters; there was Hogshead's Drug Store with the best soda and the best peanuts-in-the-shell in town; there was the Newsshack which carried a full range of magazines, but making its money on the ones filled with pictures of G-strung, big-tittied girls hunching the arms of sofas and sticking their asses and tongues out enticingly toward the readers; and there were the three movie houses: one for the Gs and PGs, one for the PGs and Rs, and one for the Rs and Xs. There was more, of course. But the life of most of the boys at the academy on the hill filtered and flowed, spun itself through and around those places.

First to the Newsshack. Robbie glanced at *Time* and *Newsweek,* flipped through *Esquire,* then spent a little time with *Playboy* before getting on back to the girlies. Mostly a reminiscence with him. Since Rose, he hadn't needed the girlies so much, but he smiled to recall how little it had all changed. There he had been four years earlier, had found the shelf as they had all found the shelf, had homed in on it as they all had. He grinned, Robbie. It was there four years earlier—the baby fat on his cheeks a-quiver, his soft hands a-tremble, the fire in his loins beginning to burn— that an upperclassman had frogged him on his arm and, leering, said, "No rats allowed downtown with hard-ons, fellah."

He had looked down, and there it plainly was. Worse, it had been oozing as well. The stain in his trousers. A mere spot, but so clearly there on his light tan pants. And no rain coat. Not even a jacket to take off and drape, as though casually, across his arm. He had bought a newspaper instead. But not even the embarrassment of having been seen could counteract the visions of giant boobs and thick, kinky triangles of hair: it throbbed all the way back up the hill to his room where it went off before he could drag his soiled undershorts from his hide.

Robbie still felt the prickle. Rose or no Rose these last two years, the prickle was never far. No matter how cool (as he tightened his sphincter and belly muscles looking at the girlies one after the other, casually, calmly), no matter how detached, he knew the prickle was always there, ready.

The movie started at two-thirty, the last house to hold to a weekday matinee as a regular thing. Robbie had planned to go regardless of what it was, but hoped it might be pretty raunchy. Still, it really didn't matter. Rose was out of town, after all. Up to Washington—"D.C., the nation's capital," she had told him with a perfectly straight face—on a Greyhound bus with the rest of her class taking their senior trip. That left Robbie stranded in town with permission and nothing much to do. Wishing now that Rose was there with him. Knowing that probably she was going to get planked by one of the local swains in sight of the Capitol or behind Mr. Lincoln or in Mr. Washington's smokehouse at Mt. Vernon or in some other exotic place with her gum going *snicker-snack* as she made up riddles to while away old grunting time until the action got to fuck-ee fuck-ee, as she always put it.

He paid for his ticket and went to the candy counter. Behind it was Zella, a friend of Rose's, several years older. Pneumatic, he thought.

"How much for the kisses today, Zella?"

She jiggled at him, smiling. She knew him, all right. "Nickle each," she answered, inhaling as she shook her head to make her hair swirl for him in the dim lobby.

He leaned forward over the counter as though to look more closely at the wrapped sweets. Then slowly he raised his face to look deeply into her eyes.

"I don't mean the chocolate ones, Zella." Deep and husky-throated.

She jounced out a hip and looked away from him, the flesh of her breasts shimmering in the dull light.

"Dirty thing," she said, and crossed her arms. Which made her breasts shimmer even more.

He pointed to the chocolate-covered peanuts.

"Them, Zella," laughing.

"Sixty cents, Robbie."

He held the three quarters in the palm of his hand. She trailed her long fingers across it to get them.

Clink into the coin tray, and smoothly the nickel and dime were pressed back into his palm.

"Tsktsktsktsktsk," he rapidly chided her. "And your best friend out of town, too. Shameful temptation. Shameful."

She stuck her tongue out at him quickly. And smiled.

Then into the cave of seats.

It was an R chiller-thriller with lots of tittie lusted after by blood-sucking plants—a gooey liquid dripping from extensile, swelling stamens—whose blossoms pulsed their way toward the jugulars of their victims. Prime meat for quick releases to the late-late shows across TV land.

Robbie ate his chocolate-covered Goobers and watched. And thought of Rose.

The year before—the fall of his junior year—he had reached his growth, and he had thought: *I am sixteen and a virgin.* So he let a friend introduce him to Rose, a girl in the local high school. She was delighted. As was Robbie.

On their first date they had supper at Chris's, then went to the town park for a walk. Robbie was primed to make as much idle chatter as necessary, but none was needed. Rose took care of all that. And between her barrage of chatter and the *snickersnack* of her Ju-Ju-Fruit chewing gum, there was little Robbie needed to do but hold her hand. It was unending, her stream of words. Usually it was about TV programs she had seen the night before—or the week or the month or the year. It was all a giant, never-ending TV show to Rose: the plot summaries, the descriptions, the constant backing and filling in of information about the characters in the series; the casting ahead and the looping back to catch up, surround, and enclose every possible, every imaginable detail that had flickered into her life from the tube. Robbie walked amazed at her, amazed that the first night until she touched him, put her hand between his legs to feel him, he had hardly noticed it—stuck in amid her recapitulations—when she said, "You got a hard-on yet, Robbie?"

But it didn't matter that he couldn't stutter an answer, because she had found that he did.

"Ooooh," she squealed in a tone as canned as the enthusiasm projected by the actors on one of her beloved Alka-Seltzer commercials. She led him over to a swing, one of those with double seats facing each other across a short platform. They sat on the same side, and Rose took his hand to her breast and began rubbing it for him.

"Do yourself a faaavor," she said.

Snickersnack.

And kissed him juicily on his cheek. Then down with his hand to feel between her legs.

Snicker. Snickersnack.

"Tryyy it, you'll liiike it." Again giggling.

Then before Robbie quite knew what had happened, she had mounted him across his lap, had him out of his pants and into hers almost before he could even offer to help, and was saying, "Know why a beggar wears a very short coat?"

"Uh . . . uh . . . ," he tried to respond. "Uh . . ."

"Because it'll be long enough before he gets another. Get it?"

"Uh . . . uh . . ."

"Oooooh! Fuck-ee fuck-ee fuck-ee," she whispered very heavily in his ear as she hugged him tight. "Ooh, aaah," she finished.

And was off. Leaving Robbie feeling rather like a raped flagpole.

Though more pleasurable, subsequent nights with Rose were never significantly different. Only the riddles. Robbie didn't bother to keep an accurate count, but he strongly sensed that she had never asked the same one twice.

Once, it was way out past the academy in a thick grove of woods and underbrush. ("When did the lamp stand? When it heard the gas pipe. Get it?") And on several occasions it was on academy property itself. ("What key will never open a door? A DON-key. Get it?") But more often, it was in or near the park. ("When is a pen knife very noisy? When it won't shut up. Get it?") And during the winter months there had been a number of times in a car Rose was able to borrow from sources she never chose to disclose. But more often they used Zella's little walk-up fire trap of an apartment—just a room and a bath on the second floor of a shabby house in town. That was the most convenient place. Zella worked the candy counter at night, and the owners of the house apparently stayed transfixed before the tube, which was more than loud enough to cover any noise from Robbie and Rose upstairs. And there was a private staircase—a set of metal steps that acted as a fire escape as much as anything else—on the outside of the house.

But no matter where it was, it was always the same: riddles and *snickersnack* until time for him to come, and then she grabbed him with both hands tightly clutching his rounded, football-toughened rump and squealing *fuck-ee fuck-ee fuck-ee.* Until he was through. Then it was *oooh, aaah.*

And done with.

She obviously had a home, and it obviously had a TV set. But Robbie never saw either. He couldn't get to town more than once a week during season, and never more than twice a week the rest of the year. And there were always dates with girls at the local Southern Institute for Young Gentle Ladies—still the official name for the girls' finishing school nearby. He and Rose always met somewhere in town. It had been a lovely two years for Robbie.

And every Saturday night it had been, "Feed me good, Ressie, I'm heading for town."

"Um hmmm," she'd say, her wig shining black, perched like a hooded hawk ready to be set loose.

"Um hmmm," without her usual banter. Watching him, seeing him grow up, big, strong. Boy-man.

"Um hmmm." Knowing.

"Um hmmm."

"That all you got to say, Ressie?" a boy in the line asked once.

A forced smile from one side of her face. A cutting of her eyes at him. Silence.

And Robbie had just laughed, scooting his tray on down the line, taking great gobs of food. Robbie had just laughed.

She would be home, then, Ressie. After the evening meal was served, after her cleanup on the line, she could go home: a bedroom, a front room with the stove in it, a bathroom. Living by herself now. Ever since her daughter got married. Three years.

Home where she took off her wig. She would shake her head and run her fingers through her hair. Then after stripping from her uniform, a bath: a quick shower to get clean, then a long soak for the water to wash over her smooth thighs, her belly, her breasts. Then out and into her nightclothes. By then it would be nine o'clock, usually. And she had to be up the next morning by half past five to be back on the line by half past six to make sure everything was right for their breakfasts. The boys ate at seven.

Saving the best for last: the brushing. She would sit at the little table in her bedroom and flip the switch that turned on the lights rimming the three-glassed mirror just like the backstage dressing room mirrors in theaters in movies. She had gotten it for Christmas once. Long back. A long time back. Wallace had given it to her before he went to Korea that spring. And she would look at herself as she brushed her hair straight back. Head-on, three-quarter right, three-quarter left. Brushing and brushing and brushing her hair back. It was black and white now, her grandson said. Not gray, but black and white. She brushed it and looked at herself: her skin, her missing front tooth, the full swell of breast beneath her pajama top as she brushed her hair back. Not kinky hair so much. Rather straighter. Indian? A slightly almond look about the eyes. Brushing, brushing. A puffiness showing at the bottom of her cheeks. The gaining sag to her face. She would smile and stare at the gap in her teeth. Smile hard, staring at the gap, her cheeks, her eyes. Brushing, brushing.

From the time she was nearly eleven she had bled each month, and from the time she was nearly fifteen she had bled each month, and two weeks later would tonk for two or three nights. Beer, usually. Maybe a little gin. But a lot of dancing. A lot more dancing than drinking. With Wallace, usually. Nearly always with Wallace who seldom saw very much of her during the rest of the month, seldom took her out or home either one. And when she was pushing seventeen, a daughter. Then Wallace lived with her most of the time until he got drafted and went to Korea. Then came back to her once during basic training. Then again after basic and before going down to Kentucky to learn how to operate radios. And then before he went overseas. The night before he left, he hit her in the face and knocked her tooth out. He hit her again, and one side of her face was partially paralyzed. She wouldn't let him sleep with her.

"I'm goin' away tomorrow," he'd said. "I'm goin' to Korea, woman!"

Didn't matter. She'd crossed her legs.

"You crazy, woman?"

Didn't matter so long as he didn't kill her, which he wouldn't, or hurt her baby, which he wouldn't.

"What the hell's wrong with you? What the hell do you want, woman?"

Don't know. Nothin'. Don't know.

He grabbed her up from the bed.

"Woman!"

"Nothin'."

He hit her and knocked her to the floor.

"Woman!"

She shook her head and spat blood.

He yanked her to her feet.

"What the hell's wrong with you?"

"Nothin'."

He hit her again.

When she came to, he was cradling her head in his lap, his hands shaking as he wiped her face with a cold, wet towel. His voice cracked and trembled. Sweat poured from his face. He looked very handsome to her, the beads of sweat draining into his thick mustache, his eyes blinking, his hands on her, trembling.

"What you want, woman? What you *want*!"

"Don't know, don't know." Her head lolling away so she wouldn't look at him.

When the war was over he never came back to Stannings, Virginia. She didn't think he was dead. She never heard that he was. But he never came back.

69

So she kept her legs crossed and raised her daughter.

Brushing, brushing every night before the little dressing room mirror he had given her, watching herself.

Watching her daughter grow. Doing what she could for her. As much as she was able to, there. Watching her grow, marry. Watching the child grow.

Watching herself in the mirror rimmed with lights. Brushing, brushing.

And then Robbie came.

Saw her in yellow with a small child in tow, her hair loose down on her neck, loose and graying and only somewhat kinky, her dress full-skirted and clinging around her thighs and belly as she faced the occasional wind gusts of spring. Ressie, with slender, silver earrings tinkling in her ears like fairy bells in the wind.

Her dress yellow but not flashy or shiny, not shimmering or golden either, but mellow and still bright, bright and complementing the color and texture of her skin, each setting off the other, and both set off by the little boy hopping and prancing in her shadow. Robbie looked down at him, then back up at Ressie planted squarely before him, her legs slightly apart, her head back.

"Hey, Ressie. I hardly knew you."

She smiled, her lips still mostly covering the gap in her teeth.

"Oh yes," she said, her voice gentle on him as always. "You seen me lots of times before without looking." She laughed as he blushed.

"Oh? Well, uh, I'll be." He looked at the child by her. "Gosh, Ressie. Is he, uh . . ."

"Naw. He ain't mine," and she closed her eyes in a full laugh. "Nawsuh. He my gran'son." With love and pride as she flicked a hand through his hair and brushed lint from one of the shoulder straps of the boy's navy blue suit.

"Grandson?"

"Um hmmm." She stared up at him, her lips slightly pursed but curling up at the corners as she watched him struggling with himself to ask her. Or not to.

"I didn't know you had grandchildren, Ressie," he finally said.

Then, with a stab at late tact, "You look too young," and he grinned largely. And yet, his cheeks quivering from the strain of his smile, as soon as he said it, it seemed to be so.

She eyed him, the curls at the edges of her lips gone now, the smile set, her eyes on him, measuring him.

"Um hmmm," she muttered very softly. "Um hmmm." She lifted her hand to his cheek and rubbed her fingers across it ever so softly. "You blushin', Robbie," almost crooning.

He tried to keep his smile, but couldn't. She saw and looked away, down at the boy, his knees locked, one hand balled into a fist in her skirt.

"My daughter nineteen," she said down at the boy. "Just like me when she were *his* age."

"How old is he, Ressie?" Robbie looked down at the boy.

"He three."

"Hi there."

Robbie put out his hand to the child. "Hey," he said softly. "Hey there, little one."

The child kept his hold on Ressie's skirt, but stared back at the large white man, stared with curiosity.

"Arnol', can you say 'Hey'?"

"Hey," Arnold said quietly to Robbie who had squatted to get face to face with him. They shook hands very solemnly. Robbie grinned and looked up at Ressie, then back down to the child. A handsome child. He saw Ressie in his face, and her features seen so clearly now, startled him.

"Ressie," he murmured, and ran a finger across the boy's forehead and down the soft, child's curve and gulley of the nose. Then, "Ressie," he murmured again, and still with his single forefinger traced a line across the boy's upper lip.

It tickled.

And lightly across the faint down on the brown cheek.

It tickled a smile from Arnold.

"Ressie," he said again. He turned his head from the boy toward Ressie, but didn't look up for a minute. He quite simply stared at her. His head was level with her belly. He stared at her, at the full curve of her stomach under the dress, that swell running down to the fork of her legs. He stared, able to see the outline of her panties when the wind gusted and blew her skirt tight to her. Saw and knew the lace on the edges, knew the smooth, the feel of them.

He got quickly to his feet and stared down into her face.

"You shakin', Robbie," she said, and patted his shoulder as she would have done in the dining hall.

He trembled, thinking he might even fall, glad it was getting murky with the setting sun so she would not be able to see him clearly. He crossed his hands in front of himself so she would not be able to see him.

"Squatting so long," he said. "My legs have gotten weak, like. You know?"

"Um hmmm." She never looked down at his hands.

"Guess I was too glad not to be having spring practice this year." He laughed, his lips set in a smile.

"Um hmmm," and still she looked in his face, not down to his hands. She reached up and wiped his forehead with her fingertips.

"You catch a chill," she said, and held her hand out for him to see the sweat.

"Ressie," he managed to say. "Ressie . . ." His face twitched.

"Come along," she said, and turned to go. "We got to get you on home, Arnol'." She walked away slowly with the child, walking toward the edge of the park, away from the main section of town. Robbie had never been past the wooded stand at the edge of the park. But now he was able to see a few houses scattered almost helter-skelter as the hill leaned lazily up and away from the small plain of the park. Robbie walked after her, just as slowly. No hurry. She was in no great hurry. She let the boy play along the way as they got nearer to the end of the park, closer to the scatter of houses hunkering near the unpaved street that meandered like a stream all around back in through there, like a stream more than like a real road or street, like an almost natural thing. He recognized the woods. He had known them well enough at night.

Then they stopped. Ressie turned. "She live right down there," and pointed to a path that led around and down past a deserted shack and out of sight. "My daughter."

They walked another few feet. Robbie was just able to make out the details of the scene, just able to know the path was there. Then it was gone in the heavier settling of darkness. They walked another few feet. Robbie stood, his hands no longer crossed, but still before him as though he were readying himself for a boxing stance.

"And I lives right there," she raised her arm and pointed to a little house faced with asbestos brick, the roof over the small front stoop at a slight angle.

"Run along, Arnol'," she said.

The boy dashed away and down the path. It was almost dark. Robbie stood very still thinking: *Go on. Go on back, now.* Ressie didn't move until she heard him whoop from down the path signaling that he was home and safe. Then she shifted her body. She was some six yards from Robbie. He thought he saw her tilt her head toward him. He heard her voice. He heard what she said even though he never saw her mouth work, never knew that such softness could carry so.

"Gon home, now."

He heard her say that, saw her move, then, and start slowly toward her little house, dark in the quickening night.

His hand accidentally touched himself. A glancing touch was all. But he understood, then. And followed until he was at the single step up to her stoop. It was empty. Ressie was inside, and he thought he could see the faint glow of yellow from deep inside the dark house. Then she was standing in the open door, but still just inside.

"Robbie," he thought he heard her voice. The yellow withdrew, fell back, disappeared. He put one foot on the step, sure he had heard her speak his name. *Robbie.* And he lifted himself up. On the stoop.

"Ressie," he whispered. *Ressie.* He stepped the short way to the door, stood under the lintel: poised, balanced, ready to step back, back and away, or to go in. Depending.

Ressie. The name.

Robbie. The name and the whisper just the same. All one. All together.

He was before her: tall, broad, young, hard. She put her hands gently at his hips: trembling, he was. She could feel it in her

73

fingertips, clear up through herself. She moved closer still, then, her left hand easing around his waist, her right arm going up, her hand resting easily on the nape of his neck. She stood on tiptoe and was able to pull him down so her mouth was on his throat under his ear. She knew him, then, could feel him hard against her, trembling, starting to circle her waist with his thick, powerful arms; starting to pull into her, trembling, his hands still held away, only his arms starting to tighten and enfold. Whimpering, trembling. She felt him, her hands on the skin of his back, the skin and hairs of his neck, her lips to his throat and ear. Trembling, ready. But only his arms, his hips trembling, still. Still withholding his hands from her. Holding back. Still holding back.

Robbie Robbie Robbie

She opened her eyes in the dark of his throat, tears coming now.

"Robbie," she whispered against him, pulling with her hands, pushing hard against him with her body. "Robbie."

But it was all too much for him, this love she offered. Too much. And all he could hear screaming in his head, echoing round and round and round was Rose's FUCK-ee FUCK-ee FUCK-ee . . . echoing, echoing, echoing . . . Oh FUCK-ee. Oh fuck-ee fuck-ee . . .

He forced himself from her, held her away for a second, trying to see through the dark; waiting, almost, to know before he turned and was through the door running—running toward the park, running back to school, running for home. Running from Ressie and the other dark, imponderable gods of his soul.

She followed as far as the sill of her door, but stopped there, leaning against it, her cheeks wet.

"Robbie," she whispered after him. "Oh, Robbie. Oh, Robbie," her hands against her ears holding quiet the once tinkling earrings. Just for a minute. Then she turned back inside, back into her own echoes.

What you want, woman? What you want?

Drowning

• • And again he awoke in an atmosphere thick with the darkness of the early morning. He lay quietly, waiting for the heaviness and darkness to dissipate enough for him to engage his mind in his own thoughts. Those moments were touchy, when he would first wake up with it—his mind—functioning along as it wished, slushing through the dense green life it had assumed for itself. . . .

He waited until the wake of his mind fanned away, until the sea on which it rode evaporated and he could—yet again—lie still and quiet in his own bed listening to the very real breathing of his wife as she stubbornly clung to her last half hour of sleep. Her breathing: so deep, each breath so assured of being followed by another, and it in its turn, and it . . . . No end to that. No end at all.

. . . not like *him.*

And again he wanted his wife to sleep forever. That was what he thought in the mornings. It was the only thing he could think at first. And then he wished his students would not be, that he did not have, eventually, to get up from his bed to endure the looks, the mundane daily process of preparing his teeth, his kidneys, his hairs for the gazes of *them,* those outside his house.

. . . not that their gazes were any worse than those he must suffer from his wife and his children.

75

These were the thoughts that came each morning as he awoke earlier and earlier—almost deliberately so as to have more time to think them, to get his mind back up into the tissue of his brain where, inside his skull, he could exert some influence on it.

But so regular, those exercise thoughts, as regular as the expansion and contraction of her lungs. As regular as that breathing of hers—and his, and everybody else's: unwilled, unpremeditated, painless, thoughtless, and spontaneous.

Breathing.

. . . not like *him,* the lanky black man who would not breathe, whose wiry musculature failed for no good reason to do what it should so naturally and rhythmically do: pull in air, push out air; inhale life, exhale waste.

His wife's breathing pattern was interrupted. She wriggled onto her back and licked wetly at her lips as sleep slowly, quietly fell from her. She turned her head toward him, her eyelids starting to drift open. It was time, once again, for people to be waking, arising, strolling, or screaming through another day.

. . . but not *him,* the dirty bastard. Not that black athlete who went thirty feet down and wouldn't breathe again.

. . . not him.

The general din of the classroom chatter ebbed slowly to silence as he called the roll carefully, tediously pronouncing each name as though it would be the last time human ears ever would hear the word or hear of the student. They answered each in his turn: loudly, softly, affixed by a 'sir,' surly, comically, with a 'present,' or flatly. That done at last, he drew a sheet of paper from his text book.

"All right. If you will take out a piece of paper and a pen . . ."

The groans from the class were muted by now, the increasing number of pop quizzes coming to be expected and even accepted as a part of this teacher's methodology; but the groans remained only partly because of the pressure of QUIZ.

Satisfied that all notes were well concealed, he asked the first question, a simple matter-of-fact question about their poetry assignment for the day. After a pause, he repeated the question slowly, making certain they had plenty of time to write their answers down.

Then a second question, it too repeated with adequate time for answers. Then a third question, and on until he had asked ten. After they were finished, he repeated the entire list, gave the students another three minutes to make any changes or corrections desired, and asked them to pass in their answers. By the time he snapped a rubber band around the thin packet of folded answer sheets, twenty minutes had elapsed.

Originally, his quizzes had been short-answer questions, but that had left too much time in the period, so he had begun to require that all their answers be in complete sentences. Then he wanted to make certain they couldn't complain about not having enough time to answer, so he repeated each question—as well as the entire list. But that still left him thirty minutes of class time to fill up.

It wasn't always so bad. He sometimes could read a number of poems to them, or he could pass the quizzes back, giving each person's paper to someone else and have them graded in class. Or he could start asking questions of his duller students, questions he knew they would be unable to answer very readily. Or he could let them out five minutes early, or even ten if he didn't do it too often. But whatever he did, he did it to fill up time so that he wouldn't have to talk to them, wouldn't have to look into their eyes or into their faces.

But always there were days when the quiz device didn't work, and then he would have to lecture, to actually speak to them. On those days he spoke as rapidly as possible, as loudly as he could short of screaming. On those occasions he got so wound up that he could barely stop: sound was what he came to need then, noise and activity, anything. But the more he fed himself, the more he needed, so the less good it did him.

His class had finished grading the quizzes and had passed them back in to him so he could record the grades in his roll book. He carefully studied his watch, then, counted slowly and precisely the number of minutes remaining until the bell would sound, shattering the fragile little fifty-minute worlds humming and thriving, spinning or falling, up and down the hallway. He held his watch in his hand four minutes, transfixed by the precise jerk of the second hand as it minced its tiny way around and around as though it were trying to work up enough speed to sweep and whorl the air enclosed under the crystal down into a vortex of time spinning furiously, growing larger and larger until everything and everybody would be caught in it.

When the bell clanged in the hall, the class departed in order, and he was left to hurry, during a free hour, to the Student Union to drink a cup of coffee and smoke a cigarette, his watch ticking steadily in his pocket: carefully, obediently, precisely adding second after second to the unrecoverable past.

He poured the sloshed coffee back into his cup, then carefully folded a napkin into a square and placed it on the saucer to soak up the remaining liquid. He drank several sips quickly before lighting a cigarette, then let the cup sit to cool.

The Union was not full—he would leave before the ten o'clock press—so he was able to sit at a small table by himself. He looked around cautiously, hoping he wouldn't catch the eye of any colleagues or students, but he did see two or three of *them*, the boy's friends. One lurched to his feet from the booth they were sitting in and went to the juke box to continue the bellow of soul music screeching from the machine. The boy returned to his seat where he was passed the sports section, now almost a wad of ink and newsprint struggling to look like a newspaper, but closer to its previous form of pulp.

He found himself staring intently at the boys and was made aware of it only because his cigarette had burned down to his fingers. He dropped the remnant to the floor and gulped at his coffee which had cooled so much it was almost undrinkable. He looked down at its surface undulating gently under his touch, and it seemed oily and splotched like unhealthy skin, black skin . . .

The boy was a first-string defensive back. He was tall, rangy, quick, hard-hitting. He was good. And he tried other things, too. Fencing. And he was good at that. Or intramural softball. Or track. Or baseball. He had been all-state batting champion two years running in high school. A natural athlete, a natural competitor (as the sports writers said later). But he couldn't swim.

One fine day in late spring, another year nearly gone and only one more season ahead to work for a pro tryout, he went for a walk with half a dozen friends around the nearby manmade lake stretching like an amoeba for thirty miles: scene of family fun, camping, picnicking, boating, fishing. And swimming. They were tired and wanted something to drink and eat from the concession stand. To walk there they would have to have followed a big crook in the lake for a mile and a half. But if they crossed the lake, the little eighty foot neck of calm water in front of them, they would only have to go about a third of a mile. In they went, all but the natural, the one boy who couldn't swim at all. He stood on shore taking the ribbing from his pals who were splashing along, already about half way across. He looked up the trail that patiently wandered with the lake's edge. He felt his clothes sticking to him from the sweat of his hike. He looked at the deep, cool water roiled only by the capers of his friends, now two-thirds of the way across. He listened to their taunts.

"I can't swim, though," he said just loudly enough for his voice to carry to them.

"What?" they yelled back.

"I can't swim," he shouted, admitting his failure—not publicly, not from the roof tops, but where it hurt most—privately to his friends.

"Who can?" they joshed back at him, and the first one walked up out of the water on the other side as the others clowned, cooled by the calm, deep water.

His feet were hot, and the hike around the trail would make him late for his Coke, and it would hold them up. Besides, he was a natural athlete . . .

"Chicken," they finally called, as eventually they had to.

79

. . . and a natural competitor.

He looked at the water: so deep, so calm, so heavy. But no tides, no waves, no currents; nothing but eighty feet, just twenty-seven yards. Hell, man, he could run that far in three seconds. With the pads on. And in just two more he could slide off a blocker, get an angle, and bring a man down. Hard. Hell, this was nothing.

But it was water, and he couldn't swim.

It was only because of adrenalin pumped through him by his fear that he got as far as he did before he had to gasp for help. But his buddies were out and waiting. In the middle he stopped his frantic paddling and called again. His friends stood on the shore and cheered. *Hooray, hooray. Help, help.*

"Help me," he yelled, but it was swallowed, forced back down his throat by the calm water, tasting very faintly of engine oil.

Hooray. Oh, Daddy, hep me, hep me, they sang from the shore as their friend waved his arms in violent protest against the cooling water.

Then a scream they would never forget, a scream that finally pierced their teases and hoopla, a scream that shattered their safety on the shore forever:

"Save me!"

So he dove into the water just after the head went under. He must have asked a question of them. He must have said, "Can't he swim?" And one of them must have answered, "No, he cannot swim," because he vaguely remembered something like that passing between them.

He heard the shouting from the concession stand, and being finished there and on his way anyhow, he had come up behind them, quietly watching the boys whoop it up. He recognized them as students he had often seen in the Union, lolling around playing bridge, gin rummy, or sweet-talking their women. But he heard the call for help and was frightened by it. So when he came up close and saw the boy beg for the last time to have his life, saw the stunned, slack-jawed expressions slowly pull the blood down from his friends' faces, he had his shoes and khakis off and was at the spot, it seemed, before the shock of water had slowed him down. He looked quickly back to shore to get his bearings, then dove.

Down he went, looking left, then right, circling in quick darts. Then up again to blow for air, a lot of air, because he had seen him. Then down again.

The boy was going straight down, his long arms stretched out, his elbows and knees bent, his hands fixed like the claws of an eagle setting itself to light on a tor. He scooted after the form, got directly above him, and grabbed for hair. But he couldn't get a hold. He tried a second time, but pulled his hand back as one of the claws shot up to grab for the touch from above. A third time he tried to get the hair, couldn't, got an ear instead, and was starting to pull so he could get his hands locked under the chin. But both claws suddenly were around his wrists, and he was still going down. He shook to free himself, but his ears were hurting and he was out of air. He fought again. Finally doubling himself into a ball, he brought his feet down on the boy's shoulders as hard as he could, broke the hold, and pushed for the surface.

By the time he got up, he had tasted the waters of the lake himself. He gasped for a second and was about to go down one more time, when he choked slightly on the vomit burning up through his throat. He threw up his soft drink, gulped air again, and went back down.

Down, far down, he felt the cutting pain in his ears and knew that he was lucky nothing had popped already, but below him, half reclining on the bottom, was the long shape of the boy. He was moving only as the water gently swished him.

He circled again, got behind the form, and was terrified. If he got into a fight down there they would both be lost. He saw the long arms, awkward and useless looking as they hung suspended from the body which was ever so slowly sinking into the silt. He moved in closer, terrified now by the silence. He lurched forward and got a full nelson, then tried to push up from the bottom. But the silt was too loose, and all he could do was to paddle up, paddle and know that if his air gave out he would have to let go. And then it would be too late.

There was no fighting, but his ears were popping and the pressure in his chest and throat were numbing him enough so that he was no more than a bundle of muscles and responses: his eyes were closed to the darkness, his legs were chugging automatically, and they rose closer and closer to the surface. When they reached the light and air again, the world had changed. He opened his eyes, but couldn't see. His head was throbbing so painfully and his ears were assaulted so violently with sounds that for a second he wanted to dive back down.

Then he felt hands on him and heard shouts and screams.

He finished pulling the boy from the water. He got him up onto the shore, and, still unable to speak, his chest still heaving for air, he made one of the friends get down on all fours while he tugged and pulled the gray shape across the friend's back. He pumped at the shape for all he was worth—wildly, ecstatically, maniacally. Then he got the shape flat on the sand and pushed and pumped until he was a part of the shape himself. He even flipped the boy over and tried mouth-to-mouth resuscitation. At last he lay down.

It seemed ages. His head still hurt, and the sunlight pierced his eyes like brilliantes of hot steel. At last his breathing was easier, and he heard a man's voice say, "Thank God! I thought we'd lost you both."

Eventually he was able to understand that when the rescue squad had arrived, the Negro boy was already dead, and that they had been working twenty minutes to save him. He had gotten the boy to the top himself. The boy's friends estimated that he must have been under the last time for four minutes: not bad, someone in the gathered crowd had allowed, for a prof who wasn't in particularly good shape.

For a while the tragedy of the drowning was balanced nicely by the heroism of the teacher who had tried to save him. But the world had changed that last time. When he had finally broken surface with the dead man locked to him, he had pictured himself settling into the soft quietness of the silt, his limbs floating this way and that without effort, without reason. He even saw each finger, each segment disassociated from the joints, his whole body kept together only by his skin. So for the next several weeks on campus, the awed stares and admiringly pointed fingers kept giving way to the euphoric picture of himself dangling fluidly, half floating, half reclining in the precious silence of the eternally soft, yielding, and undemanding bed of the lake.

Dinner that night went off well enough in spite of his having forgotten that he was supposed to go out. So he and his wife arrived a little late, though not late enough to cause dinner to be delayed. Including themselves and their hosts, there were five couples— just enough so that there was plenty of conversation without his having to take any real part in it.

"How," his host asked him shortly after dinner when they had all seated themselves in the living room. "How is that article you were blocking out coming along?"

He looked at the man for a moment, his face still loosely set in a companionable sort of way. He was answering, he knew, to a man who was close enough to the department chairman to do him good or harm, and he knew further that this man seldom had people from the department over for dinner without reasons best known to himself.

"Well," he heard himself begin to reply. He was not full, for he had eaten relatively little, and the effects of the single, quick bourbon before dinner were all gone. But the room seemed stuffy and he felt gorged.

"I wasn't," he continued blandly, "blocking out an article." He paused to see if anything would happen. As he expected, nothing did. "I had said I wanted to see if there was anything there worth writing about." A second time he paused while watching the flabby smile of his host twitch ever so slightly at the cheeks from staying locked too long in a forced position.

"I don't see much point in trying to write up something that doesn't really make any difference. Do you?"

"Oh," his host answered. "I thought you'd said you were actually ready to start in on the writing. I must have misunderstood. Of course it *was* a good while back. But," he exhaled wetly and comfortably with the presence of a man who no longer had to cadge or curry, "I'm pleased that you're still working around to something."

He smiled broadly at the pudgy face of his host, fully aware of the veiled reprimand to get to work if he ever expected promotion and advancement. The conversation then veered sharply away from him as he had planned, and he was pleased that it was even easier than repeating pop quiz questions to his classes.

'How is my article?' he repeated silently, sliding inch by inch down into the quietness of himself.

How was what he had wanted to know, too: the initial question, the final question he had asked himself and them until the little circle of its phrasing had been completed.

It had not raised itself, precisely, at the first cool splash into the water. Then, it had been vague and formless, like the body at the bottom of the lake. It was not until after he had known who it was that it began pulling itself together as something to be asked. Then, it was eddying deep in the crinkles of his brain, the wonder that a man so physically gifted could sink away so quickly.

For a time he had mulled it over silently, and later mused aloud to his wife that it was a peculiar little irony of life that the physical man should die performing (attempting to perform) a physical feat. He even had discussed this facet of the affair with the boy's friends sitting around a big booth table in the Student Union. They agreed at first, then talked the matter over, then agreed at last that yes, it was a kind of fitting irony, the way he died; they were all agreeing, after several weeks, that Housman was right about his athlete after all: that their friend had died a sort of proper death, really.

And it helped some.

But the answer was never totally satisfactory, because it dealt with fact, not cause; so that question *How?* remained.

"How," he finally asked, only after several weeks had passed and a perverse rapport had been established. "How could he have just gone down like that?"

"I guess he just panicked," one of them responded automatically.

"Panicked? But how could a big old boy like that panic? I mean, does it make sense to you?"

"No," the answer slowly floated back. "Not panic, exactly. Just for a second, you know? More like, well, like . . ."

After the impotent gestures of the hands in the air were finished, he broke silence.

"Like what?"

"Well, I mean, he *did* go in, you know? And that seems pretty . . . pretty *courageous* to me."

It was then he understood a little, but not enough to leave off. He sensed a shifting of things, but put it out of his mind. After all, these were now his friends: he sat with them, talked with them, had even had them all out to dinner once.

The word *courageous* drifted across his ear once again. Not *brave,* a term more likely to be heard from their lips, not *gutsy,* an even more likely word. But *courageous.*

"Courageous?" he questioned, then smiled as he looked down at the brown stained paper napkin under his cup of coffee. "Well, gutsy, maybe. But not courageous, surely."

With that, the artificial bonds between them began snapping. He had been around too long, now. He was not one of them, really. He was a teacher, an adult, an outsider to their way of swinging. A nice enough guy, and gee, we appreciate what he tried to do and all, but . . .

. . . he realized later, he was putting their dead friend down. He was telling them that their friend—now enshrined as a legitimate portion of campus folk myth—was closer to being foolhardy than heroic. Worse, that he had gotten sucked in on the oldest head fake in the world: *Chicken,* they had cried, then stood watching him charge head first and legs churning, only to be double-teamed out of the game for good.

Too, they were young, younger by twelve years or so than he, and more resilient, more capable of forgetting. But with his greater maturity, he puzzled to himself, by then sitting alone at a small table in the Union, why couldn't he maintain a more philosophical attitude? Was it the boy's foolhardiness, he asked himself, that kept after him and after him? He moved into the contemplation of it all, asking the questions of himself, examining himself.

Until even his wife told him to hush up about it.

"My God! The boy's been dead for three months and you nearly drowned trying to fish him out. That's all there is. If you keep on this way they'll think your brain got waterlogged on the bottom."

After that conversation he had his first consciously sleepless night. He had smiled to her, told her she was right, of course, but she shouldn't be so short with him. He was, after all, a minor philosopher, being an English teacher and all that, and his work was contemplative more than active. They kissed, she apologized, they went to bed, and he lay quietly awake able at last to conclude things for himself.

Chiefly: how the boy could be flawed enough to sink was not important. He was sorry he had injured the boy's friends about that, but it probably was just as well—even right, because he had had to work through that erroneous position to find the true flaw in his situation which was, naturally, his own failure. He was thankful to the boy, in a way, for through him he had been shown something about himself, something important for him to know, something he might never have learned otherwise. Still, he hated the man for dying. His wife was right: he did get waterlogged down there, never did come up. In a very important way he was still down there, because the picture of himself settling into the soft quietness of the silt was not only with him, but clearer and more immediate each week. It was his vision, his insight into his true self: disjointed, disassociated, reasonless. More: it was what he wanted.

But though it was pure vision, it was, like the visions of all prophets, unattainable. He wanted very much to have saved the black man, but had he succeeded, he would not have had the vision of himself. So when he kissed those cold pink lips, the mouth-to-mouth resuscitation, he sealed the unthought of, unasked for, unknowable bargain for knowledge: he knew himself, he knew death.

What had he wanted in life? Fame and fortune, of course, as

does everyone. With him: whatever fame and fortune comes to scholar-teachers.

What were the possibilities now with three years in the University, one minor publication, and a middlin'-sized article seeping slowly through his mind? Approaching zero. And what could he do with the knowledge for which he had almost died to obtain? Nothing.

How is the article coming along? Badly, thank you, but it will be done by the end of my fourth year by which time I will accept a generous and gracious letter of recommendation from my esteemed colleague and chairman of the department to a smallish school somewhere in the East where I will spend the rest of my life silently and secretly doing what I must do. Knowing what I am, yet I must wage war against myself. I must not die.

He smiled quietly.

"You look like the cat that ate the canary." It was the voice of the host, the smile on his face making him look uncomfortable, suspicious.

"The cat has many lives, and I have many secrets."

They went through their bedtime ritual and turned out the lights. He yawned loudly as his wife snuggled down into her pillow. He waited patiently, so very patiently as he had learned to do, until he heard her deep breathing, felt the bedclothes moving ever so slightly with each of her breaths until he was convinced she was asleep.

Then he started to work. In his head he wrote articles, stories, jingles, poems; he addressed the faculty senate, the student government, and the literary club; he recited the Bible and Shakespeare:

The multitudinous seas incarnadine,
Making the green one red.

He chuckled softly. They are not incarnadine. Not even very green, except near the top. They are brown, very very brown. And they are calm and still, very quiet and beautiful.

He stirred himself. Tying himself to his mast of wakefulness, he listened to the rythmic flow of air in and out, in and out of his wife. He no longer cared whether she slept forever or not. It didn't matter any more. *He* did—the black man—and that was enough.

No. He could never go down there again, no matter how much . . .

No. Better not to think of that. Better to stay awake and go blind in the sun.

Downstairs he heard the grandfather clock ticking strongly, not like the frustrated vortex of his pocket watch, but steadily, implacably measuring out the infinity of time, and demanding of him eternal wakefulness as the price for his knowledge of his involvement in death.

The Phone Call

• • "Don't you think we *ought* to call them, Ferris?" She stood near the phone awkwardly, like a little girl.

Ferris looked up from his chair where he was finishing a cup of coffee before going over to the store.

"Naw," he answered quite deliberately. "Naw, I don't think we *ought* to call them."

Sharon shifted her two-year-old to the other hip and took a step away from the phone. "It sure would be nice for them, though."

"*Nice,*" he echoed almost testily without looking up.

"Well." She trailed off and took another step away from the phone so he wouldn't think she wanted it too badly. "Well, it sure would be nice. I mean, the way they put us up for the night and all. You know?"

She got red in the face as she realized how insistent she must be sounding to him.

"Well, then," Ferris said, and for half a minute that's all he said as he watched Sharon shift from one foot to the other, just like their boy caught with a chore undone. "Sharon, there's lots of things would be *nice.*"

She nodded her head slightly as he turned back to his coffee. She understood that that was the end of that: they would not call her

89

half sister Sarah June and her husband Jack. They would not call to thank them for putting the four of them up. They had taken a vacation—the first one since their marriage—had driven to the Smokies for three nights of camping out, and on their way back they had swung down through Moses, Mississippi, where they had both been raised. She had gotten to stay with her sister only because even Ferris couldn't turn down the call to *family*. Once. But he couldn't stand Alabama—or Alabamians, either. So that one visit was most likely going to be the extent of it all, unless Sarah June and Jack came up here to Arkansas, which wasn't very likely. She had to admit that. And she *had* thanked them for the night in their house with the letter mailed before they got out of Huntsville the next day. And that was that. But she'd had such a good time . . .

She wanted to see more of her sister.

She jiggled Missy on her hip.

"I know you didn't get on too well with Jack," she said.

Ferris finished the last of his coffee. "That's right," he said. "Didn't like him much." He got up and stepped into the kitchen.

"I figured," she said. "Uh, how come, Ferris?" She followed him and watched as he washed his hands in the sink.

"Oh," he shrugged, "I don't know. He thinks because he played football at Alabama he's special." He dried his hands on a tea towel.

"Well, though, he's a principal of the elementary school now. Got his M.A. in education while he was coaching at the high school."

"Um," Ferris said. "I know. He told me all about it."

"Oh. Well, I sure did enjoy Sarah June, though."

Ferris stopped at the front door. "Him I didn't like. Her I *dis*liked."

"Well," she said, "I sure did feel . . . oh, real close to her, and I'm sure sorry you didn't like him better. He seemed real nice to me."

"He is, I reckon. Except he's one of those guys who thinks that football's about the only way a boy can learn anything."

"Ah." She shifted Missy.

"And when I said I thought a boy could learn discipline and honor and fidelity to high principles from reading a history book well or by learning how to use the periodic charts in a chemistry lab as well as by playing some kid games, he looked even funnier— like he'd never heard anything so strange in all his life. Which from Alabama maybe he hadn't."

"Oh, Ferris."

"And then he asked about why if I felt that way I kept playing baseball, and I told him, 'One, I like to; two, I can; and three, it helps keep my belly flat.' Then he started laughing so hard I figured I didn't have any more to say to him. Which didn't seem to matter because he pretty well likes the sound of his own voice anyway. Sharon, that child isn't ever going to walk if you don't learn to get her off your hip and put her feet on the floor."

"Aw, Ferris. She's my baay-by. Oh, you want a light lunch today with your game this afternoon and all?"

"Yep."

He was out and in the car then, starting it, letting it idle as Sharon toted Missy out to say bye-bye to him.

"Sharon," he said just before he backed out the drive, "Baby, you just sometimes expect way too much out of life."

Ferris popped his fist into his mitt, flexed his calves automatically to bring himself practically to his toes, rested the outer heels of his hands on his knees, and contracted all of his muscles into knots as he watched the motion of the pitcher out of the corner of his left eye. As the arm came across and the blur of the ball headed toward the plate, he tightened up even more, was on his toes ready to leap up, dash left, fling himself right, charge forward, or backpedal. The batter started to offer at the pitch, but checked himself just in time.

"BAW CHEW!" the plate umpire roared with the rumble of a man disgusted with the pitch.

Ferris unwound and wandered in two tight little circles almost casually, checked the runner at first, caught the eyes of the second baseman and shortstop as they checked him, all of them making sure the others remembered it was D-P time with the one on and the one out. And with a one-run lead late.

Then as the pitcher started screwing his lungs and legs and arms and back and fingers into their nervous balance again, so did the others.

Count: two and one.

Batter: a bingle hitter, a sprayer, a bunter, a bad-ball hitter; the kind who'll drive you crazy all the time and beat you half the time; not much power—only two doubles during the season, the rest singles, bingles, Texas Leaguers, safe-on-errors, infield hits, and fielders' choices; wild. Can't depend on 'em.

Ferris popped his hand into his mitt.

Swing like Mantle and top the ball just like a perfect bunt so you don't have a chance to get to it.

He flexed his calves.

Give 'em nobody out and a man on first and you charge in to grab up that bunt that has to be coming, and he pops it right over your head into short left on a checked swing so you end up with one on first and one on third and *still* nobody out.

He rested his hands on his knees.

Gimme a Somebody or a Nobody, but Lord deliver me from the Anybodys.

He was on his toes and charging automatically to scoop up the bunt, look quick to see if there was a chance to cut down the head man, or to get the sure one at first if there wasn't.

Bunt he did, but foul it went.

So they had to start winding up all over again.

Register:

Count:	two and two
Field:	man on first
Outs:	one
Score:	one up on them
Inning:	top of the ninth; we get another crack if they tie or go ahead; it's all over if we can double them up right here; but hold that ace to second if

there's still a chance for the double play with
the next batter.

Special Conditions: with two strikes the bunt ought to be off.

Ferris moved back even with third. He popped his mitt, then
backed up a few more feet. The runner on first was jumping around
like he thought he was Joe Morgan. The pitcher threw very deliberately to first.

"OK," Ferris yelled out to the rest of the infield. *OK,* he talked
to himself: a lazy throw over; he'll chunk it twice more, than a
pitch, then two more times to first quick if the pitch doesn't get
anything done.

He forced himself very carefully to go through his entire routine
of readying for the pitch he knew wasn't coming so their first base
coach couldn't get tipped about a pick-off play. That had always
been the hardest thing for Ferris to learn: how to use his own tics
and habits so well that he could use them on his opponents.

The throw over. Very fast. Very good.

The runner danced around some more. Ferris watched him as
much as he dared. He was doing very well, too.

Ferris popped his mitt. The throw over. Close. Mighty close,
but the ump's arms were spread wide. SAFE.

"Ah we had him," Ferris yelled over. *OK,* to himself. Two and
two. Ferris saw enough to know that the runner was holding first
about two feet closer than he had been. Good. Two feet can be the
difference between our holding him to second or his getting to
third. Or busting up a D-P or being the front end of one.

Ferris flexed his calves. Two-two. That's the count, boys. That's
when Aaron hits 'em out. That's when they're dangerous, boys, because a pitcher wants to blast it on by them 'cause he sho don' like
to run that count out full.

There was the hesitation at the belt as the pitcher checked the
runner one last time at first. His arm came back, the runner leaped
like a jackrabbit toward second, the arm came around, and Ferris
felt himself charging the plate. Why, he really didn't know, but for
every stride the base runner took toward second, Ferris matched

him with one toward home. The ball came in—a beautiful hanging, change-up that a Nobody would have swung at before it was within six feet of the plate or a Somebody would have held up on and knocked the stitches out of. But this one had squared around with the two strikes to bunt. If he missed or fouled, he would be out. He didn't, but it popped high. Ferris dug. Again. Once more, his arm stretched out as far as he could get it and still keep his spikes digging in. The ball plopped just into the mesh between the thumb and forefinger of the mitt. Ferris squeezed ever so slightly to hold it in: too tight and it would squirt out like a watermelon seed. He came to a full halt, calmly picked the ball from the mitt, and almost casually tossed it to first base for the double play. The base runner—already at second—stood and watched the last half of the action with his hands on his hips and what in a twelve-year-old would have been tears in his eyes.

"Good game, boys," the coach called. "Let's clear off and clean up. Nice game, Ferris. Nice game."

They all patted him on his rump or his shoulders as he jogged toward the dugout. But, then, he always played nice games. For five years running he had been All-League Third Baseman, and for three of those years, he had earned the Mid-Ozark League's Golden Glove for being Best Infielder. And everyone *still* said that he should have been playing Southern Association ball—at least—for all of those years.

But Ferris didn't like to think about that.

Ferris liked to think that the best thing about these home games was that he could take off his spikes, slip into his loafers, get in his car, and drive right home. He didn't have to spend the night in some overcooled motel or drive all night to get back. And best of all, he didn't have to eat some stranger's durned lousy cooking.

Everett was in bed reading himself to sleep with his baseball rules book. Missy was asleep in her crib at the foot of Ferris and Sharon's bed. Ferris, his face showing neither amusement nor indignation, was hunkered down in his chair watching TV. His shoes were off. Sharon was in a straight chair near him, hand-stitching the fancy front of Missy's little dress.

"Everett sure was proud of you catching that ball," she said.

He turned his head slightly, but never took his eyes from the tube. "Ummm?"

"He was practicing on the batting exerciser thing you brought him from the store all morning."

"Uhmhmm."

She continued to sew while he watched the tube.

"He says he wants to grow up to be a baseball player like his daddy." She smiled warmly.

"I run a store," he said after a moment.

"Well he knows that," she replied, vaguely miffed. "But you play baseball, too."

"Oh."

"Yes, he said this morning he wants to be a real Big Leaguer." She felt the smile make her cheeks tic a little. She kept her eyes carefully on the stitching as she waited for his reply. It didn't come quite as soon as she had expected; so she thought he might not bother to catch her up on what she had said.

Very patiently, though, he did answer. "I'm not a Big League baseball player."

She nodded her head as he spoke each word.

"Oh, I know, but it's all about the same to Everett."

He turned to look at her as a Message of Interest took the place of the program.

"Well, Sharon, I reckon I ought to talk to Everett about that before church tomorrow, because it's *not* the same thing."

"Oh gracious, Ferris. All I mean is he knows you tried out for the Majors and that you play now, is all."

Ferris stared at her for a minute as she tried to compose herself, but she had looked up and lost her focus on the stitching, and when she looked back down, she couldn't see properly. She left the sewing in her chair as she went to the kitchen to get a glass of ice water. When she came back, Ferris said, "You're sure jumpy today."

She twitched her mouth and tried to smile. She shrugged.

After about ten minutes of them both watching TV, he said, "You'd gab for an hour on that phone and it would cost us a lot of money we don't have."

"We wouldn't *gab* in the first place, Ferris. And in the second place, it wouldn't have to be for anything like an hour. Probably no more than ten or fifteen minutes. If that."

"Then it's hardly worth it. Write her a letter if you have to."

"It's just not the same, Ferris. How much would it cost for a quarter of an hour. A dollar? Two?"

Ferris stirred slightly in his chair and flexed his toes inside his white socks.

"I guess."

"You mean we can't afford a couple of dollars?"

"Sharon, if we can afford a couple of dollars for that phone call, then we can afford a couple of dollars for more meat each week and a couple for butter and a couple for movies and a couple for all kinds of other things we can't afford."

"But you said the business was doing so well you almost couldn't believe it this year."

"It is."

"Well, then . . . ?"

"Sharon"—his voice was starting to get an edge to it—"I'm one of maybe a dozen merchants in this whole town who can say that. Most of them, their business is off. Money's tight again. Times are getting hard again, Sharon. This year's been good. Next year may be awful."

"But last year was good, too, you said. And the year before that. And you bought that new place out on the highway. Bigger and all." Her voice trailed off.

He sighed deeply. "You want a lesson in economics?" He bugged his eyes at her. "Ever since you've seen that woman on the trip you've been nagging me about the craziest kinds of things, Sharon."

She fiddled with her fingers, shook her head slightly, and said, "You think I can't understand an economics lesson, Ferris?"

"That's just the kind of thing I'm talking about, Sharon." He was as close to shouting as he ever came when off the field. "You've been getting very pushy since you were around her." He raised his

hands, palms up, in a gesture to include everything. "I have pro-
vided you all with decent housing, decent food, decent clothes.
And now after one night with her, you're getting dissatisfied with
practically everything that comes up. That's why I don't want you
to call that woman."

"*That woman?* She's my sister, Ferris."

"Your *half* sister."

"We had the same momma."

"That may be, but you sure weren't raised the same."

"What about the economics lesson?"

Ferris sighed. "I could buy that building because there was
enough *business* money saved up for it." He looked at her.

"Well?" she said.

"*Well?* Well what?"

"Is that all?" and she twitched her shoulders in a nervous little
shrug.

"What more do you want?"

"I don't know. What more is there? That's the shortest lesson I
ever had. I thought economics was supposed to be very complicated and all."

"It's not."

"Then how come the government pays so much money to all
those Harvard professors and things in Washington?"

"That's a waste of money, too. All you need to know, Sharon,
and all I need to know either, is that if you've got enough money in
the bank to buy something *after* you've paid off all your bills and
after you've put some in savings, *then* you can think about spending
it. The *business* had enough money to buy a new place because the
business had a firm offer on the old building *and* there was to be
enough cash coming in from selling it *and* the business had saved
twenty-five percent of the purchase price from profits *and* there was
enough cash coming in from the balance owed it so that the *business*
could afford to buy what it's bought because that would bring in an
increase in income, which will be more than the increase in notes
for the bigger place over the old one."

She was bobbing her head up and down.

"*But,*" he went on, warming to his new role as teacher, "when

97

you don't have money, you don't let yourself have stupid daydreams about how to spend it."

She waited until he was quite through.

"But Ferris"—and she touched his arm with her hand—"two dollars for a phone call?"

He looked tenderly at her as he reached over and took her hand from his arm. "I knew you wouldn't understand it, Sharon."

Tears gathered in her eyes.

"Sarah June and her brainy husband can call you, maybe. But I haven't seen them do it yet. Sarah June and her husband—who has some money from his family, don't forget—can take trips to New Orleans and Biloxi and Mobile, maybe. That's what she seemed to be talking about all the time. But there is no cause, Sharon, no *sense* in your getting tied up with people like that. Because they've got more money than we do, and because they live different from us. All that woman can do for you is make you see how much you don't have. And that's that."

"Ferris, for heaven's sake! I didn't say a thing about New Orleans or Biloxi—or Mobile either. All I'm saying is that I haven't seen my sister for over ten years, and that I wasn't around her very much before that, and that when Momma died I didn't even get to go to her funeral because I was in the hospital with Missy, and I wanted to see my only blood kin again, and I did and I liked her and I want to get to know her better because I don't have any real friends, and I don't think that *that's* such a terrible durned thing that you have to be so mean about it. Or so ugly about her. I don't, Ferris. It's mean and ugly and just plain un-Christian."

She broke into tears and, clutching her sewing, cried herself into their bedroom, hoping that church the next day would help straighten her out.

The sun shone gloriously, it was hot, the sky was blue and high: a perfect Sunday, Sharon felt. In spite of the running tiff about the phone call to Sarah June, she was in a good mood as they all got in the car to go to Sunday School. Everett began his usual complaint about his Sunday School teacher, a Mr. Seaman who owned and operated a 7-11 near the Negro section of town. Mr. Seaman smelled sweet, Everett informed them. And he lisped.

"That's his teeth, son," Ferris said.

"They're false, Everett," Sharon put in, "and we shouldn't make fun of people with afflictions. I might have to have all mine out someday, too."

Ferris looked puzzled. "Afflictions?" he murmured.

But Everett's eyes brightened. "Hey!" He remembered. "The footballers are going to be in church today."

"Oh that's right," Sharon said.

Every year near the end of summer, the high school Baptist athletes and often other members of the Fellowship of Christian Athletes witnessed at a service. This was done before the season began so that the college footballers there at the university could witness after their first two wins when the town's hopes were once again rejuvenated in anticipation of a conference championship and a national ranking.

Ferris slumped. Durn, he thought.

"What's wrong, Ferris?"

"Oh," he answered.

"Oh," Sharon said. "But you don't have to introduce them *again,* do you?"

"No," he sighed. "They asked me, but I told them I wouldn't. Just plain wouldn't."

Sharon sighed in sympathy. "Well, I guess it's nice, though. Them wanting you and all because you're an athlete, too."

Ferris gave her a stern look. "Why can't they just have a picnic for them if they want to do something nice for them?" He slowly shook his head as he pulled into the parking lot of the College Avenue Baptist Church. "And have them all at the same time. I swear to goodness I get sick hearing those boys tell how they quit smoking and drinking and whoring after they found Jesus."

Sharon's face reddened, and she glanced quickly back at Everett and Missy. "Ferris, shhhh."

"Well, I do. And they always ask me to do it." He slammed the driver's door after making sure the other doors were locked.

"That's because you're an athlete and run The Sport Shop."

As they got to the entrance of the Sunday School building, Everett dashed off with a group of his friends, and Sharon held Missy by the hand, ready to take her to the nursery.

Ferris stopped her with his fingers on her shoulder. "I'm *not* an athlete, Sharon. I like to play baseball is all, and I'd have thought everybody would have finally understood that by the time I was thirty-two."

And he was off to the men's class.

After Sunday School they went to church. Sharon felt that the Bible lesson hadn't helped very much that week. Sitting in the pew with Everett between her and Ferris, and Missy still down in the nursery, she knew that the question of the phone call still hadn't been resolved, and as she remembered the dream she had had the night before, she was afraid it might never be. All night long, it seemed, she dialed Sarah June's number: With great care she had spun it out—the 1, the area code, the seven digits of the number itself—only to have Ferris gently put his finger down and break the connection. Over and over, time and again.

Ferris is right, she reasoned with herself. You live within your means and you don't owe for what you can't afford. And Ferris was good and right to be that way. Just think what some women had to put up with. Like Momma . . . And she was proud of him for it.

They stood for the first hymn.

But the money doesn't really seem to be the most important thing to Ferris. It was Sarah June and Jack and the way they lived.

Sharon and Ferris took their seats and listened to the announcements about the Ladies Aid rummage sale, Youth Fellowship meetings, Foreign Mission reports, Home Mission reports . . .

It was the way they lived and *thought,* she realized, and she felt a coldness in her stomach: much the same feeling she had had when Ferris had asked her to marry him. She had told him she would have to ask her mother about it.

"Are you in trouble?" was the first question her mother asked.

"No."

"Do you love him?"

"No. I don't know. No, I don't guess I *love* him, exactly."

"Does he love you?"

"No. Well, I don't know. He's asked me to marry him."

"Has he ever tried to mess around with you?"

"Ferris? Naw."

"Is he a good man?"

"Yes, I think he is."

"How old are you now?"

"Nineteen."

"Then you'd better marry him, I reckon. You're getting on and God knows when you're likely to find another good one."

She felt suddenly out of place and strange. Then Everett was tapping on her elbow and Ferris was looking at her. Quickly she bent her head for the prayer as the others had already done.

Sharon, you want too much.

Probably so, she thought. Probably so, but she wished church would be over and she could get up quickly and walk out the front door, could go away somewhere—out in the woods in a little cabin, maybe—a place where she could be by herself with no Ferris, no Everett, no Missy. Maybe she would take her memory of the one stillbirth and the two miscarriages; maybe not. But certainly no telephones to keep tempting her to disobedience, tempting her to call a woman miles away, the only woman she knew, really, who could be her friend, her only real friend in the world. Or maybe she would even be able to walk out and go to a man who wanted her love and who wanted to give her his . . .

. . . *Oh God,* she prayed very hard, her eyes tightly closed, her hands clasped, *please help me avoid the sins of temptation. Please, God. Please please please . . .*

Everett was tapping her elbow again, a grin across his face. The prayer was over, and the parade of sixteen- and seventeen-year-old Christian athletes with the pimples and confessions had begun. She sneaked a look at Ferris who sat staring, a bit glassy-eyed, but otherwise giving no clues as to what he was thinking.

"I smoked at eleven . . . ," one of the athletes confided to the congregation.

Said another, "I drank a swallow of beer, and then another, and then . . ."

And a third, "I had unwholesome thoughts."

The smoker was fourteen, the drinker sixteen, and the lad with unwholesome thoughts a full-grown, boy-man senior.

Ferris sniffled a discrete yawn and figured they must keep the actual tales of whoring for the mostly adult revivals nowadays. Not like when he was a boy in Moses. It was no-holds-barred at Confession-Witness time then. Of course he also knew some boys who'd make up sins. Even did it himself once, then had to admit later that he'd lied. But small as Moses was, there was not much in the way of sports, so there wasn't much chance of getting so many athletes together at one time like here—Christian or otherwise. There was the seven-man touch football team, the basketball team, and the baseball team where you had to learn to play just about every position, including pitching. And the joke used to be that Moses was so small they got the State C League to alter the rules so that they could use at least three outside boys—if they hadn't graduated more than a year before—to help field a complete team.

He looked down at his family. Everett had gotten bored with the boys because they weren't saying so much to him—except once when a reserve quarterback recounted the time he had sent up a silent audible to Jesus as he flipped a quick pass out to the flat that got gathered in by another good Christian who ran eighteen yards for the winning touchdown . . .

. . . and Sharon looking like he'd hit her.

Ferris put a hand up across his eyes and closed them for a minute.

She *does* want too much, he told himself. *Everybody* wants too much. His daddy was right. His daddy was a hard man because he was right about so many things.

Ferris went to college because in Mississippi the scouts are always out, and even if he was from Moses, it was clear to anybody with one eye and half a wit that he could play baseball. It wasn't to Ole Miss. Or even to Mississippi State, which is almost always good in baseball. But it was college, it was in Mississippi, and was free with the scholarship.

"Do you want to go to college, son?" his father had asked.

Ferris didn't know how to reply: he neither did nor did not want to go. He looked at his father's eyes nearly closed by wrinkles, his lips set.

"I don't know."

"It will be hard, I expect. You might not make it."

"Yessir."

"Schooling like that is very different from farming or cruising timber."

"Yessir."

"A man good at one might not be good at the other."

"Yessir."

"Don't expect too much, Ferris. A man who expects too much can get hurt bad."

"Yessir." Automatically. Nothing new in all of that. He had been raised on it.

"And a man who gets too disappointed can get so's he can't do nothing at all."

"Yessir."

"It can turn a good man sour."

"Yessir."

He neither liked nor disliked college. He liked playing baseball. He didn't think it was nice to be called a jock, though. Pro scouts came next, but he stayed in school until the spring of his senior year. Then it was on to the Braves' training camp where everybody was very good. Where even the rookies were all very good. After the season he would go back to school to finish the work for his degree, because that was what he had left home to do.

"So," his father had managed to say before he left for the training camp. "You're going to be a ballplayer, then?"

Ferris couldn't speak when he saw him. It didn't seem possible that this could have happened in less than three months: already bedridden, already *old* since Christmas. Sharon had told him, had tried to prepare him for this look at his own father so suddenly wasted with cancer.

"If I can make the team, Daddy."

"Do you want to, Ferris? Do you really want to?"

"Well I like to play, all right. I sure do."

"There'll be niggers up there," more asked than stated.

"Well, they like to play, too, Daddy."

"What if you don't make it, Ferris?"

"I reckon I'll have to go to work, then." He laughed once.

His father slowly turned his head away and a sigh seemed forced up through his throat as a slight groan.

Stunned at the sight of his father, his laugh caught in his throat. Stunned and wondering, as his gaze crawled down the body of his father and stopped at Sharon standing quietly, patiently at the foot of the bed . . . Wondering, trying to remember what the importance of the smooth, hot feel of leather on his left hand had been in the face of this . . . this . . .

His father turned back to him.

"I get to set up three hours a day," he said. "But not all at once."

Ferris opened his eyes. The high schoolers were done now and the choir was singing "Just as I Am."

That's it, Ferris thought. Just as I Am. His hand tingled from being in one position for so long.

Just as I am
Without one plea
But that Thy blood
Was shed for me

That's it. Just as I am. Do your work and what happens happens. If it's good, you can be pleased. If it's bad, you can be displeased. But it must be work. And all the rest is . . . is . . .

He looked down at Sharon just as she looked away from him.

. . . and all the rest is phone calls to people who live a long, long way away and can't do you any good.

They all stood for the benediction, were blessed, and it was over.

That afternoon he watched TV. It was AAU Track and Field. Exciting races. More exciting than baseball with all that running full steam each time. But in baseball you got to run *and* throw *and* hit something. And it lasted longer.

He thought about the pop-up again. Just like the one that last day with the Braves during spring training. The last day and he had made it in spite of everything. He was headed for Richmond and Triple-A ball, and if it all went well and he got back in form, he'd be in Milwaukee within two years. That's what the management had told him.

Then that guy bunted with two strikes.

It had been nearly the same situation as the one the day before, only no one was on base and it wasn't the ninth inning. A crazy play. The kind you get in baseball lots of times—even with the best of players. Like Mickey Mantle catching a fly ball and holding on to it while he started trotting slowly to the dugout. The base runner on third scored because he knew that when Mantle caught that fly ball it was only the second out. It wasn't his fault if Mickey hadn't paid attention. A crazy play that can happen to even the best, only when it happened to Ferris it was the last day of a miserable spring for him. And since he had quit after that, had gone back to Moses to sit with his father to shed desire like his father shed flesh, had written a letter of resignation and not gone to Richmond—then or ever—the story got told a little bit differently from the way it had actually happened.

The play itself: one out and nobody on, the Braves ahead by two in the top of the eighth. Then the bunt.

He had charged in trying to make a play out of it, but had fallen down instead. The runner saw that and never stopped at first at all, but had pushed off from the bag in as near to a right angle turn as you could make going as fast as he was going, and was well on his way to second by the time Ferris picked up the ball and threw it . . .

Ferris shifted in his chair.

. . . threw it into center field. Fell down and looked silly, then threw the ball away to look stupid on top of it.

Durn he was fast.

Scored on a bunt because the center fielder couldn't believe his own eyes: couldn't believe the batter would bunt with two strikes in the first place, next that Ferris would be sprawled awkwardly on the ground, and last that Ferris—again—would have thrown the ball out toward him in center field where it rolled dead thirty feet away so that he couldn't even touch the thing until the guy was half way home.

Scored on a bunt.

Ferris stretched his toes inside his socks and sucked in a quick breath.

That was the play, and he'd never bothered to tell anyone that the story that had spun itself up around it, that had been stretched— like the play itself—from a bunt into a home run was anything less than what everybody wanted it to be: which was that he had been so bumfoozled he'd just trotted off the field right then, showered, dressed, and gone home to marry Sharon, sweetheart from his youth. For some back in Moses, Mississippi, it had been good for a few *haw haws*. For others there had been some sorrow that he hadn't made it. Sorrow and a bit of surprise.

Ferris still clenched his teeth. That was all right with him what people thought: that he'd failed, that he'd been cut because that bush-league, bonehead play had capped a lousy spring when all he could say for himself was that he was in better shape than anyone else.

A lousy spring. He couldn't remember the intricate series of signals the first and third base coaches kept throwing at him: he missed the signs for bunts, steals, pick-offs; his timing was off; he couldn't get his bat around at the plate; he couldn't get off his heels at third to charge the grounders humming at him.

"Concentrate," the coaches finally were yelling. "Concentrate, concentrate."

He couldn't. In the field, at bat, on the bench, in the chow line, all he could see was his father's face, its mouth gaping and twisted down on one side as the sigh—half groan, half belch—came crying out onto the pillow.

"Ferris?" It was The Man himself talking to him. "Boy, what's wrong? We've had scouting reports on you for nearly four years. What's wrong?"

He told them what he knew they would understand. He told them about his father in Moses falling away with cancer. And the pain. He told them he could feel that pain in his own stomach when he sat down to dinner, could even feel it crawling up into his throat at night when he tried to sleep, could feel it . . .

They let him go home, of course, at last understanding what had been wrong, what had been eating at him. He didn't stay but three days . . .

No, it was easier to let people think he'd been cut. They could understand that. They could understand simple failure. Good people, they had had enough of it themselves, most of them. The only regret he'd had was that he'd let people bad-talk baseball. And the Braves. And it hadn't been either.

He watched the race on TV carefully.

His father hadn't died on that visit. He hadn't died until deep into the summer, but it was after Ferris got back to the camp that the guy scored on the bunt. An exhibition game with the White Sox. As a matter of fact, he had been back in the camp for a week. Been playing good ball, then, too.

Ferris yawned in front of the tube. It was over, and semipro was good enough for him. It was done. Except he *had* finished the game out—two for four at the plate, too. But he had *not* left the field after that play. Naturally. As another matter of fact, he'd had three more fielding tries and had handled each of them as neat and clean as ever. But it was easy then, because he'd already made up his mind.

That night Sharon started a letter to her sister in Huntsville. Ferris watched her out of the corner of his eye or when he looked up from his TV. She spent nearly two hours writing that letter: page after page of it. Then when she was through, Ferris looked at her.

"Finished?" he asked.

She nodded her head.

"Well, I'll mail it in the morning from the store if you want."

"No," she said.

"It might get off a little earlier," he added.

"It doesn't matter," she said. Then she took the carefully written sheets and very precisely tore them in half, then into quarters, and dropped the pieces into the wastebasket.

"Why'd you do that, Sharon?"

She looked at him perfectly dry-eyed, but her head dropped forward and her voice sounded tinny and faint.

"I don't guess I could take any real pleasure in it knowing how you feel and all."

She got up. "Good night, Ferris. I'm going to bed. I'm tired."

Ferris sat in his chair for a long time before getting up and going to bed, too. In minutes he was nearly asleep, but suddenly he was wide awake straining to hear and see his father again as he had that last time back in Moses.

From early April until early June, Ferris stayed with his father nursing him: talking to him, interpreting the increasing grunts as the old man's ability or strength or will to speak diminished almost daily.

. . . and watching him, noting the increasing ash around the spark of his eyes, the longer and longer periods he had to wait before his father responded when he spoke.

. . . and shaving him every day, then every other day, then even less often as the skin—drying, growing more sallow and sensitive every time—flaked and peeled until, near the end, the scrape of raw blade across his skin seemed hardly able to draw blood and the old man's skin felt . . . abandoned. Abandoned and ill-used.

And all the while, Ferris was sloughing off the trivialities of his desires. Stripping layer after layer of himself away until—at his father's last uncontrollable gurgle—he was down to the hard discipline his father had always demanded of himself and that Ferris now and in his own turn was training himself to live with: that hard denial of desire, that frame, that musculature of survival, which wouldn't brook either the massive spasm of terror or the nagging tics of anxiety about failure, because there was no hope, no thought, no concept, even, of success; his soul conditioned like the athlete's body, rid of all excess . . .

And at the end, he leaned his face to his father; in the caress of a near kiss, his lips brushed his father's ear as he whispered, "Too much, Daddy. I wanted too much."

Then leaning further over to place his ear to the old man's lips, listening for the reply. Listening . . .

He understands.

Ferris was kneeling at his father's bed, his knees aching with the pain from the wooden floor.

Whispering again, his lips pressed lightly to his father's ear. "That isn't right, Daddy."

"Unnng," his father grunted, his eyes opening one last time to scan his son's face. "Unnng."

He understands.

The pain from leaning over was kinking the muscles in his back; his thighs and calves were practically numb from staying crooked for so long; and his throat and eyes and head . . .

"I'm sorry, Daddy," still whispered, but more mouthed and barely audible.

"Unnn unnn."

"I'm sorry," soundless now, now only the pain in the knees. Only the pain.

"Unnng . . ."

Ferris closed his eyes and relaxed again.

. . . understood and *approved,* by damn!

Ferris slept.

The Man
Who Walked Pigeons

• • "Here, lovey. Come on, my sweet. Don't go getting spooky, now."

He inched forward painfully in a duck waddle.

"Come on now, my sweet. Let's get you back in your cage."

He heard the washing machine in the kitchen upstairs nearing the time he would have to help it through its drain and spin cycle. If he wasn't there to crimp the hose at just the right times, the whole thing would overflow.

"Come along now," he crooned. But she fluffed her breast feathers out, and with a saucy *coor-coor* strutted quickly away from the corner he was urging her toward.

The washing machine stopped.

"Drat," he muttered, knowing he had only forty seconds to get up there to nurse the flow.

"Come, love," he said again, and he very nearly had her calm enough to be picked up when a two gallon jar of mayonnaise exploded behind him.

"Oh no," he said as she flew up to the open window, perching tenuously on the sill, undecided as to what she should do next. He groaned to his feet, knees clicking.

Coor! as he raced for the steps with ten seconds left.

Coor! as she flew out the window and up to the ridge of the roof with a great and nervous whapping of her young wings.

The dryer could take care of itself.

"Coo, coo," he called in quite a good imitation of pigeon sounds. "Coo." He let the bright golden kernels of corn plink into the tin feeding pan. "Coo," he called to his rooftop. But she merely puffed herself up, called down *Coor,* and paced fretfully back and forth.

"Problems, Mr. Loftis?"

"Hmmm? Ah, Mr. Miller. Yes. You see she's new and doesn't really know her way around yet. And young, which means a bit fluffy, you know."

"Fluffy?"

"Ah, spooky. Nervous. Young and new. Inexperienced, I suppose you might say."

"Oh. I understand."

"Um, virginal and shy, if you will."

"Oh?"

"Well, I very nearly had her, but the mayonnaise exploded and I had to go tend to the washing machine."

"Another one?"

"I'm afraid so."

"That's three in the past month, isn't it?"

"Oh no. Just two, in actual fact. But a ketchup went the month before, yes."

"Henry," and Mr. Miller put out a hand to stop the plinking corn for just a moment. "Why don't you ask Mrs. Terramin to come get her food out of your basement?"

"Oh well, it's not really in the way down there."

"But you spend half your Saturday mornings cleaning up."

"Not really," he laughed. "It may seem that way, but it's not all that much of a bother."

"Well, it's your basement and all that, but it has struck me that Mrs. Terramin is imposing a bit much. After all . . ."

"No, no. Not at all. The food's really perfectly good, and now that she hasn't thirty boarders to cook for, she has to store it someplace, doesn't she?" He paused. "But I must admit it has crossed my mind to put it in the Good Will or some such thing." He looked down at the corn in his hand.

"You mean she wouldn't even know if you did or not?"

He shrugged.

"Well, then. I mean, it's been six months, after all."

"Yes. Yes, it has." He looked away from his neighbor and back up to the roof as tactfully as he could.

Plink plink.

"Coo," he called softly.

"Hmmm?"

"What? Oh, Mr. Miller. Yes. And besides, I've gotten on with Mrs. Terramin for so long that I'd be afraid that if I mentioned those things she'd think I *wanted* for her to come get them out. And in fact they really *aren't* in my way. All that's down there is that and the pigeons and their food. And the iris bulbs. And a few sacks of fertilizer and stuff. And the goldfish tubs, of course. But that's only in winter, after all."

He was aware of a distant but heavy thrumming drone.

"Have you cleaned this one up yet?"

"No. Not yet. I really want to get Freya back first." He smiled quickly.

Plink plink plink.

"Coo, coo, coo-oo."

"Last time you were three hours cleaning up."

"Was I?"

"Sure were. I kept track while I was doing the yard."

The heavy drone was much closer now, and he could distinctly hear a *whack-a-whack-a-whack-a-whack-a-whack-a* under it all.

"Coo-coo, my love," he called a bit loudly.

"I mean, two gallons of mayonnaise all over the place."

"Come, love. Come now, my sweet."

Plinkplinkplink.

"And all that glass."

Whack-a-whack-a-whack-a-whack-a-whack-a

"Come, Freya. Come . . ." But the rest was drowned by the heavy noise of a flight of three helicopters passing rather low.

"My God," he said as he watched Freya disappear into a ball of feathers.

"Ah, ha," remarked Mr. Miller loudly. "I guess they're getting ready to land over on the school field for the ROTC boys," and he nodded and smiled vigorously.

"FREEEE-yaaa," Henry called, but she was gone: flown away, fled from the roof like a shot.

"Oh, drat! Dad gum it all! Damn it anyway!"

"Can't you get her?" Mr. Miller shouted in his ear just as the roar of the helicopters ceased when they dipped behind a hill to land.

"Oh, poor thing," Mr. Loftis responded, his eyes following her panic-stricken flight. "Look at her. Bless her heart, she panicked because she thought they were hawks."

"Hawks?" Mr. Miller echoed.

"The helicopters. Freya must have thought they were hawks coming to get her."

"Oh. I see," Mr. Miller said. But he was off to mow his yard leaving Mr. Loftis to follow Freya's frantic flight until he saw her roost.

"Ah, Mrs. Warren."

She eyed him through the partially opened door.

"One of my pigeons has flown to your roof."

Her eyes turned up, then quickly back to him.

"I want to get her off, you see. So I've brought these other three birds to turn them loose." He lifted the carrying cage around so she could see better. "I think she'll join them and follow them home. To my house. Then she'll be off your roof. She's new and the helicopters frightened her."

Mrs. Warren involuntarily shrank from the flutter inside the cage.

"On my roof?" she said. "You got a pigeon on my roof?" and Mr. Loftis was certain he saw her thinking hard of all the defiled generals and statesmen whose statues she had seen in pictures, statues with pigeons squatting boldly on their heads.

"Just one, Mrs. Warren. And, uh, well the very top of the roof, really."

"You'll get him off?"

"As quickly as possible. I just wanted to make certain you understood what I was doing in your yard." He smiled very broadly at her, very reassuringly as though she were a new tenth grader coming into his class a week after the term had begun.

She glanced again at the cage, nodded, and closed her front door. He heard her snap the deadbolt.

"What are you going to do now, Loftis?" Mr. Miller asked.

Mr. Loftis didn't answer right away. He kept looking at his four pigeons resting comfortably on the ridge of Mrs. Warren's roof. He snapped his fingers in vexation.

"Durn," he muttered, knowing full well that all his shirts would be full of wrinkles because he hadn't been there to get them out of the dryer and hung properly on their coat hangers right away. If you don't do it right away, you might as well not do it at all, he fussed silently. He snapped his fingers as though quieting a too-noisy whisperer in study hall.

"*Durn* it," he said again, thinking of the papers he had planned to grade that morning so he would be free to watch Atlanta on television that afternoon. Though Aaron had long since bested Ruth's record and been gone from the Braves, Mr. Loftis's personal fidelities ran deep. But now he'd either have to iron the shirts, or rinse and spin and dry them again. *If* he could ever get the pigeons away from Mrs. Warren who kept peeking at him from first one window and then another.

"Loftis?" Mr. Miller said.

"Oh, *what?*" he snapped.

"Maybe the corn again?"

Mr. Loftis looked at him, feeling the dull barb of Miller's wit.

"Maybe," he said noncommittally. "Have you finished your yard, Mr. Miller?"

They started back down the street together.

"No, just taking a little break," and he smiled.

"I see." Without another word he turned into his driveway and went straight to his basement to think. Maybe the corn would work.

It didn't.

He had ironed his shirts and was in the middle of cleaning up the mayonnaise when the telephone rang. He set the sponge gently in the bucket of warm water, wiped his hands on the dishcloth tucked neatly in his belt, stepped carefully around a pile of glass slivers he had already swept up . . .

Yes, yes, he was saying clear up the stairs from the basement. He could tell who was calling by the way it rang.

"Henry Loftis speaking."

It was Mrs. Warren.

"The pigeons are still there, Mr. Loftis."

"Yes, Mrs. Warren, but they won't hurt anything."

"They're sitting on my roof, though, Mr. Loftis. Pigeons."

"Yes, Mrs. Warren. I know."

"Four of them."

"Yes, Ma'am. I know. I've had to leave them . . ."

"*Leave* them? On my roof? I have a very dark roof, Mr. Loftis."
(*Nelson in Trafalgar Square*)

" . . . leave them for just a short time, Mrs. Warren."

"They'll attract others like them."
(*The Burghers of Calais Before the Hotel de Ville*)

"I've had to come home to get some house chores done."

"I don't want flocks of pigeons on my roof. They'll settle on the TV antenna and I won't be able to watch."
(*Joan of Arc in the Place du Martoi*)

"I'll get them off, Mrs. Warren. And if they've done any-thing . . . Are they on your antenna now?"

"I don't like birds, Mr. Loftis."
(*Richard the Lion Heart Beside the Houses of Parliament*)

"We're sure to have a nice rain any time now, if they've soiled your roof."

"And I'm having guests tonight."

He gently squeezed his tongue between his teeth so he wouldn't slip and make the obvious rejoinder.

"I'll be down to get them as soon as I can. I'm in the middle of cleaning up some mayonnaise, and as soon as . . ."

"What? Another one, Mr. Loftis? That's three this month."

"Just two, actually . . ."

"You ought to tell that old lady to come get all that stuff out from there."

"It's really no problem, Mrs. Warren."

"Three in a month?"

"Two, actually. One was ketchup."

"You should tell her."

"Yes, yes I suppose. Look, Mrs. Warren, if you can hold on until I get through . . . See here," he had had an inspiration. "Mrs. Warren, your house and mine are alike. A bit, anyway. If you were to open your garage door, they likely would fly down there, you see . . ."

"In *my* garage? What's wrong exactly with *your* garage, Mr. Loftis?"

"Nothing at all, Mrs. Warren. They're on your roof at the moment, is all, because they're confused. Our houses look a bit alike, and if they think they're on *their* roof—that is, *my* roof—which I suspect they *do* think, then they might well fly down through the open door because . . ."

"Not in *my* basement, they're not going to fly down."

"Then I'll just have to think of something else, Mrs. Warren. And in the meantime, I've got the mayonnaise . . ."

"She's senile, that's what."

"Well, it's really no problem, Mrs. Warren. But it's liable to be another hour yet."

It was an hour and a half later that Mr. Loftis checked the knot on the twine one more time, still surprised at himself for having been so dull-witted about it all along.

"Not chaffing you is it, Odur?" he said to the pigeon before him on the floor.

Stay dull like that and the tenth graders would be all over me, he chortled silently.

"Come, young man," he said. And with Freya's mate tucked securely under one arm, and the ball of stout twine clutched in his other hand, he set out for Mrs. Warren's house.

"Just like a kite," he smiled down at Odur. Then he froze. Thoughts of Benjamin Franklin's experiment suddenly paralyzed him. He glanced quickly to the sky, then shook his head and smiled to himself. A perfect day. No problems.

So simple, he thought, walking up his drive. Out on the street he looked both ways. No one was around, which did give him a slight sense of relief. Everyone was probably watching TV or else in their back yards planting their survival gardens.

Mr. Loftis walked toward Mrs. Warren's house smiling openly. But as he got nearer, he realized something was terribly wrong. Then he saw what it was. He ran the last two hundred feet, Odur fighting the sudden bounce and jounce as well as he could by pecking at Mr. Loftis's tightly clutching fingers.

He was running up to her front door, but veered sharply when he spied her coming up the drive toward him.

"They're down here, Mr. Loftis," she called.

With another quick glance at the empty roof, he hurried down to her.

"I was terrified," he said, trying not to gasp too heavily for breath right in her face.

"I opened the garage door like you said," Mrs. Warren answered.

Mr. Loftis was on his knees smoothing the feathers of his pets as they strutted about cooing their pleasure and relief.

"Why, Mrs. Warren." He looked up at her with delight. "Thank you so much." He giggled his pleasure. "I do appreciate it. Especially since you don't, well . . ."

She lifted her shoulders in a shrug, but her head was turned away from the birds just slightly. She was not comfortable being so

close to them. And such large ones. Yet, though her head was partially averted, her eyes stared at them as though she were transfixed, like a person watching something horrible, but unable to
turn away.

Looking up in his happiness, Mr. Loftis saw.

(*The Twisting, Buckling Heave and Crash of the Colossus Toppling
Into the Harbor at Rhodes*)

"I had to," she muttered.

"Had to?" he repeated. "Had to, Mrs. Warren?"

"Of course 'had to,' Mr. Loftis. What would you have me do?"

He felt a nearness, a neighborliness for Mrs. Warren that he had
never felt before.

But she never looked at him, and once he noticed it, he found it
slightly disconcerting.

"A poor widow whose only little girl will be in your class next
year?" she said to answer her own questions. "Of course, I opened
my garage to your . . . your . . . WHAT!" she exclaimed, pointing down near Mr. Loftis.

He turned to look, and there Odur, so pleased to be reunited
with his wandering mate, was topping Freya vigorously right on
Mrs. Warren's garage floor.

"What! WHAT! *WHAT!*" she was calling, her finger still
pointing at them.

"Really, Mrs. Warren. You . . . really!"

He absently flapped his hands at the pair, half-heartedly trying
to get them to un-couple.

"Really, you needn't have done this for that reason."

But Odur was undaunted by the meager display.

"*Really.* That's most insulting, Mrs. Warren."

"It's dis*gust*ing," she replied watching.

"Well, not disgusting so much, I don't think, Mrs. Warren. But
I must say," and he got to his feet, "I really must protest that if you
think your aversion to my birds in your basement would have had
any effect on my academic integrity towards your daughter, then
you are very much mistaken."

"Mr. Loftis. You will take them away, won't you? She's my only daughter. My only child. I'm just a lonely widow. What if she should walk in and see . . . *them?*"

"Well?" he said puzzled. "Them?"

Mrs. Warren suddenly slumped, a great sigh coming from her. "That will just mean more and more, won't it?"

"More and more?" he echoed.

"Pigeons," and she gestured feebly at the floor.

"Why, yes, I dare say it will," he responded. "That's what I raise them for."

"You really want more," she stated in a flat and unbelieving tone.

"To race. Yes. People buy them."

"Did you get your basement cleaned up from the mayonnaise?" she asked.

"Yes," he smiled.

"You'll take them away now?" She looked exhausted.

"Yes, yes. And again, thank you, Mrs. Warren. But you really needn't have."

He held the ball casually in his left hand, while in his right the twine trailed loosely down to Odur's leg. "At least," Mr. Loftis said gently, "not for the reason you said."

He led Odur to the door leading out to the driveway.

"I still think you should tell her," Mrs. Warren said.

"Ah, well," he answered as he opened the door and stepped out. "It's really not all that much trouble."

Mrs. Warren shrugged.

"Come on, my loves," he cooed.

There was Odur, with the twine on his leg, followed by Freya. Behind her in a line were Borr, Heimdall, and Loki.

Mr. Miller saw them coming down the street. So did Mr. and Mrs. Caldwell, who had been pushing their great and heavy lawn sweeper; Mr. and Mrs. Cool, who were out eyeing their great oaks and estimating the number of leaves they would not rake up again that fall; Mr. Holt, throwing two frisbees with his three daughters; Mrs. Bryant, outside making certain the painter understood the full extent of his work; and the Hauns—all seven of them—standing there looking.

They followed the Loftis parade without a word. They were all very quiet. The only sounds were Henry's feet slapping the macadam road, and the scraping of the five sets of pigeon toes with an occasional *flup-flup* of wings from Freya, or a coo of delight from Loki.

Atlanta had been rained out.

Besides, Loftis thought, his head high, his eyes straight ahead, probably none of them cares about Henry Aaron any more anyway.

The All-Time Master
Grand-Master of Solitaire

• • I hate to deluge you with improbabilities, but I once won seven singles solitaire games in a row. It wasn't in competition—my record there was five—so it didn't count, but it goes to show what can be done when one *will* decide to do something.

One event—*fact!* if you must—certainly doesn't a deluge make, but at the least let it stand as a sort of synechdoche.

I came upon my calling at an early age—sufficiently early, to be candid, to qualify as a prodigy. When I was barely able to see the top of a card table while standing upright, I spied an idle deck sitting in its box. Not only was it idle, but, as it developed, it also was virginal. The box was sealed with a little stamp much like the tax stamps that seal the bottles of Chivas Regal. I plucked the box from the table and stared, absolutely rapt, at the printed design. It replicated the design on the backs of the cards within, and to say that I had never seen anything so thoroughly intricate in seamless patterning before is the utter understatement of my life. Years later, an acquaintance to whom I was relating all of this for some reason or other, remarked with a chuckle that I had early been hooked on Baroque. Till then I hadn't thought of those typical designs as Baroque so much as Art Nouveau—Beardsleyan, though there are those who would consider him Rococoish, I suppose.

In any event, I stared at that box, savoring every moment's delay. I caressed it, my little fingers following the delicate tracery of the design. Finally, my fingers found the seal. All that was needed was for me to snap it open and whatever glorious contents it held would be mine.

But even at that snatch-and-grabbish age of three or four, I wasn't a snatch-and-grabbish sort of person. I carefully carried the box up to the kitchen where my intention was to get one of Mother's keenest paring knives. I even had opened the drawer and had a hand looped into it when I realized that a paring knife wasn't the instrument for such a job, nor was the kitchen an appropriate place. I've nearly always had a *sense* about such matters.

So I stole into my parents' room—I say *parents'* but it really was my mother's—and searched about her secretary until I found her letter opener. It was ivory from India, yellowed with time, carved all over with elephants following one another trunk to tail across a curved bridge. Mother opened her mail with it. It was perfect.

Back in the living room at the card table, I prepared myself for the moment. A neat, downward pressure with the blade and it was done.

I set the ivory opener on the table and thought the box felt lighter, somehow, as though some essence of its contents was now free, loosed upon me by Fate.

Not that I actually conceptualized it all in quite that way at the time, I dare say, but it was working on me whether conceptualized, articulated, or no.

At last I eased up the flap and tilted the pack so the cards slid out with a little rush. And there, of course, was the next obstacle, for such prizes are never won all at once. The cards themselves were wrapped in cellophane. It crinkled at each end under my touch; yet I could slide it around ever so slightly over the cards. I understood that removing that thin wrapper was not the same as the outer seal. This was the true inner *sanctum*. I was as precise as I could manage to be, but a small corner of the cellophane tore under my hand even so. I opened only one end and let the cards slide free. I placed the deck reverently on the table while I gazed with awe at the now empty wrapper. It was a sacred thing to me then. I felt as though I had witnessed a birthing, with the cards the child and the cellophane the uterus—a far-fetched bit of imagining, I've been told, but I recall it as though it were yesterday, and I recall it as being that awesome.

Since then, as you might imagine, I certainly haven't taken that long to open a deck of cards, still—though I virtually never buy new decks any more—when I *was* buying them at such a prodigious rate during my active years, I never touched that wrapper without a moment's hesitation during which my fingers remembered that first time.

Having controlled myself for so long, however, I finally proved to be as human as most. I snatched the Jokers away, laid out the cards in a standard version of Klondike, and played with a passion and a fury that in my own heart I knew equalled the passion and fury of the little Wolfgang Amadeus Mozart when he first toddled to his father's klavier and, running his pudgy hands over the keyboard, understood not merely that he could *play!* Almost any clod could *play*. But understood that *he knew music!* In just such a way I understood that *I knew Solitaire!*

Do not ask how I could shuffle. Probably I didn't. The deal itself, after all, is a shuffle. And do not ask how at age three I knew how to lay out the cards properly. I *knew*, is all. I *understood*, is the point. Doubtless those who prefer *facts* would assert that surely I must have watched someone play before. Just as doubtless that would be *factually* accurate. But it is irrelevant. Facts always start out so bravely, with such force and vigor; yet they end up being so raggedly and pitiably irrelevant. In *fact* I probably had watched my father, or whoever he was, play a game once. But should we persist in that kind of logic, we would expect children to heave footballs about like Otto Graham or bat off home runs like Joe DiMaggio simply because they had seen it done once. Nonsense!

I was a wonder from the very beginning.

Genetically it probably was my mother. Environmentally it most certainly had to be. She left me with a great deal of time to myself. Long before all those creatures who ran about with their poor bosoms sagging pendulously beneath their quaintly lettered T-shirts, my mother was what one now would call "liberated." During most of my younger years she played in Phil Spitalmi's All Girl Orchestra. *Girl,* by the way, on occasion was stretching the point a bit, but play she did. Fifth viola.

Those were wonderful days for me. Virtually their only competition was Evelyn and her Magic Harp. Or did Evelyn have a Magic Violin and play with them? Never mind. The only *fact* of importance is that with Mother out playing fifth viola I was allowed to be alone a great deal. Father I remember only as a voice coming from the back of our apartment where he stayed quite busy yelling into the telephone. I think he talked long distance, took orders, and tended further to business by getting on a train and going away for long periods. Try as I might, I can't recall what the man looked like (though I was a wonder I never claimed to be miraculous: those claims came some years later during the height of my career and were devised by reporters bent on out-coining each other with catchy phrases). To the best of my knowledge there wasn't a single photograph of him in our home. And the only time I can recall *seeing* him was once when he had finished talking over the telephone in his office. I peeked through the crack between the door and the jamb, and there he was sitting at the desk holding a framed photograph in one hand, while with the other he held his head and, I believe, moaned loudly once. Later, he got on a train—I presume—and never came back.

"Not to worry," Mother had answered brightly one day after I noticed his absence. It had been some months.

Genes and environment, then, were essentially Mother's. I say genes, because my artistic bent obviously came from her. She never yelled into telephones or moaned. And the viola was but one of her many accomplishments. It made a living for us for a number of years, and when she felt one of those great *sea changes* rolling over her, she took up the organ. At first I hadn't understood why impressions of dank cathedrals, my mother stuck way in the back somewhere somberly pushing out wearying and never-ending bits of gloom, settled heavily on my mind. It was all to be like a great long moan, I feared. She was going to go the way of Father, or whomever.

"Mother," I queried after those nightmare visions had disturbed my usually productive sleep. "Don't you miss the orchestra and the stage with all the bright lights and people clapping and all?"

It was the eve of my first Final Play and, frankly, I felt that my limelight (I was being much heralded as the Bad Boy of Solitaire who, bad boy or no, would bring America the Golden Ace for the first time since Aaron Glebe in 1889) somewhat dimmed her luster by comparison.

"Ah, Benedicte," she answered, her hand caressing my still-downy cheek. "I shall never have left it."

Of course the only reason for all the hoop-la was my age: a precociously mature fourteen—a veritable walking nocturnal emission, actually—but some things either were taken for granted or left unsaid in those more innocent days. My mind hardly ever *dwelt* on Solitaire back then, any more than one dwells on breathing or walking about. *Golf* and *Double Golf, Accordion, Spider, Klondike:* these were all such familiar versions of the game to me that I seldom paid much attention to them.

Some may think Solitaire a mindless game devoted solely to whiling away idle moments in encounters with pure chance. Far from true. The varieties of the game seem virtually endless, and *chance* is not necessarily any greater a factor than it is with bridge or poker. After all, anyone who is a good bridge or poker player can best an inferior player who has a superior hand. But to pit oneself against oneself—ah! *that* is competition at its ultimate keenness, especially when the *oneself* one plays is myself.

Actually, I was far more concerned with Elizabeth Taylor in those days. Though it had been two years since she had fallen from her horse in *National Velvet*, I still could not shake the memory of her being taken unconscious from the track to the infirmary. What agony of suspense filled me as the camera's eye, closing up onto the doctor as he fumbled to undo the buttons of her shirt, caught his stunned look of disbelief as he saw—*he,* mind you: in those innocent days *he* saw, not *we*—as he saw her lovely, budding breasts.

Off, then, with her cap, and down about that face—that even then was launching a billion dreams of glory—fell those thick auburn tresses. Her soft swelling breasts were as real to me as though I had seen them with my very own eyes: as real and perfect and untainted, as virginal and pure as that first deck of cards I had held at age three. Oh, Elizabeth! How we have loved you. Every magazine article about you, every picture of you riding your horse or feeding your little pet squirrel, we cherished; every time you announced that you didn't have any boy friends and were more interested in horses—those fortunate, noble beasts—how hope surged once again, how our blood quickened, how . . .

Such thoughts as those precluded any serious concentration on Solitaire. Mother tried in perfectly monstrous ways to get my mind back in the channel it should have been in, but to no avail. I was in the Final Play. Those don't come up every day, of course. Or every year, either. They come up less often than the Olympics, for all of that. The rest of the time it's all local and regional stuff, then a complex matrix of play-offs followed by those champions resubmitting themselves to those beneath them to ensure that the truly best survive and work their ways to the top. And it isn't until the finest four in the world have demonstrated their worthiness to represent the Game that another Final Play is called.

I, of course, represented America, and the burden couldn't have fallen on more competent shoulders. Mother, however much she knew that, still had a mother's fears that "this Elizabeth thing" (as she referred to it) should so batter me emotionally as to make me look foolish.

Actually, I should make clear at this point that according to the laws of the Solitaire Players of the World, Grand Masters are not in any official way construed as representing the countries of their nativities or their current domiciles (that's very nearly *verbatim*) it being assumed that *Solitaire* must be represented solely by the individuals who work their way to the Final Play. Thus it is theoretically possible for a Final Play to be among people of the same nationality. It has never happened, however, and people—the common currency of their pride being what it is—will allow a certain amount of nationalism to swirl in the wake of one who goes to a Final Play. This was especially true during the worst of the Cold War when sober and responsible nationalism sank to such absurdly jingoistic depths.

Each of the four Masters has to play each of the other three in various ways, involving numerous instances of numerous Solitaire games *plus* variations on those games *plus* various permutations and combinations of those games *and* of double games with points being earned or deducted via penalties of various sorts. At the end of a full week—seven days, mind: none of your piddle-about forty-hour weeks for us—of play, the Master Grand-Master—we don't say *winner*, much to the amusement of most—is named and awarded the Golden Ace, his name to be carefully etched on it at a later date. He is then charged to keep it safely until he delivers it personally to the next Master Grand-Master, should it not be himself. Only one player prior to myself ever was awarded the Golden Ace twice, and even then some thirty-seven years and four Final Plays intervened. That was Ivan Spaastich, a truly brilliant player, part Russian, part Boer.

My first Final Play was in New York City in 1946, because at the time it was one of the few still unbombed cities worthy of a Final Play. And though many people were amazed at the quality of play—exceptionally difficult, exceptionally competent—I was not. In my youthful naiveté it seemed perfectly reasonable that when so many people had been stuck out on isolated army posts or been forced to languish in prisons and such, they would have had plenty of time to take up and sharpen their skills. It was, according to the SPOW *Recorder* (the semi-official organ for the Solitaire Players of the World), "the most cutthroat Final Play" ever seen.

My first opponent, for instance, opened with some disarming banter about being a Bahrainese by birth, though now a naturalized Jew—whatever he meant by that—living in a station at the Metropole or some such nonsense. His accent was very thick, so I may have misunderstood some of what he was saying, but he smiled at me and I certainly was on to that sort of thing.

Good he was. No doubt about it, but I bested him at every turn and managed to work myself into a positive swivet about becoming a groomsman for the Taylors. Or perhaps a tack keeper. I had an exquisite vision of my tenderly caring for Elizabeth's saddle after her rides—saddle soaping it all up into a huge and beautiful lather, wiping it off, making certain it was totally clean—or of taking her great stallion out to give him his cool-down walks. That dream plus variations on it occupied my mind for most of the rest of the week. I hardly remembered the various plays at all. And when it came time to improvise a new game, I whipped one out so fast it was down before I hardly knew I had started.

The judges gasped in awe and asked, "What do you call it?"

Quick as a wink I replied, "Elizabeth Regina."

They misunderstood, of course. But that didn't displease me, I must confess.

Mother, naturally enough, was ecstatic. It was the culmination of a glorious week for her personally. Not only was she basking in the reflected glory of my first Final Play mastership, but only that week she had been moved from third organist at the Roxy Theatre to second assistant organist at Radio City Music Hall.

"Do you know what that means?" she said to me during the whirring of newsreel cameras and flacking of press photographers' flash bulbs. Her eyes glimmered with joy.

"The Rockettes?" I could barely speak, my elation was so great.

She nodded, the tears held back only by the intense inner discipline of which she was so capable.

"I won't be playing for them, but I'll be playing all weekday matinees and one evening."

"Oh, Mother!" I couldn't have been happier. Then for the first time that I could recall, my own eyes glimmered, for her hard work, her dedication, her *strength* at ever pushing herself forward, her positive refusal to be down much less out, made this most recent accomplishment of hers so much greater than mine. I, after all, had *done* nothing. I *was* Solitaire. There was no real work or discipline or dedication or resolve to it.

"Oh, Mother!" I repeated for lack of being able to muster anything further by way of showing my pleasure. I gave her a great hug during which, for just the briefest moment, she was Elizabeth, shining from the exertion of her race, a smudge merely highlighting that incredible complexion, her body still redolent with the aroma of her great horse Velvet . . .

But the newspeople would have me, and away we were whisked for the interviews, never mind the lateness of the hour.

I have wondered since how years so filled with the golden rays of purest pleasure could also be so abysmally shriveled with the clutch of chilling despair. I have wondered how often others—*knowing* that something is not to be—still manage to keep their hearts beating with the totally irrational assumptions—not hopes or desires or wishes, mind, but assumptions—that the thing desired will come to pass anyway. I *knew* Elizabeth Taylor was not going to come to me, to visit the youngest ever Master Grand-Master; further, I *knew* she wouldn't be sending a telegram or writing a letter or even dropping a post card casually into a mailbox. Yet each day's mail was a crushing disappointment, bringing the same depressing gloom and sense of loss as the previous day's.

Because of Mother I had passes to very nearly all the movie houses in town, and I got to watch the Rockettes virtually as often as I desired. I loved to watch them, but I also loved to watch Mother rise up out of the floor of the theatre, her hands directing and controlling that monstrous organ capable of such vast ranges of mood and temperament. Mother skipped from the delicate pipings of Pan at the gates of dawn to the fun-filled accordion tones of "Lady of Spain," and thence into the expectant staccatos of the fourth movement of the overture to *William Tell*, replete with the klot-a-ta-klot of galloping hoofbeats: withal, a marvelous machine.

What Mother loved best, I think, was working out the transitions. Playing the primary tunes was a mere nothing for her—a simple, straightforward, and professional working out of the necessary organ techniques. But the little musical bridges had either to be improvised, which she loved to do, or worked out, which she also loved to do.

At home in the evenings, while I might be laying out a Fitz-maurice variation of that extremely difficult game *Canfield,* or while practicing a Yeovil attack against a game of *Forty Thieves,* Mother often would sit across the card table from me, her eyes staring above my head, her hands set upon the table. One might have thought her to be in a trance or readying herself for a seance. But no, she was merely getting the details of her musical bridge laid out in her head just as surely as I was laying out the cards on the table. Then with a smile that emanated from deep within her great soul, she would move her fingers across the surface of the table, even to the point of playing, in her mind's eye, the many banks of keys. And she could be seen to reach out—or over—to manipulate the various stops.

She especially enjoyed working out those transitions between kinds of music most would *never* have thought in any way compatible. One of her favorite and most successful, in my opinion, was a shift from Bach's "Fugue in C Minor" to "Sleigh Bells Ring, Are Ya' Listenin'?" by way of a variation on the theme of the "Rinso White! Rinso White! Happy little washday song" common at the time.

Though music always appealed to me primarily in the deepest emotional way, I nonetheless loved to watch Mother *deal* with it. I also loved to be in the theatre when she stretched her still-shapely legs out to place her dainty feet on the bass pedals and make, it seemed, the whole earth tremble.

The next several years were passed in this way. I spent much of my time giving lectures and demonstrations, directing workshops, *et cetera,* and, naturally, keeping myself busily engaged in the various local and regional and area and national and continental contests. It was a busy time, and though I truly was exhilarated by the rush of events, still, the wonderful moments were those when I could return to our little apartment on West Ninth Street and once again see and trail my fingers across the Golden Ace as it shone like a beacon from our mantlepiece.

Eventually, the pace of my life picked up considerably. It was becoming evermore apparent that another Final Play was in the offing. There was no serious doubt that I would be there, and the necessary other three Masters had pretty much emerged in 1956. I would gladly tell you who they were could I remember, but I can't. One, of course, was a Russian—a thoroughly schooled but terribly mechanical sort of player with no real class: he positively *grunted,* for Heaven's sake, when he played a card, and slapped the poor thing down like some German playing pinochle. The others I forget. After so long they all tend to meld into a single pack merely to be shuffled and dealt with.

Basically, a horrible ambivalence was tumbling through my breast. I had fallen in love, to state the matter as calmly as possible, with Ingrid Bergman. Oh! She *was* Anastasia. She *was,* she *was,* she *was!* Never has there been such regal bearing in a woman. Her nose all squared, her face strong and powerful, its features firm and in control, yet with lips that promised the tremblingly sweetest of kisses. I had been burning with desire for her ever since the earth stood still in the sleeping bag with Gary Cooper in *For Whom the Bell Tolls.* "Roberto! Roberto!" she cried back to him as they forced her to safety on their handsome Spanish mounts. "Roberto! Roberto!" as Gary Cooper turned to face his doom, the machine gun rattling at the enemy—us. The fidelity of the woman. Of course Elizabeth was my very first love, but Ingrid was my second. And when she *became* Anastasia just as I was trying to polish my style for the upcoming Play . . .

It was almost too much. I wanted to remain faithful to Elizabeth. I really did. But the choice was too great for someone like myself. I nearly worried myself sick over it. At one moment I thought there were those of us with souls so great that one overpowering love was not enough, that we could never be fulfilled as simply as the common herd. The next moment I had plunged from those dizzying heights of power and assurance into the slough of despond where I wanted to clutch my breast lest my throbbing heart burst its bounds. It was then I would demand of God why He tortured so mere a man as I with loves sufficient to overwhelm Titans. Up and down, up and down. I assure you, I hardly knew where I was or what I was about when Mother practically led me down the steps of that great silver plane when we arrived in London for the second Final Play of my life.

I know I can't have made sense when interviewed at the terminal by the British Press. I've seen newsreels of it since, and I looked the perfect dolt! Fortunately, Mother was able to stand them off and get me away to some relative seclusion. The very next morning was the first day of Play, and many wondered whether I ought to have come earlier to get used to the damp and chill. But what could chill me? I wanted to know. That first day's Play was incredible. I was in such a tizzy: angry, is closer to the truth of the matter. *Anastasia* was on my mind. There had come that smooth-talking beast pulling out his silver cigarette case, removing a cigarette from it, tapping it ever so slowly. Then he actually started to *light* the thing. But she was too quick for him. "Who gave you permission to smoke in my presence?" she snapped, her eyes positively piercing. "Who are you?" he replied slowly, but not smoking, his voice still defiant, but nonetheless awed.

Who are you? indeed! She is Anastasia, you idiot. Anastasia Nicolaievna Romanova, Grand Duchess, youngest daughter of Nicholas II. *That's* who she is, you fool . . .

. . . and before I knew it, I had laid out my opening game of Klondike in four point eight seconds, itself a new World Record. I went on to win that and the succeeding four games shuffling and riffling the deck so quickly, setting up the games so speedily, and playing with such precision—there are films of it, and in all five games there was never a single instance which even my greatest enemies could suggest by any malicious stretch of the imagination constituted a hestitation—that the five games were finished in three minutes and twelve point two seconds. My hands flew so that the judges had to slow down the film to make certain there had been neither errors nor hesitations. Five consecutive perfect games, another World Record by two.

"He must be spent," I heard someone whisper in awe when it was over.

Spent? Never! Say, rather, I was exhilarated. Intoxicated! Totally at the peak of form. The others, *au contraire,* were absolutely useless the remainder of the week. They faltered. They missed plays. They were incapable of improvising off of set hands. They couldn't pay attention to their own games for sneaking quick little glances over at my long and nimble fingers which not only shuffled and riffled and dealt, but also picked up and manipulated the cards with a grace, style, and—if I may say so myself—wit in the presence of which those other Masters had never previously sat.

On the last day I was so far ahead on all counts that I could have sailed for home and still won. However, I didn't. I stayed and, I must admit, feeling the throb and verve of my matured, youthful vigor, I put on a show for them all. By noon, the other three Grand Masters simply stopped their own pointless fumblings and, God bless them all, scooted their chairs around to watch as I finished out the Play's requirements.

When it was over, there was absolute silence in the Great Hall. Then one of them—the Argentine Cowboy of the Pampas, now that I think about it—reached out and with the most reverential gentleness took my left hand—the one I actually deal with. Cupping it in both of his, he bent his head and, his thick, bristly, fierce-looking moustache partly tickling and partly prickling, kissed my finger tips.

I was touched beyond description.

"Well," I said, trying to busy myself back to the surface of everyday events. There was but one further official duty, and that was to present myself with the Golden Ace, which I did. I felt rather like Napoleon must have felt as he took the crown from the very hands of Pope Pius VII that cold December day and—to the trembling amazement of the gathered multitudes—crowned himself Emperor of the French.

I couldn't have known it at the time, naturally enough, but the heady days of my life were left there in the Great Hall when I went through the symbolic motion of passing the Golden Ace from my right hand to my left as the throng broke out in a *Huzzah!* the tumultuous nature of which normally was so alien to Solitaire.

And if you now detect a certain reluctance on my part to proceed directly to the next and for me last Final Play, it is not because I am all that inclined toward reticence. Rather, it is because it is now all retrospect and can be seen so very much more clearly. At twenty-four, one is in one's fullest vigor—at least in certain ways. My Play in London had been . . . how shall I describe it? I can't, really. So let me merely cite several representative reviews. And please *do* understand: I am not trying to be boastful, merely informative and thorough so that my later years can be viewed with some greater insight.

From the SPOW *Recorder:*

Never in the recorded history of World Solitaire has anyone seen the sheer physical dexterity, stamina, strength, and purity of form as demonstrated in this Final Play.

From the *New York World Telegram:*

The performance from start to finish was absolutely breath-taking . . .

From the *New York Times:*

After the opening game, one wondered what possibly could come next. But come it did: play after play, game after game. It was inventiveness, it was consistency; it was consummate skill in all phases . . .

From the *Times* of London:

Benedicte, having amply demonstrated ten years ago that a *Wunderkind* could do more than dominate a Play (even to include the Plays of Ivan Spaastich), left many observers wondering what possibly could be left this time 'round from a performance that had been so ingenuously bold. We found out, right enough. Where he had been merely bold, he was now virtually flippant; where he had been merely brilliant, he now was a starburst of brilliantes, each point of which outshone the other Grand Masters; where he had been merely powerful, he now was absolutely overwhelming; where he had been . . .

Ah, but it serves no greater use to quote further. After returning home, after ensconcing the Golden Ace once again on our mantlepiece, after wandering about the City again, taking in its smells and sights and sounds, its very *feel* as though I had been away thirteen weeks rather than thirteen days, after all the obligatory unwinding and interviews and meetings with all the local and neighborhood clubs was over, I started into a period of emotional decline.

Certainly I wasn't aware of it as it was happening. And certainly I kept as busy as ever I had, looking forward (in a tolerant sort of way) to the next Final Play. But as the years went by as they so remorselessly do, a certain heaviness of spirit began closing in on me. It wasn't oppressive, mind. At least not exactly. But one's twenty-fifth birthday does something to one. When one recognizes it as a quarter century, why then it partakes of *history.* One's sense of time and one's perspective can reasonably be expected to alter.

. . . and then thirty years. Think of it, I thought. I felt fine; I was healthy; my vigor in the game was as great as ever. And yet . . .

. . . and yet I felt a certain *dash,* a bit of *elan,* a touch of the *flippancy,* as the *Times* had used the word, was draining away. And I awoke one night as I seldom ever did—at least not in this way. I awoke one night soundly drenched with perspiration. I sat bolt upright in bed. I heard nothing untoward. My little night light was burning merrily, and I *saw* nothing to give fright. But I *was* frightened.

I didn't dare mention this to Mother, because it would cause her to worry, and goodness knows she had plenty enough to worry about as it was what with the theatre organ business going into a decline as it did and her having to reach very deeply indeed into her purse of inner resources to keep ahead. She was up to it, quite naturally, but it was a struggle.

Too, the City, one could see with greater and greater clarity, was going steadily and rapidly downhill. On my own thirtieth birthday Mother was approached by some creature or other in a highly improper manner, and she already forty-eight! Oh, nothing came of it—thank Good Fortune for that—but it gave us both an unpleasant turn, nonetheless.

I tended to stay in more than was my want—or my habit—contenting myself with relatively brief strolls down to Washington Square or wherever. But it wasn't the same. The Square once had been the delightful preserve of nannies with their precious charges, prams being gently rocked or lovingly pushed about. And there were older men who played chess at each other with a silent ponderousness one could hardly believe. Lovers used to stroll, and the weather was always perfect in Washington Square.

But the nannies' little charges had grown up into those Flower People things or whatever, the nannies were long gone, and the lovers—Well! There certainly never was any doubt that they were lovers. One had continuously to be alert to the indecent advances of all sorts of strange persons, persons who wanted to fill you chock-a-block with illicit drugs, or sell you nasty photographs of people engaged in positively frightening activities, or—my God!—offering themselves to you for the same purposes. There was simply no longer any *rest* to be had there. And barricades got erected periodically, and loudspeakers blared out with people chanting obscenities on all hands. One would have thought himself in Paris during the Terror, for goodness' sake. It seemed the world of riot and confusion would force its way into one's life like it or no.

Still, one keeps going. Once on a Sunday in early October, I took a deck of cards and Port-a-Lap-Board (a device of my own invention) and set out to play a few hands in what I hoped would be the calm of those golden autumnal days.

Hardly had I gotten under way when I realized I was not alone. Peering over my left shoulder was a creature with matted hair and beard and what looked to me like a leftover daisy sagging woefully from behind his ear, remnant of God knows what kind of orgy from the night before. He was shoeless, and rather than by a proper shirt, his torso was covered only by an undershirt.

"Ooh," he said. I must admit I was startled, but I played on.

"Like, Man," he said after a good play.

He moved around from behind me, which alleviated my concern at least somewhat, and squatted before me. I played on. Several deft moves later my observer offered, "Wow! Like, Man, you know?" and he looked up at me with eyes genuinely impressed.

I shrugged ever so slightly as I continued dealing out another game. He cracked his knuckles soundly once, a request, I took it, to be invited to play. Then he—almost shyly, it seemed—touched my Port-a-Lap-Board.

"Ooh, Man," he said. "Like Wow!"

At first I thought he must be mad, capable only of babbling such gibberish. But I gathered it wasn't quite that. Oddly, though, I found myself running through one of my better set routines. We all have them, as when gymnasts go through what they call exercises to music. I simply found myself doing it. And then I started another. It was the presence of an audience, you see, a highly appreciative though essentially untutored one.

"Like, Man," he tried again, raising his eyebrows at me while making circular motions with a hand. "You know?"

I didn't, so he tried once more.

"You know, like," and he spread his hands out over my board which I had designed myself so that Double Solitaire games could be accomodated.

"You know?" he said. "Like, Man . . ." and he gestured again.

"Ah," I responded, able at last to garner meaning. "Do you wish to play a game of Double Solitaire with me?" I spoke as clearly as possible in case his hearing was as defective as his speech. I shall never forget the look on his face. He positively glowed.

"Cool," he said, and we played.

It must have been two solid hours that we played, and much to my surprise he knew quite a few games. Further, he wasn't half bad, though of course he was nowhere near me in any respect of the game. Still . . .

"Your fingering," I said. "You could be quite good if you, well, chose to attend to it."

"Man!" he said. "You dig deep."

With that, he arose from his knees, reached out slowly to very softly shake my hand, and sauntered away. It was only then that I became aware of the rather considerable crowd we had attracted. Some, no doubt, were merely curious. But it was perfectly clear that others had been able to keep up with what was going on. Many were of the bearded sort, with smelly sandals and all, but one actually recognized me.

"Benedicte," I heard him whisper.

I acknowledged his recognition with a discreet bow of my head. The small gathering applauded with great courtesy as I folded up my Port-a-Lap-Board and made my way through the fresh, sweet air toward home.

So life went on, as it always has managed to do. There were the new games to devise, the basics to keep fresh on, the various new clubs and associations to sponsor, the textbooks to write or revise, new loves . . .

Yes, you may well have understood that already.

New loves. Oh, God, I queried once quite seriously. Why do you make us so prone to temptation?

It was Katherine Hepburn, as you might have imagined. Spencer Tracy's Dearest Kate. *The African Queen, Suddenly Last Summer, The Lion in Winter*. There simply was no end to what she could do. I had admired her for years, quite naturally, but it took those years of growth and discovery to bring me 'round to where I could at long last admit I loved her. The realization had been growing in me for some time—the closer it appeared there soon would be another Final Play.

It certainly would be inaccurate to assert that I had "emerged" as one of the four Grand Masters, because I never had left the top of the deck, but three others were emerging, and all of them, I realized, were good. Terribly good! I also took considerable pride in knowing that I had spotted them as early as 1965, ten years before my last Final Play. It would be a tough go, I knew, and the odds most assuredly were against me. Even that internationally known oddsman Angelo the Cretan was silent until the very eve of the Play. The Old Magician (as I had been long-since dubbed by the *New Yorker*) would have to rely as never before on age, experience, and that one thing that always had set me apart: that I *knew* Solitaire.

So it was that, coincidentally, my mystical gift, my *Kenntnis* of the Game was coming full cycle at just the same time that I understood the true nature of passion and desire in my personal life.

As the time drew near and the Four were made public, as the site was announced—Salzburg—as the Play was coming, I knew one thing ever more clearly: I was going to win this Final Play. Winning two had been done. Winning two in a row had not. But to win three! And to win them in succession! Think of it, if you can. How many Mark Spitzes have won seven gold medals in three consecutive Olympiads? How many baseball players have pitched what they quaintly call perfect games three times in a row, or in three consecutive World Series? Well, but truly comparable examples simply don't exist. I knew I would be declared Master Grand-Master.

That's all there was to it.

I knew what I knew, and for the very first time, I was calm. As I walked down the center of the *Getreidegasse,* the street on which stood the house in which the little Wolfgang Amadeus Mozart had lived and composed and played, I was as unruffled as ever I had been in my life. One can't ever say, always, precisely why certain things are. There are so many reasons, usually. I was calm because I knew what I knew about my life, which was Solitaire; I was calm because I was forty-three, not twenty-four or fourteen; I was calm because I knew that after this Play I would retire from active competition; more than all that, however, there was a *serenity* within me. Walking by my side, Mother was absolutely regal! She smiled and waved to the throngs like Maria Theresa, the very Archduchess herself. But it was the spirit and calm maturity of Katherine Hepburn that washed through me, that gave me the sense of interior *Gemütlichkeit* I carried throughout that positively grueling week.

One, it occurs to me, can describe a soccer match replete with overlaps and headers and scissor kicks and all the rest. The same holds true for all other athletic events in which people must, perforce, get along with one another in order to accomplish scores and wins and all that. There is even a means by which that sluggish game chess is noted—just as surely as are musical scores. But chess, though some perceive it as a solitary pastime, is still a competition between two people: one must check one's opponent's king. And though people do, apparently, play against themselves to keep in practice, that really is impossible, for it requires one to pretend he is unaware of what he himself intends.

Solitaire, on the contrary, and Double Solitaire games not withstanding, is still a much more highly personal sort of thing. This holds true in spite of competition. Runners, for instance, race the clock, which is to say, finally, themselves. So it is with Solitaire. It is a means by which one attempts to better oneself rather than best an opponent: hence its classical purity.

Solitaire, however, has its own system of notations, most of which become quite thick with complexity—like the printed notations of a choreographed dance. Still, Solitaire people read these notations with the same reverence, awe, or simple interest as chess people read game resumes.

Here, for instance, was my opening Klondike win:

(H) A-8 (C) A-7 (D) A-9 (S) A-10

10(D)	Q(D)	K(S)	K(H)	K(D)	K(C)
9(C)	J(C)	Q(H)	Q(S)	Q(C)	
	10(H)	J(S)	J(H)	J(D)	
			10(C)		
			9(H)		
			8(C)		

This is a simple thing, of course, but will do to show what our archives look like.

As for scoring, a highly complex method of tabulating points has been developed over the centuries (we Solitaire people being an ancient race). One gets points for winning games; one gets points on the basis of cards played (or how few remain unplayable); one gets points additionally on the basis of the complexity of the game.

But one can get points deducted as well. For example, if one could have played the 3(D) up to a 4(C) (that is, a three of diamonds up to a four of clubs), but failed to see it, points are deducted—*unless* (you begin to understand why competent judges are necessary) unless the player did in fact see the play, but chose deliberately to ignore it for a specific *Reason of Misplay*. In that case, the player must state at the time of the play his intention to bypass—and why. Obviously, even with just four players, the din could become most distracting; so there has grown up an intricate complex of hand, finger, and facial signs and signals to indicate whatever needs indicating. Such signals also obviate the need for linguistic experts who might misunderstand a spoken explanation of play. To us it is all no more complicated than the serious bidding at high-level auctions in the showroom of Sothebys, or whomever. But to an outsider it can look rather like the most elaborate mass of tics ever assembled—especially with three judges, each armed with note pads and pencils, staring intently at each player.

Then there are points to be gained for the playing out of games set up by the judges; points to be awarded for inventiveness, the creation of variations on old games; points to be awarded for intricacy of pattern play (such as I had been doing in Washington Square when the hairy chap arrived); and points to be awarded for the *style* with which one is able to manipulate the deck in laying out the games, keeping neat rows or stacks or whatever. At the end, the player who has amassed the greatest number of points is declared Master Grand-Master and is charged with the care of the Golden Ace until the next Final Play.

I was named Master Grand-Master.

It sounds so simple, doesn't it? I was named Master Grand-Master for the third consecutive Final Play. So much for *facts!*

The issue was not resolved until the very last game. Not, that is, according to the point count. My opponent was a brilliant young man named Anthony Alexander whose mother was a gorgeous lady from the Isle of Patmos and whose father was a famed classics scholar from Exeter University. Anthony had beautiful white teeth and eyes which—though gentle—possessed mystery. He was, in that regard, like me. I sensed that he, too, had that *Kenntnis* of Solitaire that I possessed, though not to my degree.

In most Solitaire games there are times when two or three or even more plays are possible. To *guess* which play to pursue can leave one vulnerable to guessing incorrectly and thus losing; to play *always* to a pattern is to make one's game rigid and thus blind one to possibilities; to play at random or to make a play merely because it is the closest to hand is to show oneself lazy and thus lacking in respect for the Game. Most people play in those ways. Some few have intuitions. And I dare say that when I speak of *knowing* Solitaire, *knowing* those cards, all I am saying is that what I *know* is intuition raised to an infinite power.

Young Anthony Alexander had that special intuition that I had, only it was raised to the $(\infty - 1)$ power. Going into that last game we were tied in points, and our hands, as we dealt them out, drew nearly audible gasps from the judges, for they were identical, with the exception that two showing cards were reversed.

At the crucial point, young Anthony's hand hesitated visibly (visibly to the judges) and he chose to make a play that left him with four cards unplayable.

Concentrating as probably never before, I did not hesitate, and I made the play that left me with but three unplayable cards. Thus I was again named Master Grand-Master.

We arose simultaneously, and with an emotion-laden sob brought on by that week's intensity and strain, we all but fell into each other's embrace. I was both congratulating and consoling him, and as he was congratulating me, I felt in his strong embrace my powers charging into him. There was a literal shock as with electricity, a spark, a charge which we both felt immediately. He tried, out of deference to me, to withdraw himself, but I held him fast. As I did so, I felt for just the splittest of seconds that I was being held by Katherine. Then it was done. From the movies of the Play one would never have known a thing.

As we separated, our hands clasped in that symbol of our eternal union, I whispered to him, "Next time, Young Anthony Alexander, I shall be bringing the Golden Ace to you."

We wept unashamedly and embraced once more.

So now it's all over. The Golden Ace sits on our mantel waiting for me to deliver it to Anthony—whenever. Mother is as active and busy as ever. She fetched down about the depths of her inner resources and found another living. I knew she would. It's still music with her. Electronic things. She played Moogs: mini-Moogs, mini-micro-Moogs, a Moog 15, poly-Moogs; she plays ARP Odyssey String Synthesizers, ARP String Ensembles ("Phil would have been so proud of me," she told me); she plays clavenets and heaven only knows what else.

She has to travel some, but it's all studio recordings. She said the people are all so interesting. I suppose they are. They all seem to adore Mother, and though they always want her to do their Moogy business for them in the studio sessions, they convinced her, finally, that she couldn't keep up the pace on the tours. She even has taken on several *nom de* . . . Well, not *plumes*, I don't suppose. *Noms de keyboard electronique*, perhaps. In any event, she does well, and when the groups she plays for go out on their tours, fans always ask where she is—whichever of her names they know her by. And whichever group it is must always respond that whomever she is is off with some other group at that time, but surely will be with them on their next tour. Mother finds it all very amusing.

And as for myself . . .

I don't play in competition any longer. There's a certain palsy to my hands. I noticed it starting in the meaty portion of my right thumb during the last Final Play. Hardly detectable, you understand, but there nonetheless. It results in a certain tremble, a certain lack of daring in the shuffle and deal.

But during a monstrous press conference after my triumphant return from Salzburg—I could still hear the bells of all the churches and the Cathedral in the City ringing for me—the question was asked, "Benedicte, now that you have announced your retirement, aren't you afraid you'll miss the thrill of center stage?"

It was a perceptive question, and I gave it considerable thought before replying. I thought of the three Final Plays; I thought of my youthful passion for Elizabeth, my more mature love for Ingrid, my profounder affection for Katherine; and I thought how I still loved them, loved them all.

But I also thought of that gorgeous October day in Washington Square Park and that bit of, well, magic that happened there. And I recalled quite suddenly and physically that I had asked Mother essentially the same question so many years earlier.

And the two—both the question and my remembrance of that enchanted experience in the Park with the hairy chap and the gathered crowd—went quivering through me, drawing from my past and pointing the way to the future. I answered my interrogator as I had been answered by Mother.

"Miss center stage? Oh, I don't think I shall ever have left it, actually."

The press conference had been going on for an hour by the time that question was asked, and when I finished my response, the senior reporter from the SPOW *Recorder* stood to close the proceedings. The others quickly followed suit by rising to their feet, too, as he said,

"Thank you, Benedicte."

A Mature and
Civilized Relationship

• • I hadn't really liked the idea of the thing at all, but what could I do? Walter had asked me to go along, and, trusting my very best friend's intuition and sensibilities about such matters, I said, "Okay, if you think it'll be okay with Pat."

"Sure," Walter had answered me. "Sure it is."

So there I was waiting for the door to the apartment in Mamaroneck to be opened to us. I heard the latch clack out. The door swung in and there was Pat: smiling, a cute little heart-shaped apron tied around her dress. She put up her cheek for me to peck, which I did.

"Hi," she said, but before Walter or I either one could say a word, little Walter had bounded down the short hall and as near sailed into his dad's arms as a four-year-old boy can come to sailing through the air.

"Hey, big boy," Walter said, and gave him a big hug.

"Old bear, old bear," the boy laughed.

"Big ole bear gonna eat you up. Gobblegobblegobble," his dad said, and acted like he was a big old woolly bear eating the boy up.

Then he started to put the kid down, but couldn't because the little fellow held on for dear life, his arms and legs clutching for all they were worth.

Pat had closed and latched the door and stood smiling at the two of them as they went on into the living room. I looked at Pat and smiled, or at least I twitched my face at her as best I could.

"Hi," I said.

"Hi," she said back.

We stood there for a second, me shuffling my feet and looking down as though to see how shiny my shoe tips were and feeling embarrassed as all hell.

Then Pat laughed, almost like she used to, and she said, "Well, come on in, Nuck. I haven't seen you in a long time."

"Yeh," I answered. "Yeh, it's been a while, all right. How're you . . ."

I was going to ask her how she was doing, how she was getting along—the divorce, not having a man around, having to raise little Walt all by herself, and all. But I was embarrassed, still. I hadn't seen her at all in the six months since the divorce, and hardly at all since Walter came home to her that afternoon a year ago and sat down right where he was sitting now reading *Babar* to Walt, sat down while she was whipping up some eggs in a dish, say, getting ready to fry them for Walt's supper, her probably smiling then just like she was smiling now, or at least almost like it, and him saying right out of nowhere, "Honey, I have decided that I don't love you and I want a divorce."

That's how it had been, and that after spending four solid hours in town with his sister, whom he loves dearly, talking about it, her finally getting him to understand, she thought, that the fifth or sixth year of marriage was likely to be a rough one because, well, *because,* I guess. And it seemed that he had understood his sister, had comprehended that she had gone through it herself, but that things get right again if you only try to help them: that the feeling to be shut of a person along about then was as natural as the initial desire for the person had been, and that with patience and time things, well, things get right. So he came directly home, sat down, and said he didn't love her and wanted a divorce.

And now here I was getting ready to eat supper with them: Walter playing his weekly role of daddy with little Walt; Pat real collected: smiley and pretty in her cute little heart-shaped fancy-

146

dress apron preparing dinner for her no-longer husband; and me—little Walt's titular godfather—who loved them all three and didn't know what to say or do or anything.

When Walter had asked me to come with him that night, I thought he must have been kidding; so I told him I didn't think that was a very funny joke. But he said no, he wasn't joking, that he went out to see Walt, really. Visitation rights. But you mean she cooks you dinner? There? You all sit around like you were still married?

"Well, Nuck," he'd laughed real easy. "Of course. I mean, Pat and I are both adults. The shock is over. Sure, it gets a little sticky now and then, but . . ."

I noticed he never said but *what,* but I figured, Okay. Maybe that's the way to be. Now me: if I didn't love the girl any more, I wouldn't want to see her again if I didn't have to, and I figured she sure wouldn't want to see me at all. But Walter's a whole lot more Uptown than I am; so I figured: what the hell, there's always a lot to learn.

Pat seemed to sense my predicament and gave me a drink of Scotch without my asking—a pretty stiff jolt, too—so I knew she must have felt funny.

We all sat down, finally. Walter had a beer and Pat was sipping sherry. Little Walt didn't need anything except his daddy's bouncing knees. Walter was chanting,

Here we go to Mulberry Town,
Watch out, Little Boy,
You'll faaaaaal . . . . . . DOWN!

And down would fall Walt between his daddy's knees. He laughed and giggled, that boy, and just carried on like he hadn't played in a month or more. And he was being so sweet he even looked at me and grinned.

"Walt, you never did even say hello to Uncle Nuck," Walter said to him.

Walt looked from me back to his daddy then back to me. I thought I saw something fierce in his eyes for a second—you know, like he resented my being there or something—but he lowered them, and when he looked back up, his face twisted into a smile and he said, "Hey, Uncle Nuck."

"Hey, Little Walt," I said, and raised my glass to him.

At the dinner table there was never a single break in the conversation. I thought maybe that was natural enough, but I still felt a little creepy about it without ever knowing quite why. Pat would ask Walter how his job was coming along—he worked for an import-export firm—and he would say that it was fine. Then he'd ask how Walt's kindergarten was, and she would say that it was all right or fine or whatever. Then he'd tell her some little event that happened during the week, and she'd reply with a little anecdote about Walt in kindergarten or something cute he'd said during the week. Then one of them would drag me into things: Had I seen so-and-so? He was in town this week and called. Yes I had or no I hadn't.

But it didn't hit me until supper was close to over: my God, they just saw each other last week. Do they ask the same questions every Saturday night? But there was never time for conversation to lag any, because little Walt was in on everything and on top of the whole show. Finally it got so he was doing all the talking: daddy this and daddy that. I got to watching him between forkfuls of fried squash and bites of hot rolls, and I swear to God he was the best little boy in the world.

Once, he started in on silly talk like kids do. "He's poopie," or "That's fragblatch," or some such nonsense, and he'd start to get real tickled with himself. Then Pat would say, "Walt, daddy doesn't want to hear all that kind of silly talk." And he'd cut it off—I mean right now!

Or he started messing with his food and Walter would tell him real gently that he had to eat to grow up to be a big boy. I swear to goodness he was cute—and the best little four-year-old I'd ever seen, and being an uncle of twelve myself, I'd seen plenty of them. The whole time we'd been there he hadn't made a slip. He'd been good and cute and even kind.

But I got to sneaking looks at him through the meal, and finally it came to me that he was more than just glad to see his Daddy, he was more than just a naturally sharp little boy who could make lots of conversation that made every bit as much sense as how's your job fine and how's kindergarten fine. And then he caught me sneaking a look at him.

I think it might have been all right, maybe, if I had just plain been looking at him and smiling the kind of smile a no-real-kin-Uncle-who's-known-the-child's-mommy-and-daddy-for-all-through-college-and-well-past is entitled to smile. And maybe if something I didn't even know myself had been starting to surface in me I wouldn't have been sneaking those looks in the first place. But it had been dawning on me that no kid is all that good. Certainly not one who is so into things and quick headed as that little boy was. And I finally knew that the something that had been growing in me without my knowing it was showing on my face. My father, I recall, often would trace a pattern on my arm and say, "Enoch, you wear your heart on your sleeve, son." For a long time I figured that that was a failure of character, but I thought I had developed a pretty good poker face until I looked at that kid *behaving*. He was so painfully *behaving,* so desperately being good, I guess my face cracked just enough for him to see how I felt, and being most likely smarter than me anyway, he must have known right off what I didn't know yet. Because he caught me sneaking a look at him right after I'd sneaked a look at Walter and Pat, the both of them being so civilized and up to date and *mature* about what had happened: both of them—hell, all three of us—playing a game a whole lot stupider than little Walt's "poopie" talk. I realized then that Walter and Pat were the two most miserable people I think I'd ever seen.

When I looked over at little Walt and saw his lake-blue eyes boring holes in my skull, I wished I could have snapped my fingers and been a thousand miles away. Man, I mean he hated me. He hated me in the way only a kid can hate you—with everything they've got. He pulled his eyebrows down so far I thought he'd never be able to get them back up again. Then all of a sudden he threw at me, threw at me whatever happened to be in his hand to throw, and lucky for me it was only a small, child's spoon. I say lucky, but even now, sometimes, I wish it had been something big and heavy enough to have left a fat scar on my forehead instead of some gravy I could wipe right off with the napkin.

Walter and Pat looked at each other and then at me and didn't know what to do or say, it was so sudden. And of course they couldn't have known why he had done it. No, they had been so busy being civilized and *mature* with each other that they hadn't had the time to see that their son had been seen through by good ole Uncle Nuck; that good, kind Uncle Nuck was the one who had had to comprehend that their little boy had been very carefully building a sad and awful tale for himself.

I hadn't meant to do it, but it was me that busted that smart child's happy little bubble, because he saw my heart on my sleeve; he saw spread all over my face the knowledge I didn't even know I had. What I knew in my heart was what he was telling himself every day when he woke up alone in the apartment with his mother, what he was thinking when he lay down on his blanket for rest period at kindergarten, what he was dreaming when he looked up from his coloring book in the late afternoon because he heard a step in the hallway outside and his mind leaped to the hope that it was Saturday already: *If I am good,* he was making himself believe, *if I am very very good, daddy will come back to me and make things right again.*

Well, that had been something he could go to bed on and something he could get up in the mornings with. But I had smashed it all to hell and back for him when he saw me sneaking looks at his mother and father, and he knew it in his bones.

After he threw his spoon at me, his whole face started trembling until it finally collapsed. A child's tears. Good God damn!

Walter calmed him down, but when he got him into the bedroom the boy started crying again. Pat was in the hall with me, fidgeting her hands around the bow of her apron like a frustrated woman trying not to look like a frustrated woman.

"Don't go, Daddy, don't go," little Walt kept saying, trying like hell not to cry any more than he was.

But we left.

When we got downstairs Walter pulled out a handkerchief and wiped his face. I will say this for him: he was sweating like all fury and even trembling a little.

"I'm sorry, Nuck," he apologized. He was going to say something else, I imagined, but I couldn't help myself. I wanted like everything to tell him what had happened. Hell, he was my very best friend. But I couldn't, so I turned on him. I said, "Go to hell, you son of a bitch," and walked off.

Like I said, I loved all three of them—very, very much. But I think that if I ever see Walter again (which I haven't for a long time now, and which I don't either plan or expect to do) I'd have to call him what I did again. I'm sure it's wrong of me. It may be he just made me look at myself a little too closely. Still, I can't help but feel that he made me take something terribly fragile away from someone who didn't have anything solider to take around with him. Oh, I know. It would have happened eventually. The boy'll have to get used to lots worse before it's all done with. But damn it, when a fellow's worked like hell to make something that'll help him through bad times—a patch to cover the heart on his sleeve, a poker face, an ignorant hope that's got no chance of coming true—why it seems a dirty trick to rip it from him before he's tough enough to understand what it is he's lost.

Three Rivers

· · "Your violins, of course," Margaret said, one hand holding to the coiled wire of the phone.

Katherine laughed. "You pianists always want the whole world to yourselves."

"No-no," Margaret countered quickly. "Well after all, there's the cello. Be fair to me."

Katherine asked her again. "You'll come? Please?"

Margaret said nothing for a minute. Then, "I do have that Three Rivers thing coming up, and I've just *got* to start pushing him through his paces harder."

She felt the pressure of Katherine on the other end of the line, could almost see her pulling her lips in, tightening them as she waited for an answer. "But of course," she said at last.

There was a slight pause. "I know you still disapprove," Katherine said.

"Oh no-no," Margaret answered quickly, struggling to keep track of where in time she was. "I never *dis*approved. Not at all."

"But I can tell you still withhold, Margaret. Are you going to withhold yourself from me forever? There isn't enough time left for that."

"I told you I'd come, Katherine," Margaret said. She looked down at her free hand and slowly flexed it: opening, closing.

"But you're still angry with me. I wish you wouldn't be, Margaret."

"I've said I would be there." She paused. "Which have you really called me about?"

She sensed the stutter of hesitation before the answer. "Oh, Margaret, if you could only see them. They love it so. If you could just *hear* them . . ."

"Katherine, I said I'd be there." She felt the edge of bother in her own voice.

"There's one little girl especially," Katherine rattled on, talking rapidly, she realized, afraid something awful might happen if she stopped, talking only partly to inform Margaret that good things were happening: talking desperately, as though holding on—not just to herself, not just to Margaret—but to something of herself long past, something thrumming up through them that—if never resolved—had never been lost, either; something that had always been lodged securely within each of them, something that would always be with them as much as between them.

"She's so good. You wouldn't believe it. Oh, Margaret, she's . . . she's . . ."

Margaret felt it, too. But it was harder for her. She pulled the cord through her hands, straightening it, watching it coil right back up. She felt suddenly worn out—and cautious, wary that she might have to generate more energy to reinvest what little emotional capital she still had, right then.

"I'm looking forward to it," she said. She looked sharply at her hand as she continued to flex it. "Looking forward to it very much," and she smiled a firm smile.

Margaret sat at the rear of the drafty, over-heated church hall listening to Katherine lead her children and their parents through "Twinkle, Twinkle" and all the rest. She was barely able to hold down the rising gorge. There! There she was: once one of the most talented violinists she had ever known, working for ten dollar fees from childrens' lessons. Margaret clenched her hands on her thighs and wanted to scream at Katherine for having pulled back, for having made bad choices, for just plain terrible errors of judgement.

She gave her head a little shake to clear the past from it, startled to find that past still so close to the surface, as though there hadn't been any twenty-five years. But as she listened to the little ones, she understood how it could happen. More than a failure of nerve, though less than that, too.

The group moved into "Allegro" and "Gently Row" and on through the standard repertoire. Then they were done as a group. The mothers and fathers sat down and the solos began. She knew enough about the method not to expect the squawking brays usually heard from amateur violins, but she was struck at how natural the children were. So natural, most of them, that they looked less self-conscious holding their little half-sized violins than wearing their Sunday clothes.

She listened. There were the exaggerated, slow cadences. She could hear them counting in their heads. And yet there was a freedom, too: a modest daring born of innocence.

Then came Frederika. She looked as impish as most nine year old girls. She was to play a Vivaldi. She played. Margaret listened. Slowly her hands unclenched as she listened more critically.

My God, she thought. Those vibratos are good. Very good. And her bowing. She *attacks!* Those inflections. Good heavens, Margaret muttered audibly. She knows what she's playing. Really *knows* the music . . .

Then the selection was over. The others played. The proud parents and visitors—amazed that anyone under eighty could play anything at all—applauded. It was done.

Margaret was about to get up, walk leisurely down front, wait for Katherine to go through the obligatory routine of shaking hands, smiling, and otherwise dealing with the parents. But the little musician came back on stage, violin and bow held casually, professionally, naturally. She whispered up on tiptoe to Katherine who then came forward to announce that Frederika had been working hard on an extra number and wanted to try it out to see if she could get through it "in concert." Katherine smiled as Frederika looked unconcerned. The audience settled down again. The child played.

She was a child and there were childish elements to her play, but what Margaret caught was something else, whatever Katherine had been babbling about on the phone earlier in the week. This was the one, all right. This was the one, and Margaret took off her glasses and narrowed her eyes until Frederika was no more than a splotch of pink fuzz in the center of her vision. And she listened— not only to Frederika, but to herself as well, and to Katherine when they, too, had been that age: eight, nine, ten.

Her eyes closed completely as her ears did the hard work: the listening whole, the consecutive taking apart and putting together again as the tune suddenly started wobbling to a close, but sure, somehow, of its own wobbly-ness and *why* it was wobbly, and in certain knowledge in those tired but still knowing fingers that the next time "in concert" they wouldn't desert her *there,* at least.

This one will have to choose one day, Margaret thought. She opened her eyes. The music had stopped. Frederika stood alone on the stage, her violin tucked in place, her bow weaving slightly as she tried to remember where she was. A second. Two. Three. Even the audience could feel that an end had come and was getting ready to applaud the failure at the last even more loudly than it had the success earlier. Four. And Katherine made a tenuous motion as though to move forward smiling, to put her arm around the child's shoulder in a congratulatory embrace for handling well what really was still beyond her.

But the bow came down suddenly as though the little girl had seen the motion and had seen further, had seen years beyond it. The bow struck home, and the child ran through the concluding coda— a short one only some six or eight measures—almost perfectly. Almost. Her fingers were tired, her shoulder and neck weary. When she finished, Margaret saw that inner-looking stare of the child who neither heard nor cared about the clapping that followed. Margaret was up, tears starting from her eyes, gone before Katherine could free herself.

Then she was standing outside the church, her heart slamming, wondering where she would go. But Katherine found her before she could escape.

"Margaret. Oh, Margaret, were you really going to run away from me like that?"

Margaret turned. She saw the hurt in her friend's face, felt it in her own.

"No, Katherine. No, I don't suppose I was." She laughed once as she wiped her eyes with the heel of one hand. "Well, I don't suppose I could, could I?"

"Wait for me inside for just a few minutes, then we'll go have a cup of tea."

Margaret let herself be led back inside to wait until Katherine finished talking to the parents, doting relatives, and children.

"There," she said after they had seated themselves and ordered. "Now, Margaret. First, I wasn't sure you'd come. But I was so excited when I saw you . . ." Her voice trembled. "And I was so confused when I saw you rush out."

"So much came back to me, Katherine. You. Me. Us. The music. The whole world back then. It was too much there for a minute. I panicked. I'm sorry."

Katherine shrugged. "You still haven't forgiven me, have you, Margaret?"

Margaret pursed her lips, then very deliberately ate a creamed cheese sandwich.

"Um," she said, chewing slowly. "I guess not. Not really."

She sipped her tea. Katherine lowered her eyes.

"But time and age do things to you." She brushed Katherine's arm with the slightest touch. "What I really mean is, they do things *for* you, too, don't they? I mean, you're twenty-five years older, too."

"Um."

They were silent for a long time as they searched each others' faces.

"I always had the feeling it was as much a lovers' quarrel with you, Margaret. As much that as the music. Maybe more."

"Lovers' quarrel?"

"I mean," Katherine went on. "I mean a quarrel of love, maybe." She laughed softly. "Maybe I don't know what I mean. There seem to be so many hard lines drawn around everything these days. If a woman wants to be 'liberated,' she has to be a bit bent, if you know what I mean. If she wants a family, she's a traitor to her profession. If she wants a profession, she's a traitor to her sex. Nobody gets a chance just to *be* any more."

Katherine paused, then smiled. "But tell me about Three Rivers. Tell me all about it. Last year," she looked pensive for a moment. "Last year was absolutely awful. You wouldn't believe! Everything that could go wrong did: my God, from kids in trouble to hysterectomies to angry parents to school strikes to company cutbacks . . .

"Until I finally collapsed. Then I told Leonard. 'Leonard, enough! Either you put me in the hospital for a week, or shut me out on the sunporch for the week—ALONE!—and let me watch this glorious spring come over us all.' And I told him that if he wanted me to get a note from my doctor to prove I was at the end of my rope, I would. So I did. I practically moved out there with my little ear infection and my big stereo speakers.

"And one day I listened for over four gorgeous hours to those incredible people playing those incredible pianos. And I thought of you and I wondered how you were. And I wanted to see you so badly, Margaret, I literally ached. Do you believe that? Have you ever missed anybody that much? Not any *thing,* but any *body?* Have you, Margaret?"

Margaret sat quietly for a moment before saying anything. "Katherine, you are positively glowing. Even now."

Katherine giggled. "Yes. I don't know how else to say it, except that I was them—each of them—and I was the music, too, and the pianos. I was a piano. I was notes on the pages and I was the music in their heads . . . It was really incredible. I was *transported.* Of course I was ready to be, and I suspect the medicine for the ear infection had something to do with it. But I was totally receptive.

They were transmitters, and *wow!* was I ever a receiver. But I'd asked you to tell me about Three Rivers this year."

Margaret shrugged. "What's to tell? One of the finest piano competitions in the world and I've got a student in it."

"*Another* student, Margaret."

"Yes, well. All right, then, another student." She stared right at Katherine. "I'm no slouch as a teacher myself. But tell me," she went on. "Tell me about yourself. You and your Leonard. You and your children."

"Oh," she answered with a slight hitch of one shoulder. "We're fine. Nothing all that much to tell. Kate's a freshman in college and Lennie's ecstatic to be home by himself, and he's taken with being a junior and a starter on the soccer team. And they're both wonderful kids and we make a lot of faces at each other."

"Faces?"

"Faces. You know," and she twisted her face into a wonderfully hideous grin.

Margaret's own face broadened suddenly into an amazed laugh at Katherine's antics. And before she knew it, she was making one of her own with eyes crossed and mouth drawn down slowly, lips pulled back, her tongue darting in and out like a snake feeling for heat. Katherine squealed in delight and made another of her own. Back and forth it went, each improvising on the theme of the other until they had everybody near them giggling, trying not to look.

But they pulled themselves together, finally, covering their mouths to straighten them. Then, "You and your Leonard?" Margaret asked.

"Leonard? Fine. Just fine. Well, you always did manage to put your finger right on things, Margaret. We're fine, though. It *has* been rocky. You were right about that. In some ways it's been very rough. There've been some pretty bad years, actually. But there've been some pretty good ones, too. Really."

"It's always pretty good if you're not expecting too much to start with."

"I honestly can't complain, Margaret. I knew what I was doing."

"I know, I know. I wasn't trying to bring all that up again. It was your decision to make, not mine. You see? I *have* grown up in some ways. And the minute you left the apartment that day I wanted to slice my tongue out of my head. I wanted to go to the kitchen and get a knife—listen to me, Katherine—I wanted to get a knife and cut my tongue out so I would never be able to hurt anyone that way again in my life."

They were both quiet. Then,

"I do believe, Katherine, that that is the only time in my entire life I have hated myself."

The waitress came to ask if they wanted anything else. Katherine shook her head at Margaret and rummaged in her purse for a bill to pay the check.

It had been an awful scene.

"Why?" Margaret demanded. "My God, Katherine, why?"

Katherine took a deep breath. "I knew you'd be this way about it, Margaret. That's why I felt I had to wait so long to tell you. I should have said something months ago."

"Said 'something'? *Something?* For God's sake! *Something!* You certainly should have said something. Don't you have any idea how many hours a day I've been putting in on your concert the past three months? You should."

"I know how hard you've worked for me, Margaret. But I didn't say anything because I knew there'd be this kind of scene and I hoped—*had* hoped—I could avoid it."

"Why in the world couldn't you have waited another six weeks, for heaven's sake? Three months of polishing and polishing and polishing what you've been working on for a year. And with just six weeks to go you quit? Katrina, I do not understand this at all. Why?"

"To get married, Margaret. I thought that was plain enough."

Margaret stared hard at her. Then, "Are you pregnant? Is that it?"

"Oh, for God's sake NO!" she shouted. "I am not PREGnant. I just can't take it any more. It's as simple as that."

"Six weeks? Just six more weeks? Don't you understand that your entire future depends on this concert?"

Katherine's face set itself into a mask so firm and hard it made even Margaret pause.

"Just six more weeks and I would have been in the madhouse, Margaret," her voice flat. She seemed to animate herself again. "Leonard said . . ."

"Leonard! Leonard! I am *sick* of Leonard and his drivel."

"Leonard said," Katherine persisted, "that I was headed for a breakdown if I didn't back off. Now. And he was right, Margaret. I just can't take it any more."

"Breakdown. What does this Leonard know about breakdowns? Is he a doctor now?"

"Leonard is a wonderful person who is kind and gentle and who loves me and who is going to marry me and take care of me."

"Leonard is going to take care of you? How sweet of him. And is he also going to take care that there is rosin on your bow? And that your strings are tuned? And your fiddle waxed? Is he willing to take care of your music, too? *Can* he take care of your music for you? Because if he's not, Katrina, if he can't or won't help you take care of that music, then there will be no love. There will be no marriage. There will be nothing with the two of you, because you *are* music. You are not just another good fiddle player with very nice, fine competence. You are a musician, Katrina. I know what you intend. You mean to move out there to the suburbs and teach Suzuki to the children of your Leonard's *contacts!* It literally turns my stomach."

"Margaret, if you want to be enemies, I can't help that. Of course you know what music is to me. And surely you know what you have been to me. And I know that I won't be able to share a lot of things with Leonard. But we're not all the same, Margaret. We *do* have different drummers in our heads. Your drive is not my drive. You've always wanted it to be the same; so you've always acted like it was. But it hasn't been."

"Ah, he's convinced you of that, has he? He's convinced you that you're just another 'talented' person, as they say?"

"Margaret, it's *true*. What needs to happen for you to understand that it's true?"

There was a long pause. Katherine turned to pick up her jacket and purse.

When Margaret did speak, Katherine could barely hear her. "God will need to strike me deaf, then dumb, then blind, then dead."

"What?" she asked. "What did you say, Margaret?"

"I said, Katrina, that I have a tremendous amount of confidence in myself."

Katherine laughed weakly. "Tell me something I don't know."

"I mean, Katrina, that I know musicians when I see them. If there's anything in this world I know it's that. And if you throw it all up now to go be a banker's wife and an elementary teacher, then there will be no more joy in your life. And I know *that,* too. And *that* is what I cannot accept about all this."

"Margaret," she laughed. "If you think I won't ever have any more pleasure in my life . . ."

"*Pleasure,*" Margaret roared. "There you go again. '*Pleasure*' is not what I said, Katrina. I was talking about *joy.* You can get *pleasure* eating an ice cream cone. You can have *pleasure* taking a bus down to the Village. People-watching in the lobby of the Plaza can be a *pleasure.* That is *not* what I was saying."

"Margaret, I simply do not have that drive for success you have."

Margaret whirled suddenly, her fists raised, her face distorted, grotesque, and terrifying to Katherine.

"What has he done to your head, that Leonard? *Success?* My God, Katrina. 'Drive for Success'? That's banker talk. That's TV talk and he's got you doing it. You know what I've put my life into. You know the hours I've spent trying to understand what that stupid piano can do. You know what I've had to go through to get where I am. At the risk of sounding elitist and out of touch, Katrina, I like to feel that I have been grinding and batting away through art in the hope of finding out something about excellence—and about myself, to boot.

"But this 'success' you and your Leonard talk about! What a trivialization of everything you and I have spent virtually our entire lives doing. What a trivial concept, Katrina, and how unworthy of you. Success is in getting notes right. Is that what you mean? Success is in understanding—finally—what's really going on in a particular phrase. Success is managing to do something better than you've been able to do it before. But is that what you meant, Katrina? Is it?"

Katherine looked away.

"I would sell my body on the streets at night if that's what I had to do to get to spend eight hours the next day at this instrument. Is that what your Leonard means by *success?* And what would he do? What would he give to spend eight hours the next day in his cage at the bank? And if I had to sell the instrument, then at least I could buy the music and read the literature, and maybe it could at least be perfect in my head. Is that what your Leonard calls a 'Drive for Success'? Well? Is it? Please answer me, Katrina."

"You're being foolish and unfair, Margaret. You can't compare what bankers and lawyers do with what you do . . ."

"I wish you'd say that again. And again and again, Katrina, because you certainly can't compare them. Which is exactly what I've been trying to tell you."

"I wasn't finished, Margaret. I was going to say the sacrifices may not be the same, but they're there. Bankers make them, too. All kinds of people make sacrifices for their work. Artists don't have any corner on the market of sacrifice, Margaret."

They stood off from each other for a moment, Margaret's head shaking slowly back and forth, then she spoke again.

"When I was ten years old, Katherine, my father slapped my face. He was not a brutal man. He was—as you said about your Leonard—a wonderful man. He was also kind and gentle. But he was also an artist, as you know. A very dedicated artist who grew up in the proverbial old school, I guess."

Margaret looked past Katherine for a second, then continued.

"He was a perfectionist in his craft, and the result was that he was a very great singer, an artist. But he was listening to me run through a piece on my cello. It was a difficult piece for me, but I was proud because I had learned it—learned it well. And learned it quickly. I was *proud,* Katrina. By God, I was proud of what I had done.

"But when I finished I looked up at Papa, and I was face to face with a man in an absolute rage. I had never seen him look so ugly and hateful—disappointed and unbelieving, I suppose—and I didn't understand why. And then, Katrina, he leaned over—that kind, gentle, wonderful man—and with tears running down his cheeks, he slapped my face.

"It was a hard slap, and I cried out: *Papa, why did you hit me, Papa?* By then I was crying, too, not just from the slap, but from the hurt of his having done it. And he answered me, Katrina. He was as stunned and hurt as I was, but not for all the same reasons. *If you cannot love that music,* he said, *do not disgrace yourself with its performance.*"

"Oh, Margaret." She wanted to hold her, but knew there was no use. She felt empty: not sad, not guilty.

Katherine slowly put on her jacket and held her purse as she faced Margaret. She breathed in deeply. When she spoke, her voice was soft, but still under control, though barely.

"I only came to ask for your blessing, Margaret."

Margaret turned her back. She braced herself with both hands against the piano. Her voice was strong and clear. She spoke slowly and distinctly.

"I hope your marriage is very successful, Katherine."

She could not turn to look around, wasn't even sure for a long time whether Katherine was still in the apartment or not, until she heard in a near whisper, "Your father was kinder when he slapped your face, Margaret."

"But tell me." It was Katherine speaking as they waited for their change. "You don't play any more? I've looked and looked in all the notices, but it seems like years, now."

"Six," Margaret repled simply. She smiled and spread her hands open between them, Katherine surprised as always at how graceful they looked even though they were large, their tips wide and thick. "But you've gotten very unobservant in your dotage, Katherine." Katherine took them into her own, ran her thumbs across their

163

backs, felt the strength still in them. "Do they hurt a lot, Margaret?"

"Oh, not bad. Pretty constant, usually. More an ache. I guess most of the pain settled in my disposition. At least that's what my students say—when I'm not around! But I can't span ten keys any more. Not even nine now, as a matter of fact. The octave is still there, but no real power. It's not crippling, at least, this kind. I've seen people whose hands weren't anything but claws. Mine's not like that. It's up in the wrists some, though. And there's no way you can sneak up on Liszt with weak wrists."

They both laughed at the unintended rhyme.

"So I teach. Oh I can accompany without too much trouble. I can demonstrate if I have to. But you know, now that I don't perform, now that it's all reading, I've had to internalize so much. Of course you always have to before you're any good, but it's still different now. It all *has* to stay inside. When it can't come out in performance it gets even more intellectualized and theoretical. But it's useful to me as a teacher." She paused as if suddenly surprised at something she had never thought of before. "My God, Katherine, I know so much I sometimes rather scare myself."

"So you teach and have students."

"And lecture and give demonstrations and judge contests."

"I'm surprised you haven't gone into composition."

"Well now, Katherine," she said as she leaned back in her chair. "Even I have limitations." She paused. "No, composition is something else again. Composers know music on another level altogether."

When the waitress brought the change they finished their tea and left.

They stood at the platform waiting for the commuter train to arrive.

"Shall I tell Leonard you send him your love?" Katherine joshed.

Margaret's face stayed set, and she looked just beyond Katherine. "That child," she finally said. "That little girl. She's awfully good, Katherine. Be careful with her. She'll have to choose some day."

She looked, then, directly at Katherine. "As for your Leonard, you may tell him absolutely nothing for me. I shall never forgive him, Katherine. Never."

Katherine laughed. "But just a little while ago you said it was my decision to make."

"I know, I know. And it was. But he didn't help. He shouldn't have let you make it. He should have broken your heart instead."

"You mean he should have said, 'All for Art'? Honestly, Margaret, haven't you ever wished you had gotten out? Aren't you ever at least a teeny bit glad for that arthritis taking the pressure of performance off of you?"

"You tell *me* something, Katherine. Don't you ever wish you hadn't quit?"

Katherine sagged. "We all wish something, Margaret. We all wish for something we wanted but never got."

"He should have known you better. I don't think Leonard understood very much. About you, I mean."

"You say that so very seriously, Margaret."

"Do I, Katherine? Do I really?"

And again they could only look into each other's eyes, scan each other's face as though something might yet burst forth, some illuminating *answer* to all the questions they would have forgotten or not known how to ask, some spark to ignite a live *thing* that would be theirs when they needed it.

The train squealed to a stop. Margaret placed her hands on Katherine's cheeks. "Oh my dearest Katherine. You once dreamed so much . . ." She blinked, hesitating just a moment. "But you dared so little."

She drew her hands close and kissed her forehead. Katherine took those hands in her own, clutched them, and pressed the swollen knuckles to her lips.

"Goodby, Katherine," Margaret whispered.

"Margaret?"

"Goodby," she shouted from the platform just before the doors whished closed behind her friend. "Goodby, Margaret."

She saw Margaret get a seat by the window and wave.

"Write me," she suddenly yelled to her as she saw the train

start to roll away. Almost frantically she called out: "Write me, Margaret. Please. Write me . . . write me."

All the way back Margaret had been trying to figure out why she hadn't been able to answer Katherine's question. On the thirty-two minute ride back to the city, on the bus from Grand Central to her street, and up the three flights of stairs to her apartment: *aren't you even a tiny bit glad about the arthritis?*

"Yes," she should have been strong enough to say. "I *am* glad not to have that pressure. I *am* glad I'm doing what I'm doing now."

Yes, she went over it again in her head. Yes, there was a time once. I'd like to say *once,* only there isn't any single time when "it" happens. It grows and builds, I suppose, until one day you recognize it. Or admit it. Then you have to do something about it.

It was at a rehearsal for what turned out to be my last performance. I hadn't known about the arthritis, just that my hands didn't seem to be doing things right and that they seemed tired, always.

Still, I was getting it all done—the usual build-up to a performance: polishing, polishing, sharpening, going through the score over and over at night, listening less and less to the coaches as the music takes you over and it all comes more and more to be your own.

But one day was especially bad. The hall was very chilly and I just couldn't get my hands warmed up enough. I rubbed them and blew on them, went through all the exercises. Of course it wasn't all the temperature, but I didn't know that then.

Finally, we got started—it was the day we had the full orchestra and you can't keep one of those waiting but just so long—and we eventually got some heat up on the stage, too. But it wasn't going at all well. There were about three very tricky sections we had to work on full tilt. And I concentrated as much as I could, but I finally realized I was concentrating on concentrating instead of on playing.

Things were not going at all well with me and the conductor, or even between me and the orchestra. Just modest little things were going wrong that shouldn't have been by then. But a bunch of things went sour all at once—including some pretty sloppy playing on my part. And at one point—I hadn't been paying attention, I guess—I blanked out. I had no more idea than a goose where I was supposed to be. All I knew was that my hands hurt and that I was the only one playing and it didn't sound right. There were even a few whistles and laughs from the pit.

I just sat there while the conductor tried to jolly us all together again. He knew something was wrong, but I couldn't go on. All I could do was stare at the keyboard. The blacks and whites all seemed to be skittering around, shifting all over the place. I had the sense that *they* were dizzy; so I set my fingers on them like I was trying to hold them still.

The next thing I knew, Alex was leading me off the stage to a dressing room. He was clucking all the way like he does—I don't think the man has ever finished a sentence in his entire life—and rubbing my hands between his huge warm ones.

"Tsk-tsk-tsk-tsk-tsk," he was saying, and I saw he was really massaging the meaty part of my hands. And they hurt. Lord! how they hurt. I looked at one and saw the big bruise there. The other had a broken blood vessel at the base of the little finger. *Then* I heard the noise. *Then* I remembered slamming my fists on those keys over and over and over like I had been trying to make them behave and they just wouldn't. And since they wouldn't, I wanted them to sound ugly. I wanted them to sound as ugly . . . so ugly . . . I wanted them to sound as ugly as I felt.

Alex had my hands soaking in warm water and epsom salts he had dredged up from somewhere. He held them in the sink for me and massaged them while I cried and cried that I wanted to go out, I just wanted to go out.

I wish I could say that that last performance had been the *creme-de-la-creme* capstone to a brilliant and virtuoso career. Alas. It *was* good, though. Very good, actually. But as one of the critics said— I can still quote him—*A bit conservative; a bit mechancial; rather lacking that spark that has always set her apart.* He was right too. All the energy had had to go into keeping up the twenty performing years of competence and musicianship. There wasn't anything left over for spark.

But the audience seemed genuinely pleased—maybe even guessed from my encores that it was a farewell. The last thing I did was that Percy Grainger arrangement of "Londonderry Air." It's such a beautiful thing. So simple, but you can do so much with it. I never played it better. I think maybe that's when they all knew.

When I got home that night, I took a long hot bath, fixed a little pot of hot chocolate, crawled in the snug darkness of my own bed, and slept. The next morning I felt very calm, very relaxed, very sure of myself. And all of a sudden I found I was talking to my father. He'd been dead for years, but my talk with him was as real as if he were sitting right there across the table from me. I was looking out the window, down to the street. A bunch of kids were playing down there: hopscotch, keep-away, tag, whatever.

"I've practiced now, Papa," I said, looking down into the street. "Even more than you ever told me I had to." I looked away from the window and directly at him across the table from me. I swear: I knew in my head he wasn't there, but there he was.

"Now can I go out, Papa?" I asked. "Now can I go out and play like the other kids?"

There was a kind of *glow,* is all I know how to say. A kind of glow that was more than color, more than sounds, more than whatever it was. Just for a second. Then it was gone, and so was Papa.

The kids' noises came back up to me from the street. I did the breakfast dishes, tidied up a little, then went to the piano. I sat at it for I don't know how long, probably not too long, but it was a timeless sort of time. And then I spent God alone knows how long improvising the most remarkably witty, intricate, and musically sophisticated variations on "Chop Sticks" I have ever heard in my life.

I played and played and played, ending up with some jazz chord progressions even Dave Brubeck would have liked. And when I was through, I got so tickled I started to laugh. I laughed until the tears rolled down my cheeks; I laughed and laughed until I was off the piano bench rolling on the floor; I laughed and laughed and laughed until I hurt. I laughed so hard and so long I thought I'd never be able to stop. I shook and trembled with the laughing and the crying, shook and trembled until long after it wasn't funny any more.

Eventually it stopped. It was over. I got up and sat in an easy chair for a long time with my hands in my lap. They seemed to take turns holding each other, caressing each other, warming the pain away.

Later, I got up and went back to the piano. I sat back down on the bench and played a very short, brisk little Chopin Prelude.

I was all right.

Charley Billy

· · In a land where God is real and the Devil is almost his equal,
it can be understood why a sixteen-year-old boy will kill his father.
But it's a very hard thing to judge: right and wrong are both so
sharp and run so close together that if you stare at them too long
they seem to jump sides right under your eyes. "I hated that son of
a bitch." That's how Johnny Fletcher finally put it, and that's how
he'd thought it all his life, too—even before he was old enough
to think, when he'd had to know things through his skin and in
his bones.

It's hard to say whether the old man was all that bad or not. But
he was to Johnny. He was a God-fearing man who didn't understand that not everybody wanted to be as God-fearing as him. So
when he finally had it set in his head that Brother Jenkins and all
the rest of the First Creek Free Will Baptist Church were straying
grievously far from the path to Glory, he up and walked out. That
was the first thing Johnny really remembered about his father.

The day it happened was a regular church service day, rather
than a sing, so there was a sermon. One of the brothers was to take
his turn preaching the Bible, and he'd just gotten into it real good
when old man Fletcher stands up as tall and stately as a pine and
calls them down each by his name and tells them they are in league

with the Devil and don't know it because they won't listen to him, and he won't have his family corrupted by associating with them a minute longer. Then he looked down the pew and raised his family with his eyes and walked out, them skittering behind like a covey of nervous quail.

The others in the congregation turned and watched them walk out in a file, then looked to each other and shook their heads like they knew it was bound to have happened sooner or later. Not a soul stood to take Mr. Fletcher by his hand and ask him to talk about why he was leaving, but, then, no one ever could talk to that man after he had set himself about something.

Johnny wasn't old enough to remember anything about the walking out except that it happened and that he wouldn't be back in the church ever again, probably. Beyond that, all he was old enough to know was this: that if he walked clear across the field behind his Pa's house and passed through a clump of pin oaks, he would be in Alabama; that Loretto was far enough away so that his Pa didn't want to have to walk there; and that Nashville was a hymn. And what really stuck in his mind about that day was not that his father had quit the church, but that Brother Jenkins had patted him on his head before service and promised him they would sing "Antioch" before dinner.

But his Pa had walked out, so the child hadn't gotten to open up the heavy *Sacred Harp* to follow the tribble notes with his tiny voice. Instead, he had trailed behind his mother in the muddy road, one hand clutching her skirts, while she carried the baby in both arms. It wasn't but some sixty yards up the road to their front gate, and when they got back, the old man preached them a lesson on his own theme. Afterward, the boy sat under a tree in the side yard and heard "Wondrous Love" pushing up the knoll between his house and the small, square white church, out of sight, and flooding down toward him: washing, bathing, steeping him in its joy.

What wondrous love is this!
That caused the Lord of Bliss,
To bear the dreadful curse for my soul,
For my soul,
To bear the dreadful curse for my soul.

Just about everybody in that end of Lawrence County knew the old man, though back then he wasn't so very old, maybe fifty or so. But it was that he acted like an old man. He wore black all the time and he never opened his mouth except to preach out at you. He was tall and wore a full beard, and folks would say he looked like he was trying to be a Mormon or something. He was a man who hated sin, but figured there wasn't anybody else around who hated it as much or could spot it as well as him. So he figured it was his lot to get rid of it all. Truth to say, he acted like a man who had had a vision of God and had listened to His instructions. The Bible tells us it has happened before, so there's no reason to believe it couldn't happen again. But a prophet must talk to people so that what he says makes some sense. Old Mr. Fletcher never said much but things like, "Money is evil," "Man is a vessel overflowing with greed and pride," and "The Road to Glory is strewn with jagged rocks." It wasn't that people around there didn't agree with his sentiments. It was that he offered nothing better.

None of the folks who knew him understood how the rest of his family could stand to live with him. Of course there wasn't much his wife could do. She generally had one on the lap and one on the way, and Charley Billy was simple and didn't know any better about staying on or not. But the other children, as soon as they got big enough, off they'd go. To Nashville, mostly, heading right to the Opry—just like all they had to do was walk out onto the stage to sing a song and be rich—or learning to make out behind the counter in an all-night diner, or driving trucks, or whatever else they could find to do. But Johnny stayed, which was peculiar, because he was a big boy and strong, and hadn't kowtowed to his father for a good while.

The trouble with the old man was that he didn't haul off and swing from the heels at the sin around him. He picked at it. They had a worthless dog out to their place one time named Belly. And it seemed the only reason Mr. Fletcher kept that dog was so he could pick at it. He'd get that dog between his knees and pick ticks from out of the folds around its neck and throat until it yelped and howled. But he'd keep after it until he drew blood and had the hound squirming and fighting like crazy to get away from him.

He picked around the house the same way. He'd wait until his old woman had cleaned, then he'd go so far as to pull a straw from the broom and scratch around in the cracks between the floor planking. Then he'd raise Cain and get on his wife about how the lazy were always seeking ways to avoid labor. One time he even bloused her eye because instead of getting down on her hands and knees to scrub again, she told him she couldn't get the floors any cleaner than they were. That night at supper the old man explained to his children that he had been forced to punish their mother because she had tried to undermine his God-given authority as head of the house.

That kind of thing was pretty minor, really. Mostly it just shows how the old man was in a general sort of way. But there were other things that happened between Johnny and his Pa that would give anybody cause to hate.

The shrikes, for instance. When he was seven or eight, the boy came upon a shrike nest. He wouldn't have noticed it except that he heard the mama cry, and saw her swoop down from a telephone pole into a thick cluster of thistles. He knew she was probably making her nest there, so he put down his seine and started toward the thistles in a shallow ditch by the road. He got just close enough to see the bird. She was nesting for sure, which meant she would be around all summer for him to watch. He drew away quietly, but marked the spot in his mind so he could find it right off when he came back. He slung his net across his shoulders and went on home.

He spied on the nest for about three weeks. He watched the nest, then the eggs, then the chicks when they came. He watched the papa come down with a field mouse in his strong beak. And he watched the feast that followed. Until the old man caught him.

One afternoon right after he had moved slowly and quietly away from his spot above the thistles, he was walking home when he saw his father some fifty yards in front of him, striding across the field. Johnny wondered where his Pa might have been and if he had seen him looking at the birds, but he didn't think any more about it until that night.

They had eaten early, as usual, but right after supper his father left the house. Generally, he'd go over to his highbacked rocker by

173

the fireplace after supper and tell Charley Billy to bring him the Book. Then he'd spend about two hours reading, the big family Bible spread across his lap and nearly flowing off each side, and he'd mark each line as he read by tapping his huge bony forefinger on the page. He'd never read aloud, but it was easy to follow him by looking at his lips as they shaped each word.

But that evening he left the house without reading. Johnny's mother cleaned up from supper, the two older sisters sat in a corner giggling and whispering to each other, and Charley Billy settled his large, almost flabby frame by the hearth with an old stocking doll. He babbled to it like a baby, then held it on his shoulder and rocked gently back and forth. Then he'd lay it down and cover it up with a remnant of outing, only to take it up again. He was the Fletcher's third child, born fifteen years before Johnny.

It was two hours before the old man came back in. No one had heard him, but all of a sudden he was there standing in the door. He took off his hat, went to his rocker, and sat a minute with his hands folded over each other in his lap. Then he looked up and glared around the plain, square room. The girls had gone upstairs to bed; Johnny's mother was darning, her hair still stretched back in a gray bun, the dull skin on her face tinted by the light from the lantern on the big table in the center of the room; Charley Billy had curled up against Johnny who was sitting on the floor mending his net in the bad light.

"John Fletcher," the old man bellowed into the stillness.

The boy looked up, frightened.

"I caught you, boy," the old man went on. He raised his hands and began stroking his beard. "I caught you."

Johnny had a notion what his father was talking about, but he had learned to wait for the full accusation.

"When you should have been helping gather food for the family, you were idling your time away. When you could have been on your knees praying to the Lord God, you were on your belly. On your *belly!* Like a crawling thing, watching these birds."

Charley Billy had opened his eyes and raised himself up, clutching his play-pretty. Johnny sat frozen with his net still before him.

"I have removed that devilish bird and its young, and its be-fouled nest, too."

The old man stood, put his hands in his pockets, and drew out something which he threw onto the floor in front of the boy. Johnny looked down, but in the gloom he wasn't able to make out what it was until Charley Billy started pushing himself away from the spot, and with a cry ran from the house. Johnny looked again, but he couldn't believe what he saw until he touched a finger to a beak; then he saw the rest of it, what was left of the birds, squeezed until there was nothing left but the beaks, the blue-gray feathers, and the claws. He drew back and looked up at his father who, in the growing dark of the room, appeared to be a shadow standing before the unlighted hearth.

"Clean it up, boy," he shouted, his hand pointing down to the sticky mess on the floor. "Clean away the spots of Hell from this house. And there'd best be no trace of those creatures in the morn-ing—not on the floor or in your soul, either, boy. And when you've finished scrubbing away their filth, you will kneel with the Book for an hour and read aloud. Then you will be free to pray."

Mr. Fletcher sat again in his chair. His wife left the room. The only sound was the swishing of the scrub brush in Johnny's hand. And from the barn came the soft chanting of Charley Billy as he tried to sing himself to sleep.

At the time, the business of the mangled birds hadn't especially bothered Johnny. Mostly he thought it was a dirty trick. He was still young enough so he didn't know but what his father was right: that wickedness and evil were the bulk of the world, that pleasures were evil, and that anything painful or wearisome must be a kind of good because it made you aware of the weakness of the mortal coil and turned your mind to the glory of the soul and the joys of the hereafter.

But the boy's assumptions about all that grew weaker and weaker until, some years later, it came to him: It's my Pa, he thought. It's my Pa that's evil. It came to him like the answer to a problem that's been crawling around in the back of your head for ever so long, you never quite knowing you had been studying about it in the first place.

When it came, that answer he didn't even know he had been looking for, his head was filled with the chorus to a lesson he had led once:

Shout on, pray on, we're gaining ground.
Glory, Hallelujah.
The dead's alive and the lost is found.
Glory, Hallelujah.

After Johnny reached his growth he didn't have anything to do with his father. It was like an armed truce. The boy did his chores, but that was all. The old man knew he had lost something, but for a long time he didn't seem to mind because there was still Charley Billy.

Mr. Fletcher finally concluded that Charley Billy was evil, which wasn't at all silly sounding to many folks around there. But evil or not, Charley Billy was simple. He was a happy boy. He'd laugh and smile all the time. But he finally took to staying home because there wasn't any sense in his sitting in Miss Helen's classroom all day long.

It was early on in his life that he staked out the cow and the barn as his own. He fed and curried her just like she was a prize winner. He'd babble to her and pat her, and he kept the barn as clean as a Dutchman's pin. That cow just poured milk. In the house he'd play with dollies or curl up against one of the other children and doze off. He was forgetful, too, like a little child is. He'd leave his shirt out in the road or in the field somewhere, then get cold at night. He couldn't manage his clothes real well, so Mrs. Fletcher made over his pants and things with great big buttons and buttonholes that he could work himself.

He was no harm, and people pretty much liked him, but the old man got worse and worse about things. He got to thinking even more about sin and evil, and in his mind he saw Charley Billy as a curse, an affliction, a punishment. He started bit by bit to pick on him the way he had Belly and Johnny and his wife and all the rest of them.

Charley Billy couldn't entertain any notions about running off, so the old man had a built-in audience. He'd look at Charley Billy across the supper table, for instance, and say, "Ye are accursed," or some such thing, but say it real low as if he didn't really understand it himself. And then he'd grab the table with his big hands and lean forward and say, "Thou spawn of Sodom." Charley Billy would just smile and nod and cram more potatoes into his mouth.

Still, it wasn't enough for the old man. When a man is standing up in church preaching the Bible he has to have an *Amen, Brother* from his congregation every now and again or else he isn't doing much good. So when his low curse about Charley Billy being an affliction didn't get more than a smile or a nod, he'd half stand to lean down the table and smack the boy across his head a couple of times.

His father got to saying he was possessed: that, because he liked to sleep in the barn better than in the house. A barn isn't a bad place to spend some time, particularly if it's clean and sweet-smelling like Charley Billy kept that one. But Mr. Fletcher objected because he thought Charley Billy was bunging the cow.

But Charley Billy never did touch the cow like that. He loved her, of course—kept her teats real clean, patted her, and all—but he never touched her in love that way. As a matter of fact, Johnny tried to get him to, once. Johnny knew his brother well. He took care of him half the time. He knew when Charley Billy was getting nervous and excited, like a man does who doesn't want it often, but wants it big when he does.

Once, Johnny saw it coming on. It usually came with a full moon. Charley Billy would end up under a tree cooing and crooning and flogging away at himself. Then he'd be done with it until the next month. Johnny had always tried to get some of the girls he knew to lay with his brother, but they wouldn't. So Johnny went out to the barn one night after everyone else had been in bed for a good while, and he found Charley Billy in the cow's stall sound asleep. She was still awake, chewing her cud to make sure there would be plenty of milk for Charley Billy to stroke out of her the next morning.

Johnny roused his brother by shining the flashlight in his face. Then he started talking to him in a real quiet voice. The moon had been full the night before, and it still cast plenty of light.

He started talking to Charley Billy about full moons and girls, what it was like to be a man, and how natural it all was: not only natural, but a hundred percent better than sitting out under a tree alone. Then he went on to explain, because Charley Billy was smiling and nodding heavily with the sleep still in his eyes, how he had tried to get a girl to lay with him, but couldn't quite swing it. Charley Billy smiled and nodded some more. Then Johnny began to explain that this cow could do just as well. Charley Billy looked a little lost then, so Johnny stood up and moved around to the cow's rear. He got her to stand up, then he shined his flashlight right there and told Charley Billy to come over.

Charley Billy started to look sort of funny, and Johnny thought it was because he still didn't quite understand. He handed the light to his brother while he scouted around for the milking stool. He set it down and stood on it behind the cow which was looking around and starting to get a little skittish. So Johnny pantomimed what he wanted Charley Billy to do. Then he stepped off the stool and led his brother up on it.

Charley Billy stood where his brother put him, but he didn't do anything. So Johnny unbuttoned the big button and motioned for Charley Billy to go on from there. Still, he wouldn't, so Johnny tried to do like he had seen his Pa do when he was guiding a bull in. The second Johnny made contact between Charley Billy and the cow, Charley Billy roared and made the worst sounds Johnny had ever heard. At the same time, he took a roundhouse swipe at Johnny that the boy never saw, it came so fast. It landed square on the side of his head.

Johnny was taken off his feet, and he thought he must have gone ten yards through the air. The cow didn't holler but once, and then she kicked out a foot and knocked the stool flying and Charley Billy with it. Johnny was half knocked out, but when he finally got his senses back, he almost wished he hadn't, because he saw Charley Billy with his arms around the cow's neck, and he saw his brother's back shaking from the sobs. Johnny turned the flashlight off. He couldn't stand to look at it any more. Charley Billy's heart was broken and Johnny's was too, because he was the one who had done it. He turned around and left the barn, but he couldn't forget the sound of his brother crying.

It was more than a month before Charley Billy would have anything more to do with Johnny, and it was during that month that the old man started in earnest to see if he could work some salvation on Charley Billy. What bothered Johnny was that so much of his father's preaching was sinking in. It wasn't hard to see the changes take place. During the next year or so Charley Billy came to be gloomy. He pulled a long face and slouched, wouldn't wave at anybody when he was in town, and his head was down as though he was looking at his shoes all the time.

He even quit living in the barn. Mr. Fletcher didn't tell him to stay out of it, but it came about because of all the preaching. One time the old man sneaked up on Charley Billy while he was out under the tree. He didn't do anything then, but when Charley Billy got back to the house, the old man started cursing him. He hit him and cursed him some more until Charley Billy was crying and bawling. Johnny was the only one in the house to tell his father to lay off. Mrs. Fletcher was in a corner snapping green beans, and the others were still too small to do anything but hope the old man didn't come down on them, too. What Johnny got for his trouble was a big gash across his cheek where his father belted him.

Johnny didn't do anything back except to walk out of the house, leaving his mother making snick-snack with the beans, and Charley Billy on his knees in front of the fireplace while their father stood over him with the Book, reading and casting his eyes up toward the ceiling.

Other than the blood on his cheek, the clothes on his back, and a transistor radio he had snitched from a store in Lawrenceville, Johnny didn't have a thing with him when he hit the road in front of the house and started walking toward Loretto or the highway or wherever it would be that he ended up. He didn't know where he was going, and he hadn't really the intention to leave. But it looked like that was what was happening. He walked at least two miles down the road before he stopped to rest. When he sat down he took the radio out and turned it on, fiddling with the dial until he got the Grand Ole Opry from Nashville, and he remembered it was Saturday night.

He listened for a long time: Grandpa Jones, Flatt and Scruggs, Jim Reeves, Wilma Lee and Stony Cooper. It sounded good to him, and he wished he could see the Ryman Auditorium for himself. It was then he understood that he must be leaving home like the others before him.

It gave him a lift to know he wasn't going to have to put up with his Pa any more, and it made him feel good to know that he was going to Nashville. Someone on the Opry was playing a banjo, and it sounded so grand that he got to his feet, turned up the volume, and fairly danced down the road just as though he was going to arrive in the middle of Church Street before the tune was over. And when the banjo came on with its breakdown, it was so sweet to Johnny's ears he couldn't feel a thing but joy all over.

Then it was done. The announcer was selling flour again. Another group came on, but something had gone out of it. It wasn't just the ooh-ah ooh-ah background to the song, because even when the banjo had come on with its breakdown there was something in the boy holding back.

He got another quarter of a mile down the road, the radio up to his ear all the while, when that something came back on him, and the more he heard the Opry, the more the other thing was beating and beating in his head. Until he stopped.

It was the *Harp:* the *Sacred Harp* kept lining out its tunes in his head. He sat down just off the road. There he listened hard. The radio from Nashville was coming in clear as a bell, but something was wrong with it all. He'd seen some Opry folks before, seen them on stage and in person when they came through Lawrenceville one time, and he had loved it: their costumes shining and glittering with spangles, their names right there in gold script on their guitars, their cowboy hats and all. It had been a show and a half.

But there by the road in the dark of the night, hearing it come over the radio, it was a disappointment. And when he put their tunes up against the singing—the hard lining-out of gospel and God and music all at once, when he heard the tunes of each part fighting around in the same song, crashing up against each other yet all of them still on the same side and each of them coming out at the same time and winning—the Nashville music sounded awfully puny. And when he thought about Brother Jenkins in his white shirt and his one Sunday tie and his plow-tough hands, there was something terrible and fake about the spangles on the Opry costumes. Nobody around middle Tennessee really wore cowboy boots—not out in the field plowing. And there are more baseball caps seen up on tractors than cowboy hats, and the only rodeo around there was the one up in Franklin every year, and that was a made-up thing put on by rich doctors and lawyers. There wasn't anything showy about the First Creek sings, but after all, you didn't have to buy Jesus-God to fill your lungs and make a holy sound in song.

Johnny stayed where he was for a long time that night. Gradually his finger lowered the volume on the radio, until finally there wasn't any sound in the boy's mind but the heavy, plain beat; there wasn't any picture in his mind but the hand of the hymn leader in the middle of the square of singers, the hand coming down again and again and again to lead the time, the cadence, the spirit of the hymns.

"Well, hell," he said to himself. "I guess that's it, then. If it's in you it's in you and it don't drown out easy."

He turned the radio off and left it in the weeds, then got to his feet and started home again. He hated every step, but couldn't turn himself around.

It came about over nothing that hadn't been done a hundred times before: Mr. Fletcher preached out to his family. By then he had been working on Charley Billy for more than a year, and it wasn't any strange thing to see the fool on his knees crying and babbling because of it. Even Johnny was almost used to it. Why it happened that night nobody can say. Maybe it was the mist. Or maybe it was too many nights on end of preaching.

The old man hadn't been out to the fields all day. It was November and there wasn't anything for him to do out there, and it had been rainy and misty all day. The weather had been cold for weeks; then a mess of warm air came up from the Gulf and there were a couple of balmy, wet days. So everybody had been in the house all day.

The old man had done nothing but read his Book while Johnny sat up in his room whittling. Charley Billy milked the cow and mucked out the stalls like always, then sat around the house babbling to himself and playing with a dolly until Mr. Fletcher glanced up from the Book and made him put it away.

It started after supper. Mr. Fletcher stood up and said for them all to come gather around and listen to his reading.

Everybody did but Johnny, who kept on sitting in a chair by the front window. The old man gave him a long stare and said, "You need to hear this more than all the rest, boy. You come, too."

Johnny didn't even look up from what he was doing. The old man gave him another hard stare, but began to read even so. He read from Judges for fifteen or twenty minutes before he paused. Then he looked over at Johnny again.

"Come over here, boy," he said.

This time Johnny looked up at his father and said, "Why in hell don't you call me by my name?"

By the time the old man had recovered enough to answer, Charley Billy had pulled out the little stocking dolly he had been hiding under his shirt. He held it up before him by each of its flopping arms and made it jig while he smiled and cooed a little song.

At the sight of that silly little doll Mr. Fletcher forgot about Johnny long enough to reach down and grab the plaything and beat him over the head with it.

"I've told you before," he yelled. "You're not to indulge yourself with this." He smacked him again and threw the doll into the fire. Charley Billy had turned to protect himself, and when he did, Johnny saw a funny little smile on his face.

The old man had spent himself for the time, so he got back to the reading. He looked fiery, and he shouted out the verses as though it was them that had caused him pain instead of Johnny or Charley Billy, and his big forefinger thumped down on every line so it sounded like great claps of far-off thunder.

He read about Abimelech and Gaal and the men of Shechem; he read about the ambush in the field, the slaughter in the city, and the sowing of salt; he read about the burning of the people in the hold; and then about the tower in Thebez: the woman and the piece of millstone; he read of Abimelech's death: how he asked his sword-bearer to slay him so it could not be said that he had died at the hands of a woman.

He read: "'Thus God rendered the wickedness of Abimelech, which he did unto his father, in the slaying of his seventy brethren: And all the evil of the men of Shechem did God render upon their heads: and upon them came the curse of Jotham the son of Jerubbaal.'"

When he had finished the reading, he slammed the Book closed and his voice never broke stride, but went right over to Johnny.

"You, boy. You are to understand that I am the authority in this house." He was starting over to Johnny when Charley Billy all of a sudden was standing in front of him, his pants down, pleasuring himself in front of the fireplace. The old man got one look at what was happening and knocked Charley Billy down with his fist. Then he grabbed him up and the words poured out: putrefaction of the flesh, Hell's fires, damnation, the befouled condition of the temporal world, and all the time he was beating his son about the head and shoulders with his fists, his open hand: clubbing, slapping.

He beat Charley Billy until he was down on his knees crying and bawling. The old man yelled at him to shut up and to start praying that precious Jesus might—just might—hear the prayers and not put him into Hell when he died, into Hell where he'd burn and scorch and fry all the live-long day and all the eternal night for ever and ever and ever.

But Charley Billy kept on wailing and sobbing on the floor. He was on his knees in front of the fireplace clawing at himself, tearing at his shirt and chest. All the while, his father kept leaning down at him with his bony finger in his face and the light from the fire bouncing around behind him. There's no telling what he was saying, finally, because it was grunts and growls and clamping of teeth. But in between those sounds and noises it came out that Charley Billy was a sin and a punishment, that everything would have been all right if he had only died in his mother, that the world would be better off without such as him wandering around loose in it to scare folks half out of their minds. Then in a final scream, his face a smear of hate and despair, he told Charley Billy that if he was dead there would be some hope.

By then Johnny couldn't stand it any longer. He told his father to lay off. The old man was so worked up he didn't hear at first. So Johnny pushed him away from Charley Billy. Then he heard. It finally came to Johnny what his brother had been doing, or what he figured he had been doing, playing with the dolly, then with himself. And when he understood that, he had to help him. So he told his father again to quit.

The old man stood where he was, his back against the fire. He raised his finger at Johnny and told him to stand back out of his way or he'd beat him until he couldn't even crawl. Johnny was ready, though. He crouched, his arms spread, and he said, "That'll be the by-God day."

With that, Mr. Fletcher whipped his belt from his pants and started to swing at the boy, but Johnny was set. He grabbed the belt as it cut through the air at him, and jerked his father to his knees. It was a good feeling for the boy to see his father on his knees to someone for a change. It hurt the old man, too. His eyes reddened and watered, but his face was still meaner than Johnny ever remembered it. But he didn't care by them. He'd been too big for his father to take down for a good while, and besides, it was all in the open now and Johnny was ripe for whatever might come.

The old man started for the boy, but before they could make contact, Charley Billy was standing between them blubbering something to his father and looking back at Johnny. The old man pried Charley Billy's hands from his lapel and pushed him away. But Charley Billy got ahold of him again and started babbling like he was pleading for something. Once more Mr. Fletcher pushed him away and yelled, "Go out to your beast in the stable. You have been damned from birth, you soulless animal. Go sodomize your cow."

For a second Charley Billy looked as though he didn't know the meaning of his father's words until the old man screamed again, "Your cow, you fool. Go to your cow," and he showed his forearm, jerking it up and down in the air so anyone would have known what he was saying.

There was no sound for what seemed the longest time, nothing but the hissing of the smoky green wood. Then Charley Billy took out through the door, screaming and yowling into the night. Johnny started after him, but the old man laid on a clout to the side of his head. It wasn't as good as he thought, though, because Johnny was up almost immediately and gave it back just where he'd gotten it, and it was a good one. He knew that when it hit.

While the old man was on his back on the floor, Johnny reached down and grabbed him up by the skin of his neck and the waist of his britches and threw him into the fire. He got out fast enough, but by then Johnny was gone.

He ran straight into the barn, but the cow was already on her knees. In front of her was Charley Billy. Johnny saw him pull the pitchfork out of her, brace the handle against her, and push himself on to it—all before the boy had been able to focus his eyes.

When he saw what had been done, he couldn't stand it. He started to run back to the house, but there was his father standing in the doors to the barn. He didn't seem to see Johnny in front of him for looking at Charley Billy, slumped over the cow. Johnny pushed on by, went to the house, and grabbed down the shotgun from the rack on the wall. Then he flung all around looking for the shells. All the while, his mother was grabbing at him and hollering in her tiny little voice, more whimper than holler, "He's your Pa, Johnny. Your Pa." But the boy got two shells and ran back outside trying to break open the gun and load it and get his mother off him all at once.

His breath was steaming as he tried to run, but his mother finally wrestled him to the ground, all the time pleading for him not to do this thing, that it would help nothing. But Johnny was just about out of his mind by then. He clubbed her pretty hard on her head. He got up, and when he saw she was coming out of it, went on his way. In the barn, the old man was kneeling over Charley Billy.

He had taken the pitchfork out of him and set it down. He turned when he heard Johnny come running in. When he saw the boy had the gun he got to his feet, standing there tall and stately as ever. Johnny raised the gun and pointed it at his father's head, but the old man stared right back down the sight at his son. He never flinched or budged. He didn't pale, he didn't breathe heavy. He stood there looking as fierce and right as the day he had stood before Brother Jenkins and the rest of the First Creek Church and told them they were damned. There was no fear in him. There wasn't anything else for Johnny to do, so he fired.

It was done. Neither one of them had said a word to the other. The boy didn't know what else to do, so he put in the other shell and fired that into his father, too.

It was Matthew Galder, one-time sheriff and sometime lawman, who found him under the old plank bridge up the road from the Fletcher house. Matthew hunkered down and let him tell all about it, though Matthew didn't think the boy knew who he was more than half the time. But he told it all, and the man sat still till it was over.

"How come you brung him down here with you, Johnny?" Matthew asked.

The boy didn't answer for a long time. He just stared at the creek or up through the gaps in the planking. "Well," he said finally. "You wouldn't want the flies to get him, would you? They'd blow him up something awful. I seen it happen before. I seen a cat once." He licked his lips and looked down at what there was at his feet. "This old cat . . ." he said. But that was as far as he could get. All he did was sit there until Matthew helped him stand.

Matthew had thought to bring a tarp with him, and he laid it over Mr. Fletcher. Then he helped Johnny up the bank and into his pickup. "How come you toted that shotgun down here with you?" he asked.

"You wouldn't want the dogs to get him," the boy said. "They'd of eat him, you know."

Then he was quiet. He stared out the window.

"But they ain't no more shells for it, son."

"Naw," he said. "Naw, there ain't."

Matthew drove the pickup onto the road and started for Loretto when the boy asked, "Did you put a blanket over him?"

Matthew said he had laid a tarp over him.

And the boy said, "He might get too hot. He never liked to sleep with much on him in the way of bedclothes."

He was quiet again; then he started talking. "When I was little," he said, and he licked his lips like they must have been terribly dry and cracked. "When I was a little tad . . ."

But it was no use. He leaned back into the seat as the truck bounced and skittered on down the road. Matthew looked at him once and saw that he was holding his hands together real tight, and he was still licking his lips. Then he heard the boy talking again, only he was not talking to Matthew, but to himself. It was hard to hear it all, but he did hear the boy say that it sure would be good to get back home and go to sleep, because he felt like he hadn't slept in at least a week, and that after he woke up he was going to fill himself just as full as full could be on one of his Ma's big Sunday breakfasts. Then after he'd eaten and slept some more, he'd have to remember to ask his Pa what the Curse of Jotham was.

Matthew then began to talk to himself, and he said to himself, You don't mind it so much with the bums or the drifters or even the niggers, but with a boy like Johnny you hate to see it.

He looked again at the boy whose lips were moving. But there was no sound, and there was nothing in the eyes. Matthew looked back to the road, trying to pay attention only to his driving, but the boy was there beside him and Matthew couldn't help himself.

They'll never hang him, he said in his mind. But he won't know whether they do or not.

He looked at the boy whose lips were moving, whose eyes were vacant, whose hand was slowly pumping up and down in a slow and perfect rhythm. He looked one last time before he jammed his foot on the accelerator and drove as fast as he could toward town.

When Etta Reece Danced

Let others live to serve God: you must have no other life than God. Let others believe in Him, learn about Him, love Him, reverence Him: you must taste and comprehend Him, know Him, delight in Him.

William of St-Thierry
Epistle to the Brethren
of Mont-Dieu

• • Times like this she thought of herself as a butterfly, one hand fluttering at her throat, her eyes blank. Especially now that he was gone and it was over. Again. Not that *he* was over again. This had been the only time with him. *Time,* that is, in a more or less extended sort of way. Not the only "time" with a man. Oh no.

She slipped her fingers around the glass of bourbon. Bourbon and water. Sour mash, really. Things like that can matter. Now that was real, something you could get your . . . well, not your teeth into. But you could understand that because it did you in predictable ways, once you knew what was happening. Not like men . . .

She eased down from her stool at the bar and made toward the jukebox, its round of lights a silent show in the early evening, a visual promise of performances to come.

Two bits . . . *Plock!* . . . Three tunes.

Appropriate tunes, ones that wouldn't remind her of him. No spinnings that were *his.* Or *his'n'hers.* She avoided the tunes that she could say belonged somehow to *them.*

Because he was gone. Had made no promises to her, but had given her a picture. A real photo of himself. And not one of those nasty things men do when they don't care. Not a blurry snapshot with a sucked up gut and pretending to pose like Muscle Man. Or grinning with a cigar, holding out a line of stinking catfish.

But one of *him.* Really him. From the shoulders of his sports jacket up. So you could see his necktie and shirt. And he was smiling like he wanted to be nice to her, not to brag because he'd killed a boar or a shark.

Back at the bar she again slipped her fingers up and down the wet sides of her glass . . .

She'd framed it. Spent her own money to put him behind glass. She must have known even then that she would need to preserve him against age and change. There on her dresser where she could see it early in the mornings after he'd dressed for work . . .

She felt her breasts heavy across her arm on the bar. She lifted the glass to her lips.

. . . or was it to protect herself?

Either way, there he'd be: her man, her love.

The juke box stopped, its lights revolving, rotating, spinning around the perimeter of the machine. Waiting for the time of crowds and noise and fights and dates . . .

She swallowed the last. God, it was good. God . . . God . . .

She dismounted again from the black plastic stool, a finger and a smile asking for the refill as she went to the machine, another quarter held gently between her fingers, as willing to plunk a fortune into that machine as she had been to love him. She didn't want a stranger, say, playing a song that would work him back up into her . . .

She sipped like a lady on the waiting drink. The smell of it. She loved it, even when the sweet of it cloyed.

She smiled.

Him, of course. Him with his jacket and tie and real portrait photo he'd given her for framing.

Flesh. His sweet flesh, she remembered. Which was what was so different about him. Not just there being no catfish or stringy muscles rolled over with fat . . .

. . . but his flesh.

The picture was class. That was nice. She liked class. She liked a touch of that. The frame helped that.

The music spun out its lines and she hummed along, gazing at the mirror behind the bar: there was herself, almost invisible, she noticed. Hard to pick herself out of the growing crowd. And the booths behind her. She looked through the mirror at them, too. Saw them filling up with the regulars first, then the occasionals. Then came the visitors and transients. Warm. The excitement of all those bodies come together here with the swirl of ice and music and lights, the swirl of dancers.

She sipped at her drink, her fingers lightly patting the heavy bar top in time to the tune. She smiled, then took a deep breath as the record stopped long enough for the next one to clack on. She never liked that part of it. The *click* or *clack* of the machine. It always broke the spell for her.

. . . playing again, a tender ballad of love . . .

. . . in the mirror she caught herself, stopped, and focused carefully. She felt herself sag slightly. Hell, he never liked coming in here. He didn't even very much like to drink.

Her fingers fluttered at her throat, then moved on up to her face. She wiped at something in her eye and was startled to realize she was crying. She thought at first it was water on her finger from the glass.

Actually, he didn't like any of that music very much.

Actually, he preferred people like Luke Jeter who had once been a national fiddle champion. He had told her that in her place while he was listening to a bunch of his many records. She liked Jeter, too, but she liked the rest of them, or at least most of them.

"It ain't pure," he had said to her.

They were in bed and had made love. She just plain enjoyed making love to him more than to anyone else she'd ever known: husbands, lovers, the lot. It was his flesh: hard, muscled. He was wonderful to her, and he never seemed to mind that she wasn't a trim, flat-bellied little trick.

"Not really pure. It's all been debased by spangled boots. And big business got a-hold of it. It's tarnished. I have to laugh."

And he did. She rolled over and eased a leg across him, felt his manliness under her thigh.

"Folks in this town, some of them twenty years ago wouldn't hardly admit the Grand Old Opry was even in Nashville."

She eased a hand across his stomach, that thick, narrow band of hair rising up from his belly in swirls across his chest. She slowly raised herself onto him.

"Now they're proud enough. Now they count the money fast enough."

She raised herself so that her nipples just barely trailed across his chest. She felt his hair on them and she tingled all over. She felt his privates under her now. Not hard. She pressed herself onto him. He never made love to her twice in a night. Usually no more than once in a week, or even less often than that. Her hips rolled around on him. She didn't mind he wasn't hard. He was still there for her to feel.

"It was better then, too. I've got all the old records. They played better music. Jimmie Rodgers and Woodie Guthrie and all of them. None of that electric stuff. None of that rock and roll junk in it back then."

She pushed harder on him, rolled and swirled on him. She felt him stiffen some. That was good enough. He let her pleasure herself any way she wanted. Any way at all. Oh! Oh! She loved him so.

"It was pure, and the people played it because they'd grown up playing it. They never had to learn it. They'd just known it all their lives."

Ah! And there. Oh, God. He was so good to her. She gently pushed up, sat up and looked down at him naked in the bed. She patted him, smoothed her hands across his belly and chest, ca-

ressed his thighs, his calves. She leaned back toward the bottom of
the bed, stretched out and kissed his feet. Then she rubbed and
patted and smoothed him all over again . . . and again.

"But they're none of them pure any more. Not like Luke and
Jimmie and the others."

She put her hand out for the drink, but knocked the glass over
instead. A slip of ice was all there was in it.

"Oh," she said, her mouth open in a wide smile, her eyes filled
with tears. "Oh."

They brought her another one.

"Come on, Etta Reece."

She knew without turning it was Jimmy B wanting to dance.

"You got your teeth in, Jimmy B?" she asked.

"Hell, Etta Reece, I don't want to eat you. I just want to dance,"
and he gave a huge and awful wink to the others sitting near her as
they laughed.

"Come on, now. It'll be over."

She sipped her drink.

"I'll get you a beer after."

"Oh, Jimmy B. It's been a long time." She looked at him at last.
"Beer just makes you fat."

He whistled through his lips and pinched at the roll around her
middle.

"Etta Reece, honey. You just a born winner," Jimmy B said as
he led her to the small dance area.

The tune was a hard-rock-rock-a-billy something she couldn't
name, but her body knew what to do with it. They waltzed.
Jimmy B could smell a waltz clear across the county no matter how
it was disguised, and that was the only thing that non-stop teller of
outlandish tales would get up from his booth and beer for.

They waltzed.

When Etta Reece waltzed, she was so light on her feet, her body
swaying, fluid and natural as love . . .

When Etta Reece waltzed, she made you hear the swoosh of great
ball gowns, made you see diamonds woven through her locks . . .

When Etta Reece waltzed, she turned volume into music . . .

When Etta Reece waltzed, her face was beatific, and she touched them all with grace . . .

And Jimmy B—silly, toothless old man—led her like one born to sip cognac and attend princes of the realm . . .

Once around . . . Twice . . . Then twice again . . . Done.

He bought her a drink and told her a joke. The one about the shy boy who was trying to think of something to say to the little butterball of a partner he had, because his mother always told him to say something nice to your partner after you dance with her. So he danced three whole dances with her trying to think of something to say. And then he had it, and he said, "Liza Jane, you sweats less than any little fat girl I ever danced with."

Etta Reece drew back her arm in a mock threat. "Jimmy B," she said, her voice wonderful and full and low, "You are no gentleman."

He whistled his laughter at her.

"Nope." She felt his hesitation, his kindness at saying nothing about Finley this time. Then with a leap and a cackle he was back in his booth, repeating his story, talking, somehow, around the brown bottle he held stuck straight from his mouth.

She sipped, unable to keep him at arm's length anymore. Now, maybe, even willing to conjure him up. Or willing to let whatever happened to come into her head come on in. Maybe she could handle it, she thought.

Until the dreams came she loved to watch him dress in the mornings. She would lie curled under a sheet while he stood naked before the dresser and brushed his hair. She liked to watch his buttocks as he shifted his weight from one leg to the other, posing, she liked to think, for her, brushing his hair with the matched brushes so she could see the muscles knotting in his arms and rippling up and down his back. She loved the little dents and mounds they made, everything in motion even while he was standing almost stock still. It amazed her. She would pretend to reach out to rub her hand up and down his spine. She especially liked where it curved so gracefully in right above his bottom . . .

. . . and his bottom wasn't all red-pimply like most people's. It was white. So very white compared to the brown he kept from summers and summers of tanning.

When he finished with his hair, he would turn toward her to dress. First his undershirt, as he stood with one hip cocked, his body so relaxed, yet so full of force. Then jockey shorts: neat, trim. Then his shirt. Socks next. Trousers, with the shirt tucked in just so. Shoes. Tie. Ah yes, a necktie. Like the photo of him she'd framed, it was a touch of class. Then a jacket. A windbreaker, usually, not his good sports jacket. Ready to go run the machines that made the shoes.

. . . but those awful dreams, those awful dreams that ruined it all.

He wasn't actually crouching. He was actually sitting by her on the edge of the bed. It was the first dream. He sat for what seemed a quarter of an hour, crouched like a young, feral dog: tense, smooth, ready to leap ten feet and be gone. Naked as always. He never wore clothes in bed, summer or winter. Her hands patted him cautiously.

He whispered the whole time.

"I don't know if it's real," he said. "There was this voice in my dream, and it called to me." He was silent.

She thought his eyes would burst into flame. She was frightened. He looked overwhelmed with awe.

He whispered but never looked at her.

"I think it *was*," he told her.

She held his arm, then his hands. She kissed his knee.

"It was *His* voice. He was calling for me. Like He knew where I was, but couldn't quite see me yet."

Again he kept silence. She lay her head on his knees and lightly set her palms against his chest and stomach.

"He was *calling* to me."

"Oh, Finley," she whispered. "Oh, Finley Finley."

The dream came about once a month after that. But since it was so much the same each time, all he would say the next morning was, "It came again," and she understood what he meant.

There wasn't ever much for her to say to him those weeks about the dream: *it* called as if it knew he was there, but couldn't quite see him yet. And each time there would be the fire in his eyes, the look that was like something more than fear, that was something beyond what either of them could name. It made her sad.

It made her sad, but it did something else to him.

"Etta Reece, do you remember where we first met?" he asked. He neatly poured another bit of beer into his glass.

"In the church," she answered. "We met in the church, Finley."

"Do you know why I was there?" he asked. "Do you know why I had gone to church that day?"

She shrugged.

"Do you know why *you* went to church that night?" He stared hard across the table of the booth at her, his face as near to a scowl as it could get.

She shrugged again, her lips parting in a wry smile. "I wanted some ole time religion," she said, and took a swallow of her drink.

He shook his head.

"Etta Reece, this is meaningful, and you ought to take it seriously." He paused. "You came to find me." He spoke very matter-of-factly.

She closed her eyes slowly, her lips still parted in the grin.

"I didn't know you," she said.

He didn't say anything for a minute. He pushed his glass aside and leaned across the table at her, drawing her toward him with his stare so their faces were only eight inches from each other.

"*I* was the one came to find God. You came to find *me*." He set his face and slowly pulled away as though having explained all. Etta Reece stayed leaning forward, waiting.

"You mean what?" she said very quietly and solemnly. "You found me instead of God? And I found you and *you* were God?"

"Listen," he said. "Listen. I have always been looking for God. I was born under the caul, and that marked me, marked me out for something special. Listen. My mother always told me. And my father, too. They were both able to know."

"Know?"

"They could talk in tongues. They could understand the how

196

and why of things no one else could ever imagine. They *knew*, Etta Reece. They *knew*. And when I came under the caul like that, they knew I was marked for special, and they told me I would know God because He had already set His hand on me, but that there is no such thing in the world to come too easily, and so I would have to go out into it and seek Him, and that if I did it purely enough, then He would come to me—probably in dreams like He has—and you see He has."

"And so you have looked for Him with a pure heart," she said.

"No," he corrected, and looked down. Very softly he said, "With pureness of the heart's desire."

"I see," she answered.

"It is the intent that has to be pure," he said, covering her hands with his. "What I am telling you, Etta Reece, is that I mean to say we were both searching," and his eyes looked through her as though he was having a hard time making himself stay with the conversation. "We were both searching and we found each other, but each of us was just a stop on the way."

They were both very quiet. Etta Reece felt his hands on hers and then felt hers trembling under his touch, felt her cheeks quiver. Her mouth dropped open as she understood what he meant.

"On our way . . . where?" She could hardly speak.

He didn't answer. He kept his eyes straight on her.

"Don't do this to me," she whispered. "Oh, please, Finley. Don't do this to me. You can't. I won't let you."

"It isn't time, yet," he said. "Not yet. But last night . . . last night He *saw* me."

She felt herself trembling all over. Suddenly he was up and around on her side of the booth, squeezed in very close against her, his lips to her ear.

"Feel me," he hissed. "*Feel* me," and he guided her hands between his legs.

She felt him with both hands, her face up to his. Their lips touched lightly, their eyes were open and their mouths were open as they breathed into each other. She kneaded his erection, felt his thighs tighten under her touch.

"He saw me," he whispered into her mouth.

"Oh," her mouth shook softly. "Please," she said back into his mouth. "Please."

He held his windbreaker in front of him as they hurried from the tavern to her place.

Then the dreams were weekly, and they made love often.

He didn't tell her when he'd had them. She would know. Not just because he began fondling her heavy breasts or spreading her legs with his strong hands. But because she would wake up when the dream came to him. She felt it coming. Sometimes it was midnight. Or two. Or four in the morning. Once, it wasn't until a quarter till six, just fifteen minutes before he usually got up.

She could tell, because it was like there was someone else in the room with them. The first time she felt it, she was frightened. She thought someone had broken in to rob them, to murder . . .

She was going to wake Finley when she realized there was no point. It passed across her without pausing, and it lay with him. Or on him. It seemed she could actually feel a weight on the bed. And his breathing was different. Like he'd been running or doing his exercises. And not just that his heart was beating fast from that, but it was like she could see his face and there would be no smile on it. It would be more like . . .

Then words failed for her. More like what she sometimes felt she must look like just when he was making his best love to her. Something she couldn't name.

Then it would be gone. It never went like it came. It was just suddenly not there any more, and he would be reaching for her, pulling himself on top of her and plunging deeper and deeper into her as though he were trying to get *through* her to something else. Using her both as gate and path to somewhere beyond.

. . . then he'd wake up just at the end. Wake, often, with a whimper like a child waking to find a dream of discovered treasure disappearing into the daily realities of school and chores.

Other times, he didn't wake right away, but would stay restlessly sleeping. Then he would mount her again . . .

. . . and occasionally he would take her a third time.

She didn't mind. She loved him. She loved to have him throwing himself into her time and time again. She only wished she could know where he was going. She wished, shuddering as though caught sitting too near the front door of the tavern on those wet winter days in Nashville, he would take her with him. Wished she knew . . .

It went like that for a year. She took the pleasures as best she could and tried to put the mysteries behind her as best she could. But it was hard. He was so much the same: his neatness, his clothes, his preening before her each morning, his records of Jimmie Rodgers, Woodie Guthrie, Estil Ball, Boone Reid, and God alone knew whoall else. People she'd never heard of. People you'd never hear on the juke box.

At the same time, he was so different, too: where he used to jabber away, he had grown quiet. Where he used to let her do what she wanted with his body without seeming to care one way or another about it, now he had gotten tender toward her, would actually look at her as she lay in the bed—still a pretty body even if it was too fleshed out, too heavy, too weighted with time. He would look at her and run a finger tip over the eight-inch zipper of scar pointing down from her navel where they had opened her up not so much to rid her of that last child that had already died in her, but to take its home, too, so there would be no more chances for that again. Ever.

. . . would trace its course with his finger tips, then bend, even, to kiss it and stare at it hard enough, she would think, to see clear inside her where those little unborn things had had their brief spark of life. That's how Finley had put it: "Touched with the spark of life."

Then he would sigh. He seemed swollen with concern for her, but at the same time, the skin of his joy shrivelled, and most of the fun seemed to have gone from him.

The last time: it didn't come. She slept that night through, but had sad dreams, though she couldn't remember a single detail about any of them. She woke suddenly, her heart pounding like it does when you've overslept. He was sitting on her side of the bed as if waiting for her to wake up. He was already dressed.

"Etta Reece," he whispered. He put a hand over her heart and calmed it.

"Oh, God," she groaned. "Oh . . ."

"It is time," he said quietly.

"Oh no. Please no." Tears plopped to the pillow from her cheeks.

"It is time, Etta Reece, but I need to tell you about the dream."

She snuffled, her chest heaving.

"Jesus. Oh sweet Jesus," he said pausing. She saw how he wouldn't look at her straight.

"I held Him," he whispered. "I went to Him and stood so He could put His arms around me. But He wouldn't. So I clutched Him naked, and I hugged His bare flesh to mine. Then I went down on Him. I slid down His sweet frame and loved Him. *Loved* Him. Do you understand what I am saying? Do you?"

He still would not look at her.

"Do you? Can you under *stand* that?

"Let me tell you." He still whispered, but he would look at her now. "When I was a boy—just a little boy—I had this picture of Jesus. He always looked so sad to me, and His arms were always spread open like He was asking for people to come to Him, to come to Him so He could hold them and let them know that everything would be all right. I was raised to love Jesus, and that picture made Him look like He wanted you to. And I did.

"I kept that picture of Him under my mattress for a long time. Then I folded it up and carried it around with me in my pocket. And for a long time I would plan when to take it out and open it up. I would make sure I was alone, then I'd get it out and open it on my lap. It got so I'd have to be very careful with it, to smooth out the wrinkles as best I could. I would touch my fingers across those folds where it was wearing, and I could see a cross right through Jesus, and I would trace that cross with my fingers. I would rub my fingers up and down the body of Jesus, Etta Reece.

"Then one day, one night after supper and right before I was to get to bed, Momma caught me. I was sitting on the side of my bed with my picture of Jesus, and I was staring at His face and trying to figure it all out. *Who are you?* I wanted to know, all the while rubbing Him up and down and side to side. *Who are you?*

"Then Momma was standing there beside me. Her face was white like she'd been witness to an awful thing. 'Finley Finley Finley,' was all she could say.

"I snatched that picture away like it was a dirty thing I wanted to hide, and when I did that I saw what she must have seen when she came into my room. I was stiff, Etta Reece.

"'Finley,' she kept saying. And then she backed out of my room. Backed out, Etta Reece, like she couldn't trust not having me in her sight. Backed out with a moan that came up from I can't begin to tell you how deep in her and lasted for what seemed like weeks and weeks and weeks."

He was silent for a long time.

"Finley, what did they do?" Etta Reece asked.

He leaned to her very slowly as though coming back from far away.

"I don't remember. All I can recall is the two of them—the three of us—on our knees a lot. And the moans. They moaned and moaned and would now and again tear at themselves like they was trying to get rid of an itch by pulling it from their very skins. They never hit me."

She kept very still, waiting.

"And now I have been with Him."

"It was a dream, Finley."

"He smelled of sawdust. His flesh smelled sweet like from fresh sawdust. But He didn't know what to do."

He was looking away from her again. She felt she was losing him.

"You'd think that being God and all He'd have known what to do."

"It was a dream is all, Finley."

"He was confused, like He'd never had anybody want to love Him before."

"Just a *dream*."

"I mean *really* to love Him."

"Oh, Finley."

"I can't stand it," she heard him say.

"What, Finley? What?"

"I can't stand it if He has cut me off. Why did He come to me if He was just going to despise me afterwards? Why?"

"A *dream,* is all. Oh, Finley. Let *me* hold you. I know how to hold you."

"Momma saw me kissing Him when she came in."

"Let *me* hold you, Finley. *Let* me."

"I thought that after, He would be able to hold me and tell me everything would be all right."

"Oh no, Finley. That's for Etta Reece, Baby. Etta Reece is here to hold you."

"But He didn't. Maybe He can't. Maybe He can't make anything right after all."

"It was just a dream, Finley. Oh, Finley. A dream, a *dream*."

"Then I was talking to somebody. I don't know who it was, but it was somebody I understood was off to see God, somebody who was on his way right then. And it was right then I understood I wasn't, that I wasn't *ever*.

"I said, 'Tell Him hello.'

"I said, 'Tell Him I love Him.'

"I said, 'Tell Him I miss Him very much.' Oh, Etta Reece, I have never felt so all alone in my whole life."

Finley paused, then cried so suddenly and with such bitter unhappiness Etta Reece gasped. He stopped almost as soon as he started, and it struck him as so strange a thing to have done that he laughed.

Etta Reece heard his voice, then, heard it wavering, crossing back and forth between what it had naturally been raised to be and what he had so early in his life tried to make it be. And she caught the picture of him, saw him just as if she had known him when he was a little boy—round cheeked and nearly pretty, that soft, exposed, vulnerable, dependent past that men seem needing always to deny or hide or scorn—growing up with a radio through the still-remote stretches of the countryside, listening, trying to make his voice rounder so it wouldn't sound like his mother's and his father's: all flattened out and nasal, itching with the dust scratched from a red neck.

Finley listened to the radio voices of announcers, then turned the radio down, the little boy talking to a hand mirror salvaged from the trash left by a sister who had loved and left early in his life, that mirror framed in yellow plastic, pink curls of rosettes in a faded tracery on the back.

Finley listened to the radio voices of announcers, then turned the sound down, looking carefully at his mouth as he sounded out the vowels. He didn't like how fast they talked, and he didn't often listen much to what they were saying. What he studied was how they sounded.

"Aaaaaeeeeeeooooooo," all the while watching his lips open . . . spread . . . widen . . . narrow . . .

Watching, then closing his eyes to listen without the distraction of seeing, then finally watching while the sounds were just the merest whispers: watching his mouth, finally, as he moved it into every strained configuration he could manage, stretching his face, then, until he had grinned himself into someone new.

There was also the thrown-out lipstick salvaged from the heap of his sister's leavings: a deep red, a red that even glimmered to hint of depths of color piled on color. He sneaked it out along with the mirror to keep until he knew what he was to do with them. He left the comb, though.

It wasn't the hair still woven, scattered through the teeth, but the teeth themselves. Three or four in a row were broken off all the way, and several were broken half way off. He pulled the comb through his hair, his sister's hair trailing across his own. He didn't like it. It didn't get his own hair combed much. He held it in his hands and looked at it, then at himself in the mirror. He could see flecks of powder in his hair, smell the softness and sweetness of it on himself. He looked closely at the comb again and saw the tiny bits of his sister's scalp that had been pulled loose to lodge in the comb . . .

If it had had all its teeth, he thought . . .

But he had the lipstick. And still curled around the inside edge of a little white jar there was some eye shadow. He had that, too. And the mirror.

And finally he stole. The first thing was another jar of eye shadow. Then some rouge. Then another lipstick. He didn't use any of them for the longest time, because he knew they would be hard to get off and because he wasn't able to be alone all that much. But he collected them, even so, kept them hidden in a box with pencil stubs and stamps, bits and pieces of paper or broken glass he'd found, pebbles, cicada shells . . .

Then he saw the bottle of white shoe polish. He was in a supermarket in town with his mother when he saw it. They passed down the aisle with all the shoe waxes and laces, brushes, shiny shoe horns, and footrest boxes to keep them all in. He knew the white liquid right away, knew he was going to have it, knew also that he would have to be careful about it, even become wily and patient about getting it.

They circled the store slowly, his mother gathering the flour, the pork, the lard, the beans, the other staples, her attention always on the equation of volume and cost. He managed to wander off once, found his way slowly back to the shoe-care section, passed it carefully, and went on.

He caught his mother's glance as they came at each other down another aisle.

Eventually they found it all.

"A clown," he managed to cough out to his mother as she stood over his bed. "I wanted to be a clown, is all," he managed between the screams from the pain from his father's beatings. "A clown."

Etta Reece looked up into the face of that bruised and bleeding child. But before she could reach out to take his face between her hands, he had turned. And in that instant, she knew she had lost him.

"Violence," he whispered. "It is all violence. From the birth to the death." He looked over at her. "Have you ever seen a baby born? I have seen it."

She turned her head away.

"I have seen it in dogs and cats and horses and cows. I have never seen it in people, but I have looked at pictures of it. It is violent. It hurts to come out. It hurts. It *hurts* the baby—they always scream. And it hurts their momma, because she nearly always screams. It is violent. And I have seen men die. That is violent, too. Men scream in their pain. They can't breathe. They hurt. Death is a violence on us. And so is love. Making love is a violence. Think on it, Etta Reece. *Think* on it. *You* know it. You get ripped and tore. You get too dry and you bleed. And if a man gets too hot, he hurts. His balls purely hurt, Etta Reece. And think on it. Look at it: grunts and shouts and blood. Bruises. Scratches. It is a violence.

"And that isn't all. There is every other hurt in the world besides. It don't matter all cuts and bruises. People get their souls hurt, too. And that is a violence. It is a violence when your Poppa straps your legs with his belt. It is a violence when your Momma looks away from you and cries because she has seen an abomination of sin. That is a violence. And loving is a violence as great as hating because you—Hush, Etta Reece! Stop that crying and you listen because I am telling you what you need to know. Then you can *know* me. *Then* you can know me. I say that loving is a violence because it is a hurt as comes from violating other people. You violate their quiet. You violate their own business. You violate as surely as you violate yourself when you do it to yourself in the dark and the quiet and when you feel it hot and sticky in your hand it is a violence. And it is a further violence to have to get up and rinse your hand or wipe it on a rag you'll throw away. It is a violence. It is a violence. *All* of it, Etta Reece. And there's not but just so much a body ought to have to be made to endure. Not but just so much."

"Oh, Finley. Finley Finley Finley." She sat up in the bed and held herself to him, shuddering against him, grasping, pulling herself as close as she could, feeling his arms and his back hard under her hands. "What are you saying to me, Finley? That's the worst violence of all. The very worst. God don't want you dead, Finley, else He wouldn't have put you here to start with."

She felt something in him calm at that, felt a tension go from him, a softness, an almost tenderness of something. A sadness, she

205

understood, a heavying sadness drawing him from the clutch of her grip.

"And *that,*" he said, still just barely more than whispering. "He is the greatest violence of all."

"Oh no, Finley. Don't dare to say that. Don't don't don't, Finley. Oh, Finley. I love you, Finley. Oh God knows I love you."

But he fell from her, too weighted for her to hold, or her too weak to be the one who could hold him.

"And after all that," he said, his voice calm and gentle. "After all that a man dies. He might have a headstone over him, but that's not much of a monument, is it?" He looked at her. "He's gone, and it's like he'd been one of your little ones, Etta Reece. It's like he'd never been born at all."

She felt him bend to her, felt his lips on her forehead, felt them linger just ever so slightly. Then she felt him go, felt him gone.

"What's wrong, Etta Reece, Baby?" one of the men at the bar asked. "What's the matter?"

She was sobbing out of all control, half leaning against him, half falling from the stool.

"Hey," he shouted. "Gimme a hand here."

Several of the women rushed to help, patted her hands, clucked their comfort to her.

She fumbled herself off the stool, her body shaking and trembling from her gasps and sobs. She started to fall.

"God knows, get her."

"How in hell much's she drunk?"

The bartender shrugged as he tried to recollect fast enough to answer.

"Get her to the ladies room."

"No," she grunted, flopping her arms around in a helpless search toward the bar.

"Grab her purse. There, Ettie Baby. There you are."

"I want to go home," she cried. "Take me home, for God's sake. Please. Take me home."

The floor spun under her, and she would have fallen except for her friends who led her out to the street. As they surrounded her, she looked like a pinball bouncing from bumper to bumper. They got her down the street and up to her apartment and into her bed.

After the women told the men to go on, they got her mostly undressed. She lay still, letting them do with her whatever they wanted. She just waited for them to leave her alone. The bed swirled awfully.

When she heard the last *click* and *clack* of heels down the stairs, she managed to heave herself into a sitting position. Slowly she gained her feet, stood woozily before the chest of drawers. She looked in the mirror, but couldn't see a thing. Inhaling deeply, she managed to get the rest of her clothes off except for one stocking that hung down around her ankle. She shuffled the two or three steps to the dresser. Carefully, she reached up and took his picture in both hands. She forced herself to stare at it hoping the rest of the crazy world would go on and whirl itself right past her and leave her alone.

She banged the picture on the top of the bureau. Then again. At last she took a deep breath and crashed the glass against a corner of the dresser. As carefully as she could, she picked out the pieces of broken glass, then eased his picture from the frame which she banged a couple of times against the side of the chest before letting it clatter to the floor.

She held the photo near her face, looking hard at it, then kissed it. Kissed it, her mouth open to form a suction, held it to her face and sucked and sucked to pull the image from the paper, tried to breathe the image into life, to form him there with her again in the flesh.

Panting, she fell back a step. The picture was wet, crumpled, still not him, but all she had. She clutched it in both fists, embraced it, held it to her face, rubbed it across her wet mouth and tongue, across her breasts and stomach. She stumbled back another step. And another. She forced the picture between her legs and rubbed herself back toward the bed.

She fell across it, raised and spread her knees, and had him in her once more as the world spun, her face charged now with the pain, her body charged now with the look in his eyes which saw things through her she never understood, her head charged now with the ecstacy of his dreams

   . . . one last time with him

   . . . one last thrust of love as her world spun itself madly round and round and round

   . . . one final lunge before loosing herself into the vortex where she too could spin herself down to the very center of it all, where maybe she could know him forever.

Talking to the Boy

• • She was into her talk doing fine, working them up to listen to what she would read them. This was the easy part, always: the depreciatory thanks to the person who introduced, the amusing anecdote, the talking. Then the reading itself: she read well and she knew it. Hell, she wrote what she knew and what she knew was rednecks because she was one, more or less. Her without a lick of college and now teaching in one because she was a writer. Weird world, she knew. A real weird world.

And as she rattled on with her big grin, her eyes invisible if it hadn't been for pointing to them with eye shadow, circling them with dark blue, her eyes stuck way back in her head and close together like a pig's, by God! her eyes dark as pitch, black as coal, always in motion looking, searching, wary, seeing what they could see to tell her some more about this vale of tears we all must wander through before the Promised Land hoves into view: rattled on with her preamble to give her time to sort them out if she could, or at least as much as she could.

She knew what she was going to read. That was not the question. The question was more what she was going to say afterward—at the party. *That* was always the hard work in these things, the party after when all the academics wandered up smiling and nodding with their highballs, their beards already catching the detritus of cheese and crisp crackers, while their spectacles caught reflections of muted lights and of each other. Sometimes she would see herself in their glasses as she jabbered responses to their questions, smiled at their antics as they aimed to please either by telling her how good she was (which she already knew) or what her fiction *really* meant and how it fit into the current trends or, heads cocked, brows furrowed in consternation, looking concerned for her because her work *didn't* seem to fit the current thrusts toward, well, whatever. Which she already knew or, if she didn't, didn't care about anyway.

But she enjoyed it, oftener than not. At least it was a living and probably better, take it all in all, than working in the mill or fetching another cuppa for the boss.

She had seen them all now and was ready to read, and there didn't seem to be any surprises in particular: a good crowd, considering: students clutching notebooks just like there was something to take notes about, faculty wives—some looking like they might really rather be home taking a nap after a day chasing dust balls, deepdown dirt, and little ones; others looking glad to be anywhere that *was* out, even if it was there where yet another woman was making them feel slack, like they ought to have done something with their *own* lives besides breed more of their kind—and oddments of others like the old writers: a bit seedy, leaned back in their mis-matched pants and jackets like they'd heard all this crap before, which no doubt was true: the locals who had never quite made it but who, bless their hearts, were still in the same business with her—good or bad, successful or not, made it or not.

Except for the boy she had seen: mop of curly-kinky hair, a built-in smirk on his face, a scraggly scuzz of mustache perching in comically smug innocence on his upper lip, sitting with what must have been parents, they looked so on edge around him: the Lear-stern father, the apologetic mother. The boy had been careful to make eye contact with her. She smiled to herself as she responded on the second sweep-through during her preliminary patter. The third and final sweep it was still there. And suddenly she felt very sorry for him: his nice wool jacket sitting like an unfamiliar courtesy across his bony shoulders, the glazed look in his eyes, his childish need to play these games. Well.

It was a gas. She was funny. At least he was ready to laugh, anyway. There were all these people come to listen to her read her stuff strut her stuff stutter stuff. He giggled to himself and kept staring at her as she rattle battled about the booth, only it wasn't a booth, it was a rostrum dosturm frickety-fracking DIis DAis DILdus DOPEus, giggling silently again, always silently, always to himself everything to himself everything that mattered to himself because that's where he wanted to be except when he wanted to be somewhere else and with someone else except Popsydopsy and MumsyPoo who, Popsydopsy, sat there with him his arms folded across his chest and her, MumsyPoo, with hands in lap a-twisting away at a piece of paper. She always carried a piece of paper so she could write things down on it, but Popsywopsy was the one who always took the notes but had to borrow her paper and her pencil because he always forgot the bringing of his own. But as for himself, he wasn't going to take notes. They taught you how to take notes in high school and there wasn't anything in high school to be worth the waste of trees for the paper and the pencils. He wondered sometimes about the lead and poisoning the atmosphere with jet planes, though. For a long time he had not understood chemical toilets and thought that planes flushed out like trains, except when standing in stations. He was always a hit between classes on the smoking ramp when he said *Don't Look Up* like it was a flock of pigeons, whenever he heard one screaming its slice through the sky.

There, she did it again, he crooned to himself watching her watch him as she watched the rest of the world. And he wondered how she could see so much so fast WOW! she must know how to do things fast because she saw him twice and if she sees him thrice he will know something that he had never known before. Like the first time he had slept with Susie Q Sally Poo Silly Who and hadn't known what he was supposed to do and tried to put it in her belly button where it certainly didn't fit but he had gone goo all over her anyway and was embarrassed but by then it was too late. She had laughed at him for that mess and he would never forget it never, would remember it always and had remembered it later when he knew where it went and had put it where it was supposed to go enough times to control himself a little and not goo all over at the wrong time and the wrong place, wondering, still, when things were wearing off and time sat breathing furiously before him gargoyle-like, chin on hand, wings spread out like concrete demons: heavy, man, heavyheavyheavyheavyheavyheavy *time* blocking him, keeping him from getting where he wanted to be which was nowhere he could think of except away; time, though, sometimes stretching out, then, like a birthday party noisemaker curling uncurling curling uncurling to the sounding *baaaaaht* of the tin reed, then slapping itself suddenly out forever into void and chaos where there was nothing but goo at wrong times and places.

There! Thrice! And she reads to us like Mommas of yore reading to Kiddlies of yore, Kiddlies nestled snuggily in their Mommalies laps, Kiddlies curled cattily against their Mommily-Poo's bosomy-boobs listening to stories read by such soft-cheeked round-cheeked beautiful Mommilies whose Kiddliepoos *loved* their MommilyPoos.

Wondering, he remembered he had been thinking. Wondering if anybody else had ever gooed at the wrong time or not known it wasn't the belly button was the seat of all learning. And there was something else? He tried to remember that he was going to know something else if something else happened? He couldn't quite bring it up into his head from wherever. But Hark! She reads.

Funny, man. A real gas.

After, there was the applause, nicely offered and she was glad to accept it because she never could know how things might go. You read something they have read, something that has already been published and with which they are familiar and they know what is coming next and can anticipate it with you and love it when they hear it—like little chillern listening to their mommas reading stories they could long since recite, or like Christians every Christmas Eve making it through candlelight services, bladders stretched from too many drinks while the preachers tried to make it sound like the first time again, and fresh, only they out there in the pews were waiting to go back home to finish the evening with their chillern so they could read *them* the Christmas story they liked most: it was usually not from the *Bible*.

And now time for the questions, and she: hoping for students who might ask something, might stutter and shuffle and finally manage to blurt out the burning things, the bubbling, deep-down things from their own personal earths: that unimaginably, embarrassingly direct thing demanding—no matter how baldly or badly stated—that she define the mysteries for them. She could talk to that, because what they wanted to know about was Purity and Honesty and Virtue. But all she could tell them was that while it may be God who made people, it was people with all their warts and wild hairs who made Art, and they themselves would have to learn how to deal with that: the dirt under the nails, the poots of life. The ones she grieved for were the ones who wouldn't come up to her at all because they didn't want to seem pushy like the others, didn't want to impose, didn't think they had anything to offer her. She felt bad about them because they were the ones who would tell her what she really deeply needed to hear: that she was talking about *their* mommas, *their* lovers, about *them,* for God's sake: their own blessed and anguished selves and lives.

But she hated the questions from the sophisticated students because they were so sadly self-conscious, asked, she so often felt, so their professors would hear them asking smart questions, but she hated worse the questions from the teachers because they didn't really ask questions so much as make speeches and want her to tell them their theories were right, and bless them all, she didn't know if they were or not. She was not like them, they never understood: they always thought she was one of them, always thought that because she knew who invented Existentialism and what the JEGP was that she was one of them. They didn't understand that she was a redneck, that she really mostly was.

But they all did all right and so did she and after all it was fun and she liked people and they had liked her reading and she had heard some things in it she didn't like at all, while other things had surprised, had laid some joy on her the way they worked. Still, she always tried to concentrate hardest when she read from stuff still in the mill, to make notes to herself about what she had heard before the questions started. And now, she sighed inside, the hard part starts, the rumpus begins.

The host brought her drink which she casually sniffed to get a sense of how strong he thought she was supposed to be about drinking, a thing she had done well enough and plenty enough in her time but had grown a little soft on since her brother's deep despair, so deep and sad as to never, finally, be able to see a thing but death as his redemption and it without a lick of joy. But here they came, their smiles set along with hers, she pleased enough to receive them if that's what they wanted. Well.

She talked and laughed and even felt a little like carrying on, after a few sips of the whiskey, which, thank God, was weak like she had asked for. And she was striking up with them all as they came to thank to talk to theorize to jolly to be near her for being there. Then she saw the boy. There. He was pouring Dite Sprite, but she knew him better than that. Oh, dear she did, for she had looked into his eyes three times and had wanted to cry.

He was being quite the suave little man about town, she could tell. She was practiced at it, this paying attention to one thing while she listened hard for something else. *It'll get you in trouble yet, markmywords,* her mother had always told her. *Yes'm,* she had replied as often, her ears listening to the cadences of her mother's speech, the constant catch in her mother's throat, the way she raised up on the ends of words strangely: why bother yourself with the lesson when you knew what it was from the way it started out?

She always played Momma and Poppa with her brother, she was telling one of the younger faculty. He raised an eyebrow in a studied leer, but she saw the other one—caught unawares—start to flick up in real shock. She laughed and explained that they mimicked their Momma and Poppa, how good her brother was at it—

no matter that he was seven years younger than her—and how they could while away God alone knows how many hours on a Sunday raising the arguments against pride and sin and devilment generally that they had been brought up on. Not that their parents had approved, actually, though they saw the sport of it and managed not to take things *too* seriously. Usually.

Except after a while, she was hearing herself say inside herself, not to them. She looked again at the boy, nipping around the corner of his life into another part of the party now, moving, she felt quite certain, from the food-Sprite-cola-punch to skitter nearer the boozy bottles on the counter. So young so young; oh, dear, so young to be so hard.

No kick wick sick prick to all that sweetum gunk, his tongue knew. Nothing nice to put down to the bellykins to swirl through the bloodstreams of life and back up into the head where wonderful things happened after the keys had tumbled and tumblers had rumbled them loose for him to think and think and think, as the gin be-durbled itself into the fizzyglass full of fun: a sip without stir; never stir; always sip off the top and add some more real quick before anyone really noticed, with quick darting little glances left-rightleftright alert for Poppykins and MumsyPoos and others sure to share their views about the death of brain cells, collisions of worlds going in and out the same door the same time and bumping each to each against the other and not understanding or caring. Sipsipsip ahhhhhhhhhh.

And there she is rounding the corner looking like she was looking for him and sure enough here she comes to sipsipsip herself a little more. He smiled his best be-nice-to-company smile and she smiled a strange thing back to him so the corners of his mouth felt strained to keep the smile a-going. Did she know? Could she guess? Could she ever guess?

Burble durble bourbon brown and sweet then done, with water, smiled at him and went away without a word to leave a pang an ache as empty/full as not knowing where it was supposed to go and loosing, wasting his man/boy flood and feeling silly like a put-down. Oh! She sits, looks back to him awash with pains of knowledge like Susie Q Sally Poo Silly Who. He starts toward her, but is beaten. Already three surround. She stands to look them in their eyes. Be-durble gin again and drink. Quick!

They talk about Lear-stern's son who, it seems, is a poet, for the high school annual and people say he is good except for his father who says he lucks up on good lines but will not take the time or trouble to work enough to make all the lines good if not wonderful. And so he impresses without cause? No, it seems. He is good that's true, but he does not do the work though he manages to see the things to say. Like the ones about taking jeans off to dance because the jeans are too skintight. Set a trend. Create a fad. Wonderful, she thinks, and why not, after all. After all, if he sees the things to write about that's half of what there is? Lear-stern concurs, though without fervor.

And here himself comes now, fake Dite Sprite in hand, sipping from the top, no doubt, to get the full stuff in as quick as he can. Will he say anything to me, she wonders. Can I talk to the boy, she wonders. They talk about the jeans poem, and he rubs his sweated palms on his thighs. He sweats, she thinks. He smiles and talks too loud, moves in jerks, makes her feel old, it occurs to her, and her wanting mostly to feel *settled*.

Then the others are gone, watching, some of them with tics of dudgeon licking at their lips, as the two sit and talk: she back in the chair, he on the floor before her, looking up at her, his knees up, arm-wrapped. They talk, he and she, and he tells her what, and she listens and hears it all again, hears the voice telling him what she saw in her brother, precious baby brother laughing through the hours of Momma and Poppa, inventing plays and playing clowns and trapeze in the beaten dirt of their backyard, looking up, she remembered, one time looking up as a sudden puff of cool air whipped them in a dead day of August, the yard swirling slowly then quickly into a smallish column of brown grass and dust moving lazily through: a miniature tornado for them to watch in the bright and cloudless sky as their skins chilled to goose bumps at the wind devil. Innocent as a cough it summoned up their fear: they had seen the sudden monstrous scream and turn of the real thing, had felt the temperature drop fifteen degrees in two minutes, once, and had looked to see the sullen haze of dead air turn to scudding gray, very gray clouds starting to whip black across the sky. They knew what to do: get inside and pray, listen for the sirens, watch the sky and hope against hail.

Making you feel really crazygood all the time and then it is easier to understand everything which is to say to understand they have nothing to say to you that you need to hear because in a hundred years it won't make any difference anyway so what's the point? And with the good stuff there is always someone you can share with and you can talk because you talk the same and because whatthehell they'll invent a cure by then no matter: livers, lungs, hearts: out with the old in with the new, no? A real gas.

A poet, they tell me?

She is thinking she can tell him something of poetry, can tell something of her brother Boy and poetry, because Boy *was* a poem himself. Boy McClain (McClain her maiden name, of course) her little brother who had so much fun with imitations and being other people. Always being someone else, always skipping sideways around himself, that Boy, shuffling around behind a curtain or a corner only to come back out with another face, another voice, another change of costume enough to make you sick with laughing, crying till you truly couldn't stand it any more. She felt her eyes bright on this curly-haired lad with the sweaty palms who laughed too fast and understood too quickly.

But, she was saying about poems, she didn't know: that if she lived in New York City and was maybe even Jewish and even more if she was in the part of Tin Pan Alley that does those things, then she might write a ballad about Boy and the gun he put to his head, pulled the trigger: *Boom: sha-boom sha-boom.*

Oh Hark!

Which sounds like Tin Pan Alley when you put it like that, I reckon, but if I was to talk to a class of mine about that kind of thing, if I was high enough on my own ego and Sanka (No, never mind what you see in my hand tonight, Young Buck, I'm really mostly off the hard stuff: no real palpitations, but the general loosening flab of the short-winded, middle-aged centering of myself) high enough, I say, on my own ego and Sanka and if I was tuned in to my better self: coffee, then, ego, and a good ear to know my words were coming out fine and clear, strong and grand and powerful . . .

Boy—my baby brother who I loved past my own desire—killed himself by putting the bullet from a .32 caliber revolver through his well-groomed, handsome, boyish head on a back road out from Social Circle, Georgia, which is not too far from Atlanta. It was daylight. There were no witnesses. He was drunk. His head was filled with worms. (I *can* write a simple declarative sentence. I can write factual sentences that have some modest grace, style, and wit if you'll grant that the sledgehammer force of a .32 caliber bullet entering the brain can have some grace if little style and sure as hell no wit to it.)

But it is hard for me, young boy/poet with the sweaty palms and the hard looks who already knows not to mix it and to slurp it from the top quick so early in your life, and so unlike my little Boy brother who, take it all in all, probably could have used some of your hardness because he did not have enough of his own to manage very well with.

But I was saying it is *hard* for me to write those sentences. The worms, for instance: that isn't real, but in time they would have been real enough. A man and his wife, driving slowly as country

218

people do on those roads, missed witnessing by about a minute. It is recorded that they said, "Poor boy, poor boy." They were saddened, not shaken. I know, because I talked to them.

So what I am trying to say, boy/poet, is that I'd write you a ballad because ballads are about love and failure, and even if what I was saying about Tin Pan Alley sounds like it was taking on the form of a kind of shapely Shakespearean sonnet, I would still sing you the ballad because it deals with rape and murder and violence and death and failure and . . . and what really *is* your problem, my poet/boy?

But I raised the sonnet because it is so hard and so tough with those couplets that end it all, that are so durned *durned* spiteful to get right. You go write yourself some of those things, sweet pampered boy/poet, and you'll find out something you might ought to know some day. It is very hard to end things well. It is hard enough to hammer out those quatrains so they are solid and firm and strong and moving. But we almost all of us blow it at the end on those worrisome wretched couplets.

My poem to you is a ballad of violence and failure so my Boy/brother can be loose and unexplained, so I can read his story without worrying and fretting the details overmuch. It is a rough form, to be sure, but my ballad/Boy tried for sonnetry and blew it. And I have tried for years to understand why.

Boom: sha-boom sha-boom.

Ohyes. I will learn from her something about Susie Q and goo and when she laughed at me I think I could have killed her and still don't know why unless even then I knew I did not want to go to jail and be buggery buggered by big black men cock-a-diddle crazy for fresh meat, it mattering not that they would never have sent me into that place because I am a *child*—oh horridword hardtobear word *child!*

But I have all along had this *thing* to cope with and I have not been very good at the coping scene with this particular thing which I think I can talk about here and now because nature, it

219

seems, has more or less taken the thing into hand, no puns intended especially. But I needed some *cajones*—you understand? I was like little bittle bitsy robin eggs, though not blue, it is true. Still, I found myself underwhelmed by what I could find down there of a night, or of a day or afternoon either, for all that. And of hair there was so little for so long, and speaking of the *long,* that was another problem too though not quite so much so mostly it was the hair—you understand me?—the lack of hair the presence of nothing but fuzz and not to gross you out or anything like that but there is still not so much as others my own age which is one of the reasons Sports! has never had all that much appeal to me. (But why do I speak to you of these things? Why do I always speak to women of these things?) My mother wants to know and I think is sometimes sorry that I do not speak to *her* about them, that I never showed *her* my robin's eggs, though I must admit that there has been of late an unavoidable *scene* in which my MumsyPoo happened upon me whilst I was in the altogether, as her own mother seemed always anxious to phrase such matters. In the event, she saw me whilst I was bareassed and after I had my *cajones* wellwell developed, bulging, if I do say so myself, from their rather slight feathery nest in a manner sure to have pleased the Whitman bard himself.

So it always comes back to that with them.

But with Susie Q and the others I could bare myself, that being all there is to bare and most of what there is to bear, though Daddykins does not accept. But I was talking about Sports! and open showers and the boy/men who make the rest of us look so kiddiley, and of poking they know how to poke the fun as well as other things.

But there are ways to bear the burdens of having to pretend to the taking of notes in the school, there are ways to deal with the Daddykins who batted their asses for ever and do not understand the why of why *I* don't also want to follow in the footsteps and bat the ass about the world pleasing and succeeding and doing all the goodie right things just so *they* can be proud of *their* accomplishment in *me*. You see?

So it is all sipping from the top and smoking the pot and wishing for hair and broad chestedness like the bullyboy jocks who grunt and surge through schoolyards.

I was aware there doesn't need to be hair, *ma mere,* just time and place and Mumsy/Pops who leave us alone in the basements with the TVs and the fridge because we live, let us face the world as it is, in a more liberated age and we know that the young adults are all right and good kids and just learning about life in ways we were never allowed—*Doggone* it!—they mostly say. And besides, when I was their age I was what you'd call a juvenile delinquent. And besides, it's easier that way. So let the little dolls play house in the basement with the fridgefullofbeer and what the hell.

Get back to the poetry.

Mumsypoo, I think, was pleased to see my lemonballs pushing wide my thighs, the *thing* itself a-dangle. I had just taken a shower. I was facing my door and drying. She didn't know I was in there. It didn't bother me that she saw me. Why should I care? There's Susie Q and Sally Poo and Silly Who. They must have seen me, too. And why should I care? I, child of love, MumsyPopsy always say, always tell the old lie because I know that it is not the child of love, it is the child if mistake, of error, of PopsyPoo wangling his donkey dangle into Mumsy after a night of friendly wine and such to come home and warm the bed and himself. Only there were no precautions, no being careful, no being moderate. Just the same old Satan *lust* himself, a-pleasuring of themselves and a-making of poor sweet child of love Me. They were not concerned. They were not planning, they were not having a caution as they liked to tell me, as everybody likes to tell me. Having a caution. It makes me sick to my gut-e-oh to have a caution; it makes me sick to my head-e-oh to think of it: being bastard to their thoughts.

His last night alive. Befuddle. Total sweet befuddle. We all knew he was too sweet for this life, and I knew that he would some-day kill himself only I didn't want him to and I would cry and cry to my man, my good man and husband who would hold me like he did that morning when I found out about him (from a friend who called and said in low and breathy voice he had to come over and talk to me and was my Man there? Yes. Good.) and had to drive all the way there and talk to the police and talk to the couple who had found him and talk to every damn body in three counties in Geor-gia, it seemed like, even if they were all so kind as they could be, but by God! I was angry at him, at Boy McClain for going off like that and not letting anybody help. Damn him, I was mad. And I am still mad. Only he was lost, is the thing. So lost, always peering around those corners looking to see who was watching, looking to see if anyone, finally, was seeing *him,* hoping not. But to the last night: last night, first night: they were all the same nights to him, so he felt the need to make a last one, to let there be an end to it.

No one was home. He let himself in and fumbled around in his bedroom until he found the bourbon. With his hand he checked the seal. The bottle was still full. Back out in the car he unlocked the glove compartment and reached in. The pistol was there. In the dim light from a street lamp down the way he could see it. He flipped the chamber open. Full. He took each round from its cham-ber and inspected each one. Then he put them all back. He opened the fresh bottle and sniffed. He screwed the cap back on, got out of the car, and went back inside the house.

He turned the light on in the kitchen and rummaged around the pantry and shelves and cupboards until he found the ice chest. He emptied all the ice from the freezer into the chest, then carefully refilled the trays and put them back in the freezer. After a few more minutes he found the thermos. He rinsed it out, dropped two cubes into it, and filled it with water.

He turned the lights off, put the thermos carefully under his arm, holding the ice bucket in the other hand. The front door gave him trouble, but he managed it by putting the thermos and the ice bucket down, opening the door, moving the things, and closing the door behind him.

Then with the car door it was the same. He was sitting behind the wheel when he sighed deeply. He got out of the car, went back across the yard, through the front door again, and back to the kitchen where he got a glass. Then back once more to his car. There. He was ready. He drove very carefully, surrounded by his paraphernalia. He glanced down at his gas gauge: just over half full. He calculated quickly, made his decision, and drove to a filling station he'd never been to.

"Fillerup?" the attendant asked. He was a whiskery-faced, oldish sort of country man.

"Yes. Regular."

The old man nodded, glancing at the bottle, the glass, the ice bucket.

While the tank was filling, the man checked under the hood: oil okay; radiator okay; battery okay. He slammed the hood down into place.

"Check your tires, Mister?"

Boy nodded slowly, hardly aware that the man had asked him a question. The automatic shutoff on the gas pump clacked.

"Tires okay."

"Fine, fine."

"Nine point two that'll be eleven eighty-seven, Mister."

Boy handed him a twenty.

"Eighty-eight, eighty-nine, ninety, that's twelve, and here's your thirteen, fourteen, fifteen, and five makes twenty. Thank you, Sir, and hurry back and have a nice evening."

"Sure." He looked up at the man who kept standing by the car and looking at Boy.

"I'm okay," Boy said. He smiled. "I'm okay. Really."

Then the old man smiled slightly himself. "Okay, Mister. Good," but he stayed where he was.

Boy slowly reached his hand out the window. "Goodby," he said. He smiled and his eyes watered.

"Yissir. Well, goodby," the old man said and touched Boy's hand in what passed for a shake. "You sure you're okay, Mister?"

"Yeh. Sure. I'm fine. Goodby again."

"Yep. Well, bye, then, Mister."

At first he thought he would drive until the tank was empty, whenever and wherever that might be. But as he started off he understood it would take at least a little more planning than that. Not much more, but some. He headed out of town. He wanted to go someplace pretty. He wanted to go where there was a hill, maybe, so he could watch the sun rise. Florida might be nice, though. Watch the sun come up on the beach. Or go to the Gulf coast and watch it set. That would be prettier still. Or maybe he could to to Nashville where . . .

But it didn't really matter much. One place was probably as good as another . . .

He was heading south, generally.

It should be a *good* place, though. It should be a place you'd like to be. It should be *home,* probably, that place. But maybe that doesn't really matter so much, either. But it should be quiet. And nice, too. A nice, quiet place and sort of out of the way.

He fixed himself another drink. Clink of ice, heavy gurgle of good bourbon, splash of water. Everything fine. He drove very carefully.

For an hour or so he kept to the Interstate. Fifty-five miles an hour. Careful. Very careful. And enjoying himself immensely. He had wanted to take a trip by himself for a long time. Now here it was, but he wanted to be able to stay awake long enough to get wherever it was he had to be.

Wherever it was.

He finished the whiskey in the glass, put it down, reached over, and held the bottle up so he could see how much was left. Still over half.

He didn't want to get too close to the Atlanta traffic, so he turned off on a state road he knew, got through the first little town, and began to feel bleary, scared that the double vision might come over him.

He drove on: Winder, Monroe, then off through Walnut Grove, then out from there, even.

It wasn't a dirt road. Not even gravel. It was an improved county road. Boy pulled over well past the edge of the left hand lane. He got out carefully and walked around to the road side. He was off the pavement so no one would hit him head on.

"Unless they were drunk," he muttered, then giggled slightly.

He listened to the night noises as he fixed another drink. He didn't like the light in the front seat, though; so he took the bottle and the ice bucket and the thermos and glass and set them just under the front end of the car. He sat down and drank. It was quite chilly, but Boy thought that was fine. He could feel the damp around him and was glad the weather still wasn't so hot yet. At last he stood, walked a short way from the car, unzipped his pants, and urinated against a tree.

The quiet. The country quiet and dark were astounding. He looked at his watch. It was 1:30. He fixed himself another drink before crawling in the back seat of his car to take a nap. He balled himself up against the chill and closed his eyes. He thought he might go right to sleep, but for thirty or forty minutes he lay awake, sometimes hearing the *tic-tic-tic* of his watch, sometimes not. He never moved.

At last he slept.

When he woke up it was gray out. He rolled to a sitting position and looked out the window. He checked his watch. It said 5:15. He rolled the window down and put his head out. Then he got out of the car. He looked up at the sky as he went to his tree again. He stumbled several times on the way back to the car. Inside, he curled back up and fell right to sleep.

Then it was 8:30. Boy got out of the car to go to his tree once

225

more, but he had to lean against the front fender for a few minutes first. Then he heard the pick-up and raised his head as it slowly came toward him, slowly in the way people in the country often drive. In the front seat with the old man who was driving sat an old lady: straight, gray-faced, with a brightly colored dress. The old man never slowed, but looked carefully as he raised his hand in a restrained greeting. Boy smiled back slightly and nodded his head as he took a hand from his windbreaker and returned the salutation. The truck went on, and all was still again. Not even a dog in the distance. He made it to his tree to urinate again. It was an exquisite pleasure, and he thought of the sign he had seen in a men's room once: *To hell with Coke, this is the pause that refreshes.*

Pissing, he thought, pissing against a tree outdoors was one of the pure, lovely, and truly freedom-inspiring pleasures a man can have. He was looking up into the branches as he urinated, almost to the point of falling over backwards as he did. But it was feeling so good, and the leaves of the trees were so light in their color, so fragile and tender looking still; yet they seemed so sure of their eventual fullness, their eventual depths of color and cover.

Then Boy realized he had fingered himself into a partial erection. He squeezed himself a few times gently, running his palm and then the backs of his fingers against his pubic hair, then pulling downward so his foreskin partially covered the head of his penis.

He walked into the skimpy stand of trees a little way and with a stick he dug a small trench. He dropped his pants down to his ankles, squatted, and had a bowel movement, wiping himself with leaves.

He covered the trench with dirt and humus, then wandered around to find a stream if he could. He let out a great yawn. He stomped noisily until he got to the water. He looked down at it and shrugged. It wasn't the crystal pure, gurgling, sweet little mountain stream he had dreamed for himself, but it was water, even if it was mostly a kind of pond. Again he shrugged and squatted to rinse his hands. The water felt good. Cool and with a very slight slickness to it.

He took his shoes and socks off, then his pants and undershorts, squatted over the water, and rinsed himself from the bowel movement. Then he was playing with himself again, working himself to a partial erection; fondling, stroking, watching. More, and then some more. Then he was belly down on the slick, wet earth rolling his cock between it and his belly, his eyes wide open and focused on the nine square inches before him, his mouth parted in a slight smile until he was through.

Then he lay very quietly for a few minutes napping, little snippets of dreams tripping through his head: of his mother, of his father, of his sister; of naiads clothed so enticingly in their diaphanous little garments, daisy chains crowning their heads . . .

He rolled over, muddy. Again he rinsed himself as well as he could, and in rinsing he squeezed again on his penis and found there was still some feeling left, some final pleasure in it, some seed yet to be dropped into the earth.

Ah.

He put his trousers back on, but left the undershorts and socks folded by the little pond. Shoes in hand, he went back to the car. He picked up the bottle and ice bucket and thermos and glass and put them back on the front seat. He got in on the driver's side, reached over and unlocked the glove compartment. He got the pistol out, carefully closed the glove compartment, and locked it. He sat for a minute as though studying the pistol. Then he looked up toward the rearview mirror. It had gotten knocked askew so that when he looked up, instead of seeing the road behind him, he saw himself: caught the startled look on his face at the unexpected vision.

He sat up a little and adjusted the mirror so he could look at his face better. It scared him. Then he took the mirror in both hands and yanked very hard. It snapped away from its socket. He got out of the car, the pistol in the pocket of his jacket, and got to his knees next to the sideview mirror. He turned it so he could look at himself. He stared at his eyes, his eyebrows, the bow curve of his lips, the neat shape of his ears and wondered why he had been the one to have the fine features, to be the beautiful one instead of his sister. Then he used the rearview in his hands to look at himself in profile with the sideview. He studied both profiles. And the back of his head. And he leaned his head back while he held the rearview above him so he could see the top of his head. Not quite thirty, he thought. So young and already losing hair on top.

Then it was done.

One last time to the tree, then. Just pissing that time. No real pleasure. He zipped up and walked back to the car. He stood for a minute, a forefinger to his lips in a pose of indecision. Then he reached inside the car and pulled out the bottle. He unscrewed the cap and sniffed before he took a long, long swallow. It burned. There were still about three fingers in the bottom. He raised the bottle up higher than his face, lowered it slightly, poured the rest of the whiskey onto the ground, screwed the cap back on, and tossed the empty onto the back seat of the car.

He took the pistol out, placed the muzzle in his right ear, tilted the barrel up slightly, and pulled the trigger.

Boom: sha-boom sha-boom.

They never saw a thing, but they must have missed witnessing it by no more than half a minute at the very most, because they both heard the shot. Only the Missus still swore it sounded like two to her. They were on their way back. They remembered seeing him the first time.

The Mister stopped his truck.

"Dear Lord," he said. "Oh Dear Lord lookit."

"Should we get out?" she asked.

He left the engine running as he climbed down from the cab, careful of his arthritic knees. He walked stiffly across the road and looked down at the young man.

"No," he said, his voice tight with phlegm. He got back in the truck, backed and turned, and headed around again to get the sheriff.

After driving past that spot for the fourth time in the day, slowing this time, looking over where the car had been, and the body, she said—not to herself, not to her own mind only, but aloud to her husband—said, "I wonder why he killed hisself."

"Well," he answered, resuming his normal speed, pursing his lips in the habit of the old tobacco chewer who has quit, "there's plenty reasons to be unhappy."

"Yes," she said, sure as could be of the truth of *that*. "It is a shame, though," she went on, "that he had to learn so many of them so young."

"Yes." And again with sure knowledge of the truth, "It is a shame."

Talking yet, but winding it all down now, they sat as before: she in the chair, legs crossed, long skirt covering her shoes and falling to the floor; he at her feet, looking up at her, his arms still wrapped around his legs as he jounced his chin gently against his knees. Then they were quiet, still, as though waiting for something to happen.

Then just like that, it seemed, the party was over, exploding to a finish the way they sometimes do: like a great fourth of July rocket with burst after spangled burst rolling out great deep hollow booms across the sky. And they were up, too, she looking at him and wondering how long he would go until he learned to channel bitterness, to invent his own tune to dance to, to stop playing his foolish games, to stop doing his frug simply because they whistled a waltz.

And yet too tired herself, of a sudden, too shaken, she felt in her thighs, her calves actually trembling from memory, from thinking of her Boy and wondering why she was sane and he was dead, both of them with the same Momma and Poppa. And *why* wouldn't he ever let her help him? And *why* wasn't he strong like her? And *why* was he so gol-durned miserable all his life? Crying, she would find him. Crying his poor heart out over nothing. How many times she had found him like that when he was a boy, sobbing in a corner or, once, standing out back by a winter-bleak mimosa, raising his arms to her when he saw her, clutching her around the waist, frantic for her warmth, unable to speak his loss, and once, even, after he had grown too old for embarrassment, crying suddenly about his baby daughter because she would someday bleed, *bleed,* for

God's sake, bleed like a woman and become one and marry and have chillern herself and then die! Or simply staring through a window, hands in pockets—or only one by then since the other always held a glass—shoulders slumped as against doom, tears running down his face.

But in all her writing all she could do was guess at *why*, make up a *why* for herself, create a *why* to satisfy something she could never get closer to than that. It was all she could do, and it would simply have to be enough. But it was still at such a distance, at such a terrible remove, such an awesome remoteness from *him*. And would be, always.

But suddenly bending rending, not to bear this any longer, she trashing him with what he knew he could not answer to or do and there beneath her laughs and strokes he knew she held him, making him screw his head to goo too soon, asking him to stick it somewhere new that Susie Q and Sally Who could never think to do. There was a tremble in his belly as the sipsip faded from his head for her to fill, her spinning words terrible to hear, not funatall, all fullofworms and things that creep and scare. He teeter-tottered to the bar, himself awash with demons not his own.

Watch the hand as it shakes a-pouring burble be-durble before anyone comes to screw the tops on tight, to give him grim-smiled wicked looks that say he—Child!—shouldn't be doing this kind of thing and does his MumsyPoo know? And his Popsywopsy? And boozey-woozey is dear, boy. Make haste, then, use the cover of the leave-takings to drain the brain of other people, of other's thoughts, of others. Get back to self, be-durble. Get back to Susie What and Whatsie Which and Cootchie Coo. No others, only Self, only Me, not even We. Only.

Durble-durble, be-double-durble.

In the yard she made toward her ride, but swept her gaze around once more and saw him, hand in pocket, clutching the glass. She heard the clink of ice as he made his ballsy way down the street toward home, knees a-spring, sport tails a-flap, head high, butt tight, IN CHARGE, by God!

Poor boy.

In the car, windows down to the cool of the soft night, through the roar of engines, the merry goodnight brays to and from the house, the woofs of neighbor dogs wakened from memories of long-past urgent hunts, she heard the fading clink of ice in the boy's glass. She sighed and shook her head. She wanted to be home. She wanted to sleep in her own bed, to be able to reach out and touch the aging flank of her own good man, that broken-faced piece of kindness. She felt a surge of blood through her face, an adrenalin of joy as she knew—Praise Be—that she was closer to the end than to the start of it all. She couldn't stand to do all that again, couldn't stand to go through another minute of it no matter how good it had mostly been. Couldn't stand it for a minute. No ma'am. From now on was plenty good enough for her.

Clink! A-Clink-Clink.